CW01394369

John Dale was born in Sydney but grew up in Tasmania. Since returning to Sydney, he has spent time in the Attorney General's Department, taught writing at university and worked as a doorman.

Other Mask Noir Titles

DARK ANGEL

John Dale

With thanks to Noel King

Library of Congress Catalog Card Number: 95-68389

A full catalogue record for this book can be obtained from
the British Library on request

The right of John Dale to be identified as the author
of this work has been asserted by him in accordance with
the Copyright, Designs and Patents Act 1988

Treaty lyrics reprinted with permission of Yothu Yindi Music/
Mushroom Music

Copyright © 1995 John Dale

First published in 1995 by HarperCollins, Sydney, Australia

This edition first published by Serpent's Tail, 4 Blackstock Mews,
London N4, and 180 Varick Street, 10th floor, New York, NY 10014

Typeset in 10pt ITC Century Book by CentraCet, Cambridge
Printed in Great Britain by Cox & Wyman Ltd., Reading, Berkshire

For AMD,
a good mate

Diana in the leaves green;
Luna who so bright doth sheen;
Persephone in Hell

John Skelton

A dirty red carpet ran out under the feet of the poker machine players and into the foyer where a big man sat beneath a case of football trophies. He wore a red tie that matched the carpet, a white shirt, black trousers. His thinning hair was combed back off his broad sweating forehead.

Now and again the air-conditioning whirred up, only to clunk out under the strain. The big man sniffed at his shirt. It stank of this dump, of the stinking red carpet. He glanced up at the clock as the front door shot open and Jose Diaz came in pulling off his crash helmet.

'Where you been?' the big man said. 'It's ten past.'

'Spanish time, Jack. Keep your shirt on.'

Jack grunted and stepped outside. The smell of the night smacked him in the nose: hamburgers, popcorn, petrol fumes. Underage Spanish boys leaned against the club wall in white disco suits.

'Hi Jack, how's it goin, man.' They slapped wet baby palms up against his. The sweet smell of their dope loosened the tightness in his face.

He hit the streets. The night air tasted grimy, metallic. Garbage spilled over the pavement at the side of a hamburger joint and a split plastic bag oozed a foul dark liquid. He walked up Liverpool Street tugging at his shirt collar, ignoring the young dudes out on the town, the Saturday night beerskins. A school-aged girl dressed in black was puking her heart out in a shoe-shop doorway. Columns of lights towered above the city, strips of reds and blues and yellows, hundreds and thousands of them.

Jack bent down and picked a gold dollar coin up out of the gutter.

He walked on up Oxford Street. Twenty metres ahead, three tall youths in baseball caps were karate kicking a slim young man outside the Erotic Cinema. A well-dressed couple hurried past, eyes averted. Jack's feet slowed. The youths started throwing the young man up against the plate glass window and Jack saw flecks of blood on the pavement. He tried to walk around. This was none of his business. But the look in the young man's eyes pulled him up.

'Hey!' he said. 'Don't you boys think he's had enough?'

A tall pimply youth stepped towards him. 'Fuck off, mister.'

Jack's eyes went to the huge white Reeboks, and then back up to the red face.

'You a faggot-lover?' the youth said. His hand flashed to his pocket. 'You a poofter too?'

Jack tensed and backed slowly towards the city. 'Put the knife away, son.'

'Cut his dick off, Spike,' one of his mates said.

Grinning, the youth came at him; Jack stepped to one side – fast. He thrust the ball of his thumb into the youth's larynx, grabbed a wrist with his spare hand and cracked it hard across his knee. Metal clattered in the gutter. Jack hit the screaming youth in the face with his fist; blood squirted down his shirt.

Jack turned, balanced on the toes of his feet and readied himself for the other two, but they just stood there gaping like hooked fish. The pimply youth clutched his wrist on the ground.

'You broke my hand.' He was trying not to blubber.

'Go home, son,' Jack said. 'And soak it in a bucket.'

'We're gunna get the cops on you . . . y'bastard.' His two friends helped him to his feet and they shuffled away up Oxford Street, heads lowered, Hexalite soles scuffing on the pavement.

Jack turned to the slim young man who was leaning against the cinema window dabbing at his mouth with his fingers. 'You alright, fella?'

The man's creamy-white slacks were spotted with blood, his maroon shirt was ripped. 'Where'd you learn to fight like that?' he said. 'They had knives. They at-attacked me for no reason.'

Jack stared at his blond streaky hair and clean straight features. 'Maybe they don't like gays.'

The man's eyes blazed. 'If I'd had a gun –'

'They'd probably have shot you with it,' Jack said.

The young man thought that over. 'I'm Damian. Do you like Moët?'

'Never touch the stuff.'

'What do you drink then?'

'Melbourne Bitter,' Jack said.

Damian laughed and brushed at the air. 'Well, I'll buy you a dozen Melbourne Bitters!'

Jack wiped the back of his neck with a handkerchief. 'One'll do.'

They crossed Oxford Street and went into the first bar they saw. The walls were clad in mock metal done up to resemble armour. Green flashing lights made the patrons look ill. Jack took off his red tie and buried it in a pocket. He stretched his collar and glanced around him at the other heads, counting up all the earrings in sight. Damian had three in his left earlobe. For a moment Jack couldn't remember which ear was the queer one – wasn't it the right?

Damian held out a schooner. 'Do you do this sort of thing regularly – rescuing people?'

'First time.' Jack took his beer and sniffed it. He tried to ignore the foundry music piping out of the bar speakers. He tipped back his head and let the cold beer tunnel down his throat.

Damian leaned forward on his stool. 'Why did you get involved out there? You didn't have to.'

Jack rolled his shoulders. 'I dunno. You reminded me of someone. So what do you do when you're not getting bashed?'

'I'm a model.' Damian smiled. His teeth were white and perfectly even.

'What sorta model?'

'Magazines mainly – *Switch*, *Studio for Men* –'

'Never heard of them,' Jack said. He finished his beer and stood up, wiping froth from his mouth.

'Don't go,' Damian said. 'Please. I still owe you.'

'Forget it.'

'But I don't even know your name.'

'Jack. Jack Butorov.'

'Look, Jack. I could've been disfigured out there.' Damian grabbed his arm. 'Let me repay you properly.'

Jack stared at the blue eyes, the long blond eyelashes and his swollen lip. He was a handsome young fella. Most probably he could get any girl in the world he wanted. If he wanted girls, that is.

'Okay,' he said, 'one for the road. Then I gotta go. And ask Popeye there to lower the racket.' He jerked his chin at the barman.

Damian went over and spoke to the barman who laughed, but turned the music down anyway. Jack watched him leaning against the bar, his arse pushing against his trousers.

After a minute he came back and set a tray of stubbies on the table. He flicked his hair out of his eyes and swirled the ice in his gin. 'So what do you do, Jack?'

'I'm a doorman.' Jack wiped the top of his Mel Bitter.

'Isn't that kind of dangerous?'

'Less dangerous than a building site. More dangerous than working in David Jones food hall.'

'You married?'

'Was,' Jack said.

'Kids?'

'What is this, a quiz show?'

'Sorry,' Damian said. 'I'm just curious that's all. I want to know more about you. I want to know why you helped me tonight.' His eyes widened.

'Nothin to know, pal,' Jack said. 'You were lucky that's all.'

'Look. I need you to do me a big favour.'

Jack shook his head. 'Uh-uh, I'm all out of favours.'

The young man reached a hand across the table and laid it over Jack's grazed fist. 'I'm still a bit freaked. That street gang. I don't want to go home tonight. Could I crash at your place? I'd sleep on the floor – anywhere.'

Jack withdrew his hand.

'Please, Jack. I wouldn't be any trouble. I just don't feel safe on my own.'

The air was hot and heavy on Oxford Street. A man leaned on the bonnet of a Nissan Patrol with a cooked shank of lamb in his hand and a woman squatting at his feet. Jack stepped over the stream of water she was making and waved at the traffic. A cab braked and he climbed in. The driver had a black beard and wore a brown caftan. A set of wooden beads dangled from his rear-view mirror.

'Coogee,' Jack said.

Damian came rushing out of the hotel with a carton of Melbourne Bitter stubbies and a bottle in a brown paper bag. He slid into the back seat. The driver scratched his chin. 'Coogee,' Jack said again. He pointed up Oxford Street and made dog paddling gestures with his hands. 'Beach.' The driver got that and pulled away from the kerb.

Damian dumped the bottle in Jack's lap. 'You don't have to drink it all tonight,' he said. 'It's a present.'

Jack tore the paper off. 'Black label. Don't get me on the whisky, pal, I go crazy on the whisky.' He looked up and waved a hand at the driver, 'left,' he said, 'left!'

The driver swung the wheel and Jack was thrown

against Damian. The road curved past the racecourse, climbed a hill and then plunged towards the sea. Fruit bats flew low overhead and tall blocks of flats rose from the sandstone rock, dwarfing the fig trees and competing for water views.

Jack guided the driver down a side street and the two men got out. Damian paid. 'You could see the beach from here,' Jack said, 'if you had some stilts.' He led Damian around behind a laundromat and up a lane. They went through a car-port and climbed some stairs. Damian sniffed the air.

'Garbage night,' Jack told him. The lights were out in the building and Damian trailed behind feeling his way in the dark.

Jack opened a door at the top of the stairs and switched on a light. There was a rustle of tiny wings across the lino. He strode across the living room, bent down under the sink in the kitchenette, grabbed a can of something and started spraying the benches and the back of the stove.

Damian moved over to the aluminium window. A huge Moreton Bay fig tree obstructed the view of the park. Fruit bats screeched in its branches.

Jack said, 'There was a murder in that park three months ago. A young guy got his throat slit. I woke up, looked out and there's forty-two cops in white overalls combing the grass with tweezers. It made the papers, but they never found the killer.' Jack swatted a big black cockroach as it staggered out from underneath the sink. 'Got a real plague of 'em here.' He swept up the body and dumped it in the bin. He opened a couple of beers. 'Down the hatch.'

Damian took his stubby over by the pine bookcase, but Jack noticed he didn't drink from it.

'I got a lot of class fiction there,' Jack said. 'Leonard, Crumley, Chandler. I'm into crime.'

Damian nodded, 'So am I.' He picked up a boxing

trophy from the mantlepiece and read its inscription, then walked around the poky apartment, running his eyes over the marked walls, the cheap scuffed furniture. 'Oh records, you've still got records – how lovely!' He switched on the Kenwood turntable and watched it turn. 'You like living alone do you, Jack?'

'Why?'

'Just asking.' Damian hunkered down on the vinyl couch, twisting one of his earrings around in his ear. He produced a film container from his pocket, opened it and laid a line of fine white powder out on the back of a record cover. He held out a little metal tube to Jack.

Jack shook his head.

Damian bent down close to the record cover. He wiped a stream of tears away from his eyes and gave Jack a friendly smile.

Jack took a big swig of beer. 'You had many women?'

Damian sniffed. 'One or two. What about you, Jack. You had many?'

'Women.' Jack grinned. 'I've always liked them. When I was in my twenties that's all I ever thought about. The magic word.'

'Yeah?'

'Yeah,' Jack said.

'How long is it since you had a woman, Jack?'

Jack twisted the top off another stubby and threw it at the sink. It missed by a metre.

'I was just curious.'

Jack studied the young man for a minute.

Damian peeled off his ripped maroon shirt and leaned back on the couch in his trousers and Hanes T-shirt. 'How would you like to make some money?'

'What sort of money?'

'How does nine thousand dollars split two ways sound?'

'Sounds illegal.'

'Would that worry you, Jack?'

Jack laughed. He wiped his mouth with the back of his

hand and stared at Damian's sun-tanned arms. He had a lot of muscles for somebody who couldn't fight his way out of a foam cup. 'You work out?'

Damian nodded.

'Why?'

'Because I like to.'

'You should learn to box. Go over to the Police Boys Club in Newtown. Start on the bag. Skip rope. Spar a few rounds. If I was a homo – '

'Gay,' the young man said.

'If I was one that's what I'd do. But I'm not you see, I like women.'

'So you said.'

'It's true,' Jack said. 'That's why I keep saying it.' He took another big slug of beer.

Damian looked over to the door. 'You get many visitors, Jack?'

'No.' Jack shook his head. 'If I want company I can go to work.'

'Where's your bathroom?'

'I'd better show you, it's got a funny light.' He stretched his legs and stood up. Damian followed him down the hall. 'See.' Jack pointed. 'They stuck the switch under the towel rail there.' He leaned against the doorway watching the young man unzip his fly. 'This job of yours. So what would I have to do exactly?'

'It's dead simple.' Damian smiled at him. 'I want you to rob me.'

Light from the streetlamp fell in thin strips across the end of the double bed. Jack lay on top of the grey sheets in his white boxers, gazing up at the cracks in the ceiling. He rolled off the bed and stood in front of the mirror; shiny scar tissue stretched the length of one rib cage. Now and then a car cruised by outside.

Jack wiped the sweat off his forehead and padded into the lounge room. Naked, Damian was bent over a record cover. When he heard Jack, he turned, dropped the record hastily into the pile and slipped back under the blanket on the couch.

'What's going on?' Jack said.

'Nothing. Just looking through your tracks.'

'In the dark?' Jack stood at the window. The upper branches of the fig tree were swaying softly in the breeze; tiny black shadows flitted back and forth across the sky. In the bus shelter below, two broken-faced men argued over a sherry bottle. Jack undid the butterfly clip and lifted the frame a centimetre. He said, 'What were you doing out in Oxford Street tonight anyway?'

'Waiting for my sister.' Damian's voice sounded thick and heavy. 'But she never showed. Angie's like that. She's pretty screwed up. Then those hoons came along and started hassling me. Hey, Jack?'

'What?' Jack turned in the doorway.

'Thanks.'

Jack lay on his bed in the dark. A fruit bat brushed against the window and then a shadow passed across the doorway. Damian came in quietly and sat on the foot of the bed with one leg resting on the mattress. There was no hair at all on his chest. His limbs were smooth.

'I like women,' Jack said softly.

'I remember you saying.' Damian crawled in under the sheets. He pressed his head down against Jack's stomach, his face lost in the shadows.

'I like their breasts,' Jack said. He closed his eyes.

2

The clatter of the machines drove any other thought from Jack's mind. He lugged two sacks into the office. The accountant, in a cheap checked suit, was punching figures onto a calculator while Carlos, the day manager, stacked two hundred dollar-lot bags inside the walk-in safe. Nobody spoke. Just the coin-counting machines spitting out twenty cent pieces. A coin rolled loose and Jack felt the accountant's eyes on him as he picked it up and dropped it back into the sack. He tipped the sacks one by one into the machines. The noise was deafening. Sweat ran down his collar as he leaned against the wall.

The accountant looked up from his calculator, took a sip of orange juice and said, 'Twenty- seven thousand, five hundred and forty-six dollars and forty cents.'

Jack examined the dirt on his hands. He went out to the toilets, scrubbed his hands hard in the sink and came back out to the bar. The caretaker and his wife were sweeping the floor and cigarette trough, their small grandchild crawling after them. The accountant walked along the rows of pokies checking and securing the poker machine doors before he left.

In the office the manager rubbed his hands with pleasure and banged the safe door shut. He hunted out the air freshener and gave his armpits a good squirt. 'Big night tonight too, Jack. The Minister's coming to open the new floor.'

Jack moved some muscles around on his face.

'I'm going to grab a burger.' The manager looked up at the clock. 'Mind the fort.'

Jack sank into the manager's chair and stretched. A

nerve pinched somewhere near the base of his spine. He rotated his head, running his eyes along the skirting board. A thin triangle of light below the safe stopped him cold. He leapt from the chair and tugged at the metal handle. The safe swung open and he stood there staring at the mountain of money. He crossed to the office door, stuck his head out and checked the foyer. A vacuum cleaner was humming upstairs. Jack chewed hard on his lip then strode into the safe, grabbed hold of the cashbox and tore it open. He stuffed a dozen bills into his pockets and started loading up with coins. Then he stiffened. A noise – some kind of scratching out there. He heard it again. He quietly shut the cashbox and poked his head around the safe door.

Wide-eyed, the caretaker's grandchild looked up at him from underneath the manager's desk. 'How'd you get in here?' Jack said.

There was a loud banging at the front door. Jack jumped back inside the safe, emptied his pockets into the cashbox and slammed down the lid. He stepped out into the office and pushed the safe door up against the metal jam just before a voice yelled,

'Get down, get down!' Two cops were standing in the doorway waving .38s at him.

Jack dropped to the floor as one of the cops went into a crouched firing position, fanning the air with his revolver.

'Who tripped the alarm!' The cop's voice rose in pitch.

A small blue light was flashing high above the safe door. Jack looked up at it in surprise and then over at the two-year-old, playing under the desk.

Instinctively the crouched cop swung his revolver around. 'Fuck it,' he said, his hands shaking.

'Maitie! Maitie!' The caretaker's wife pushed between the two policemen and scooped up her grandchild, 'Madre de Dios!'

The cop relaxed his grip on his gun. 'I thought we had

a hold-up situation,' he said. 'Somebody could've got hurt here.'

The caretaker was waving his hands, trying to conjure up some lost English sentence when the manager barged in. 'What's going on?'

'The kid,' Jack began. He swallowed hard. 'You must've left the safe door open.'

The cop pointed at the still-flashing alarm.

Carlos turned a key in a plug on the wall. The flashing light cut out. 'There are still many problems with our new system. Thank you, officers for your quick response.' He escorted the police to the front door.

'We were in Hungry Jack's when the call come thru,' one of the cops said. 'We never had an armed hold-up before.' There was regret in his voice as he holstered his revolver.

In the office Jack grabbed a chair and slumped into it. He breathed in deeply.

'Just like in Montevideo.' Carlos laughed. He formed the fingers of one hand into a pistol. 'The state of siege.' He disappeared into the safe.

Jack heard him opening and closing the petty cashbox. Jack said, 'How come we got a new alarm hookup then?'

Carlos came out and locked the safe door carefully, a smile sliding across his face. 'Is the Committee's idea, Jack, not mine. They find in the last audit some money is missing.'

Jack shook his head sadly. 'I wouldn't trust those accountants any.'

3

The man in a black vinyl jacket next to Jack at the 20-cent machines wore his hair plastered down over his forehead. A blue crane with its wings outstretched was tattooed on one side of his neck. 'My wife very lucky,' he said. 'She always win.'

Jack watched the large leathery-faced woman playing two poker machines at once.

'She knows which ones pay the big,' the man continued.

'How does she know?' Jack asked.

The man smiled. His teeth were brown and in urgent need of a dentist. 'Some people born lucky.'

'Where you from?' Jack said.

'Before come from Vietnam. My name Pham.'

Jack downed his coffee and clipped on a red bow-tie as Carlos rushed past patting his hair with his fingers.

'Battle-stations, Jack.'

The front door swung open and a big overweight man with a shock of ginger hair was escorted into the foyer by two well-dressed minders. The man wore one elevated shoe. Carlos hurried to greet him, waving his hands with excitement and pointing out the Honours Board and a cast iron bust of Don Quixote's horse. The ginger-haired man smiled politely as he limped towards the staircase in his thick-soled shoe followed by nine stocky Committee Members and their wives in brightly coloured frocks, and then an SBS camera crew and a journalist from ABC radio fiddling with her Sony tape recorder. The foyer filled with cigar smoke and excited voices.

Jack walked over to the front desk and stood under the air-conditioning vent, checking badges. 'Special function tonight, pal,' he said to a pink-eyed little fellow sniffing his way towards the aroma of garlic prawns. Jack rested his big arms on the desk. A young man dashed in off the street in a cloud of eau de Cologne. His streaky blond hair was gelled back and he wore a silk shirt, a plaited leather wristband and sharp linen trousers. When he saw Jack he stopped and clapped his hands with delight.

'Jack!' he said.

Jack looked at Damian as if he'd been hit with a bowling ball. He glanced over his shoulders. 'What the hell are you doing here?'

Damian came over to the desk and squeezed the big man's arm. 'I'm with the Senator's party.'

Jack tilted his jaw towards the stairs. 'One of your crowd is he?'

'You're not jealous are you?'

Jack's face reddened, eyes darting towards the bar. 'They don't like *maricónes* in here.'

'Sorry?' Damian gazed up at the stucco walls. He placed a finger under his nose and sniffed. 'Love the carpet, Jack, but somehow I pictured you more in the City RSL.'

Jack shrugged. 'Weren't a lot of jobs going when I got back from Spain.' He stared at the dark bruising on the young man's mouth as a voice came over the PA: 'Jackpot on number nine. Number nine.'

'That's me.' Jack picked up his clipboard.

Damian touched his swollen lip. 'I need to talk to you later. If you're still about.'

'I'm not going anywhere,' Jack said. Damian went upstairs and Jack walked over to the change booth, placed a hand under the security grill. The Algerian girl's hair was wiry, jet black. He watched her count the fifties into his palm, her dark chocolate skin brushing his.

'*Digame la verdad, guapo?*' she said.

'*Como siempre, guapa.*' He took the cash over to the machine which was lit up and gurgling like an electric waterfall. The players had turned on their stools and were staring at the fat woman and her small Vietnamese husband.

Jack took note of the five Golden Incas in a row.

'See,' Pham said. 'What I tell you.'

The woman signed the book, her white handbag dangling from her big thick wrist like a bangle. She passed the cash to Pham who counted the notes then folded them into his inside pocket and zipped up his vinyl jacket.

'Tell her she'd better not win too much more tonight,' Jack said. 'People might get suspicious.'

Pham grinned and moved a toothpick around in his teeth.

A bunch of men leaned on the bar counter arguing in Spanish and Portuguese. Clouds of blue-grey cigar smoke drifted over their heads. Jack crouched behind them, shadowing the couple on the other side of the bar with his eyes. A whiff of eau de Cologne made him jerk around.

'What are you doing, Jack?' Damian leaned languidly on a poker machine, a full glass of champagne in one hand.

'Working.' Jack straightened, plucking at his damp shirt with his fingers.

Damian moved the glass to his mouth. His skin looked smooth and silky soft. He said, 'I want you to come to a party in Woollahra tonight. The Senator's having a few drinks.'

'Can't.' Jack shook his head. 'I'm busy.'

Damian dropped two coins into the machine near his elbow and pulled. The reels came up all different fruit. 'Do you believe in luck, Jack?'

Jack didn't say anything.

'I believe in it.' Damian nodded his head. 'Just being alive, that's lucky. That's the best luck there is.'

Jack said, 'How come you know this Senator guy anyway?'

'I've known Bryan for years. He was a good friend of my father's when he was alive.'

'I didn't know you moved in such high circles.'

'There's a lot you don't know about me.'

Jack looked at him sideways. A waitress came over and laid a plate of tortilla and tiny cubes of chorizo sausage down on the counter. Arms reached out and before she could turn away the plate was emptied. Toothpicks and red paper napkins littered the bar floor.

Damian edged closer until his shoulder was touching the big man's. 'That job we talked of.'

'What about it?'

Damian put a finger to his lips as heads turned along the bar and the official party entered through the archway, club officials scouting ahead in their maroon jackets, flicking fingers at the waiters. The Senator limped over between the low black tables with the manager hanging off his side.

'This is Jack Butorov, one of our supervisors,' Carlos said.

'Bryan Callagher.' The Senator stuck out a slab of a hand. 'Pleased to meet you, Jack.'

Jack felt the strength of the man's grip and took a liking to him. The Senator wore a double-breasted light-wool Zegna suit which lent a softness to his solid frame.

He fixed Jack with his dark green eyes. 'Young Damian told me what you did.'

Jack felt his face colour; he hoped the Senator didn't notice in this light.

'It was a brave act.' The Senator turned to Carlos. 'You've got a good man here.'

'Oh, Jack's one of our most trusted employees,' Carlos agreed.

'I've invited Jack to the party, Bryan.' Damian said. 'Is that okay?'

The Senator's mouth hardened for an instant, then he

flashed Jack a charming smile. 'Just a few drinks for the local supporters, Jack, but you're most welcome.'

Carlos steered the Senator away towards a few of the more senior members and their wives, saying in a loud voice, *'El Ministro de Canberra!'* and puffing out his cheeks.

Jack stared after the Senator, at his enormous built-up shoe. 'Nice bloke.'

'Oh yes, Bryan's very personable.'

'What'd he do to his leg?'

'Injured his spine at school. The doctors thought he would never walk again.' Damian took a sip of champagne, liked it, took another. When his glass was emptied he pulled out his wallet and tossed a hundred on the bar. 'More champagne,' he called to the barman. 'You can never have enough good bubbly, Jack.' Damian flicked blond hair off his forehead. 'Were you surprised to see me tonight? It was no coincidence me coming here. I knew this was where you worked.'

'Yeah?' Jack rattled some coins in his pockets.

'I rang round every club in town.' Damian leaned forward into Jack's space. 'You see I was trying to contact you.' He stole a quick glance over his shoulder. 'That job we spoke about. I need you to do it tomorrow.'

4

A high white wall extended down the opposite side of the well-lit Woollahra street. Topped with terracotta tiles it might've belonged to some neo-Moroccan stables, though the sign on the door said it was an art gallery. Jack stood outside a large two-storey terrace set back from the road and ran his eyes over the line of cars jammed against the kerb: Alfas, BMWs, Volvos, Saabs, Range Rovers.

Damian was leaning over a camellia bush, making noises like a sick cat.

'You can never have enough good bubbly,' Jack said.

Damian dabbed at his mouth with a handkerchief. He said something that Jack couldn't quite catch, pushed open the iron gate and climbed half a dozen steps to a tiled porch lit by a pair of hanging brass lanterns. Mozart was pouring through the open glass doors.

'Nice pad,' Jack said, sticking close behind.

Polished cedar floorboards echoed underfoot as the hall widened and carried them down to a large airy space occupied by forty to fifty people.

Damian murmured something which sounded like bathroom.

'Don't stray too far,' Jack said. 'We got to talk.' He found a patch of bare wall and positioned himself against it, staring up at the ornate ceiling and at the large paintings on the walls. Everyone else was talking in bunches of fours and fives. A big buzzard of a waiter circled with a silver tray and Jack took one of the rolled up pieces of meat on offer. He bit into its soft squishy innards as a second waiter cut in. 'Chardonnay or Champagne, sir?'

Jack took a fluted glass of what was going and examined the heads on either side of him. He recognised a radio announcer, a TV Games Host and an ex-Attorney General whose name he couldn't think of. Many of the men were business types intent on talking a little louder than each other, while the women were mostly blondes.

On the other side of the room a Chinese guy wearing a charcoal grey suit, blue silk tie, gold Rolex and gold cufflinks was listening to the Senator; in one hand he carried a soft leather briefcase with gold lettering on the front. Every few seconds the Senator beat the air with his big ruddy hands and shook with laughter at some

story he was telling. Behind them, the pianist worked her
fingers into the ivories, never once looking up from the
Steinway.

Jack ditched the grape juice behind a piece of iron
sculpture and folded his arms. He could stand like this
for hours. That's all his job was – standing, checking
badges, being a scarecrow. A man with liver spots on his
face came over, held his glass out. 'Get us another vino,
sport.'

Jack looked at him hard.

'Oh, I'm terribly sorry,' the man croaked. 'Thought you
were the waiter.'

Jack moved down past a large French window thinking
up something cutting he should've said. He stopped in
front of a big chunk of canvas fixed to the wall. Swirls of
black and orange paint growled back at him.

'Mr Frick looking after you?' a deep voice said.

Jack turned. 'Who?'

The Senator leaned a heavy hand on Jack's shoulder.
He must've weighed a hundred and twenty K's at least.
'Sometimes I don't know what to do about that young
man,' he said. He pushed out his jaw, revealing a row of
closely packed teeth.

'Nice pad, Senator,' Jack said.

A smile flickered across the older man's face. 'I wanted
to have a word with you. I suppose Damian's been telling
you all sorts of wild fantasies?'

'No,' Jack said. He felt the full weight of the Senator
pressing down on his collarbone.

'Damian's a charming boy, but a pathological liar. His
own father disowned him for it. Just thought I'd warn
you.' He patted Jack's shoulder heavily. 'If you ever need
a job, I might be able to do something for you.'

Jack opened his mouth to respond – like why'd everyone he ran into think he needed a job? – when the Senator
glanced about the room quickly and said, 'Excuse me a
moment.' He limped across to where the businessman

was snapping his briefcase shut, a flash of gold on both wrists.

Damian appeared with his hair all wet and raked back.

'Where the hell you been?' Jack snapped.

'I thought you'd enjoy it here, Jack.' Damian sniffed. 'All the celebs and everything.'

'You kidding? I feel like a water buffalo at a private swimming pool.' He jerked his head. 'Who's Callagher talking to?'

Damian stood on his toes. 'Oh that's Tony Chiu. One of the richest men in Sydney. He owns half of Chinatown.'

'He sure likes gold,' Jack said. 'You need a good pair of shades just to look at him.' He frowned, smelling scented soap on Damian's skin.

'My dear boy,' a voice croaked. 'Haven't seen you for ages!'

'Hullo.' Damian shifted his eyes.

The man with liver spots and puffy cheeks was clutching a glass of red. He looked to Jack and then back quickly to Damian. 'Well, shan't keep you now. But give me a tingle when you can.'

Jack watched the man embrace a TV *personality* dressed in Akubra and riding boots. 'How come you know all these rich old cane toads? Don't tell me. He was a boyhood friend of your father's.'

'That's right.' Damian sniffed.

'This job you want me to pull.'

Muscles tightened at the edge of Damian's scalp. 'I told you we can't talk about it here.'

'You've told me shit,' Jack said. Then turned and walked away.

Damian caught up with him in the hallway. 'Please, I need your help.'

Jack scruffed the young man by the shirt. Reeled him in until he was fronting two dilated pupils. 'Enough of the jimjam, kid. We're going back to your dump wherever it is, and you're gonna explain everything to me nice and clear.' He loosened his grip as a woman in high heels clacked past.

'We can't go to my place.'

'Why not?'

Damian adjusted the buttons on his shirt, checked the corridor. 'I think there's somebody's watching it.'

'Who?'

'I don't know. Can we go to your flat? I'll tell you everything there, I swear.'

On the porch outside Damian placed his hand inside Jack's arm.

Jack pulled his elbow away roughly.

Damian said, 'Never be ashamed of your feelings, Jack.'

'I ain't ashamed,' Jack said. An ambulance went screaming along Jersey Road, its siren cutting the air like a kukri knife. 'Damian. . .' He looked at him a moment and shook his head. 'Na, it doesn't matter. Let's grab a cab.'

The young man smiled. 'That's the first time you've ever called me by my name.'

They went down into the street. A white Mercedes SL 600 braked in front of the Senator's residence and Tony Chiu came down the steps with his leather briefcase and climbed into the back seat.

Jack watched the Merc pull away from the kerb. 350,000 bucks worth of motor car. He elbowed Damian in the ribs. 'Know what I feel like doing whenever I see rich people?'

'What?'

'I feel like going out and robbing a bank.'

'People don't rob banks anymore, Jack. It's banks who rob people now. Anyway, you're gonna do something much easier, you're gonna rob me.' He glanced nervously up and down the tree-filled street. 'This is only the beginning. How would you like to be able to give up work forever? How would that sound?'

'Like music,' Jack said. 'Like fucking music.'

5

A noise jolted him awake. He lifted his head off the pillow
and listened. Footsteps creaked on the landing. A door
clicked shut in the neighbouring flat then silence. Voices
shouted out in the street and faded. Jack thought about
getting dressed, then thought better of it. Beside him,
Damian was breathing heavily, his body tucked into
Jack's, his fingers clasped tight around Jack's cock. Jack
peeled the fingers off, slipping himself free. The smell of
Damian's eau de Cologne permeated the sheets. He lay
on his back, thinking, trying to figure it. There was
something about the whole set-up he didn't like. Damian
suddenly shuddered like a hooked eel and yelled, 'No,
please no!'

Jack laid a hand on his chest.

'Don't,' he screamed, 'don't!'

'Only a dream, fella,' Jack said. 'Wake up.'

Damian jerked his head off the pillow. The whites of
his eyes were streaked with red. His lips were cracked.

'Remember me?'

'Oh Jack, it was bad, really bad.' He swallowed hard. 'I
was laid out on this concrete slab and an old guy was
cutting into me with a power saw.'

'I'd give the nose sugar away if I was you,' Jack said.

'I'm going to. I swear it.' He shivered and wiped his
moist hands on his chest. There were goose bumps down
his arms. 'What time is it?'

'Early,' Jack said. He looked at his watch. It was 7.45.
A toilet flushed in the flat next door. Light stole in under
the torn blinds and ran along the skirting boards. Jack
worked his lower lip against the ridge of his teeth. 'I been

thinking,' he said. 'This plan of yours. You want me to knock you out in the street?'

'Only a light tap, Jack. Nothing too hard, right.'

'Right,' Jack sucked on a tooth and frowned.

'Just make it look good, that's all.'

'What if something goes wrong?'

Damian blinked nervously. 'What could go wrong?'

'You tell me,' Jack said. 'It's your plan.' He propped himself up on his elbows. A truck rumbled past in the street, shaking the front windows. Two sets of clothes had been discarded in a hasty little bundle near the door.

'Look, Jack. I can't do this alone. I need someone I can trust.'

'You can trust me, kid. But can I trust you?'

Damian slung an arm over the big man's. 'We're partners aren't we?'

Jack fixed him with a cold eye. 'Maybe.' He released a mouthful of used air. 'Whose money are we stealing?'

'I told you. I don't know.'

'But it's in your account.'

Damian gave his head a stubborn shake. 'I just withdraw the cash from the bank and place it in a P.O. box. It's a telegraphic transfer. I lend my account out to certain people and they pay me. That's the deal.'

'Which people?'

'I've never seen them. It's all done over the phone.'

The lines on Jack's forehead deepened. 'This has got more holes in it than a Swiss cheese.'

'It's true. Everybody's doing it since they brought in the new banking laws.'

The front doorbell buzzed. Damian sat up, clutching the sheets to his throat. His eyes flew to the window.

'Stay here,' Jack said. 'Don't come out.' He rolled off the bed and landed on the balls of his feet, snatched a singlet and a pair of underpants out from the heap by the door, checked that they were his and hauled them on. He bent down and felt around under the wardrobe for the thick butt of a pool cue. He padded across the cold lino, taking his time, as the ringing grew persistent.

In the doorway he braced himself, legs apart, the butt of the pool cue concealed behind his back, reached out, turned the deadlock and sprung the door open.

A big-breasted blonde stood on the landing. When she saw Jack she removed a half-bitten fingernail off the buzzer and said, 'You look like shit, Jack.'

'Thanks, Vick. I missed you too.'

The blonde stared at him, expressionless. She inhaled on her cigarette and blew a cloud of low-tar smoke into his face. 'You gonna invite us in or leave us out here with the garbage.'

'I just got up. The place is in a mess.'

'So tell me something new.' She moved towards him and a muffled voice behind her cried, 'Dahdydahdy. Dahdydahdy.'

'Hullo, tiger.' Jack lifted his son up off the floor, placed a big hand at the back of the child's spindly neck to steady it. There was something wrong with the boy. His mouth hung loose and his eyes were kind of sleepy.

Toby looked up at his father. 'I-wan-a- saep-daah. A carium. Dahe. Feeshas, dahe. Shar. . .'

'You liked the fishes did you, precious?' Jack rocked his son gently in his arms. He kissed the crown of his head.

Vick pushed past him and into the flat. She went down to the kitchen and fumbled in her red handbag for her pack of twenty-fives. She lit another cigarette, stubbing its predecessor out on the sink top. 'Desmond's waiting downstairs in the car. We're not staying.'

Jack lowered his son carefully on to the floor as if he might break. The boy tottered about the greasy kitchen, holding his hands up awkwardly.

'You got that cheque?'

He shook his head. 'Friday.'

'I need the money, Jack. Christ, you know how many

times I've been to that clinic?' She pulled at her scratchy hair. Her face looked tired, harried, sunwrecked. She said, 'These tests are driving me crazy. We gotta work out a new arrangement. You'll have to get another loan.' She flicked ash impatiently in front of her.

Jack leaned on the Lemair refrigerator in his underwear, staring at his son in the doorway.

She said, 'Desmond wants to marry me.'

There was a distant look in Jack's eyes as if his thoughts were elsewhere. He said with as much disinterest as he could muster, 'Yeah?'

'You'll have to put in another fifty a week. Just until Desmond's finished his Masters.' She dropped her cigarette onto the lino, ground it out with her shoe.

'Thanks for dropping in, Vick. But I gotta go to work now.'

Toby called from the hall: 'Mahme, mahme!'

'What is it, honey?' Vick crossed to the doorway with Jack behind her.

Bug-eyed, the boy was pointing at the bathroom door.

'Oh I see! So that's why Daddy's so busy today is it?'

'Hey,' Jack grabbed at her skirt. 'Cut the crap, Vick.'

She pushed him off, walked over to the bathroom and toed the door open.

A wet razor glistened in Damian's hand. He stood in front of the long mirror but made no effort to cover himself. His red cock looked shrivelled against the loose sack of his balls.

'Hullo,' he said.

Vick's eyes widened. She strode across to her son and scooped him up off the dirty floor. The muscles in her face were set tight as if she were on a special mission. She hardly even glanced at Jack as she passed. Just murmured out of the corner of her mouth: 'I hope you rot in hell!'

Jack stood where he was. He watched the thin legs of his son kick out as Vick carried him down the hall. The door slammed and a plant crashed over on the landing. He listened to her steps fade and then there was silence until a car started up in the street and sped away making more noise than necessary. For a while he remained where he was as if he were still figuring things out in his head. Then he went into the kitchen and got himself a beer. He took the beer over to the window and stood there drinking it. The fig tree was swaying gently in the wind; the pavement and bus shelter below were smeared with figs and bat shit.

Damian came into the front room towelling his face dry.

'I thought I said to stay in the bedroom.'

'I had to use the toilet, Jack. Did I upset her?'

'Oh no,' Jack said. 'Whatever gave you that idea?'

Damian rolled his shoulders, examined a thumbnail.

Jack stared at his young tanned body and took a long swig of beer. When he'd finished he said, 'Haven't you got any bloody clothes?'

'Sure, Jack. If it bothers you.' Damian went into the bedroom and came out a few minutes later wearing a crumpled shirt, trousers and a plaited leather wristband. He perched on the far edge of the couch and combed his damp hair back with his fingers. 'I'm sorry about your wife.'

'Forget it,' Jack said.

'How old is your boy.'

'Toby turned six in January.'

'Can the doctors do anything for him?'

Jack juggled the glass in his palm, said in a cold hard voice, 'They haven't stopped doing things.' He looked at Damian as if he was about to say something else, then thought better of it.

A siren passed in the street outside; lights flashed against the walls as the noise grew to a deafening pitch, then faded. Jack put the glass down on the window-sill and dropped into a chair. His big empty hands hung over the sides. 'Fourteen years we were together. A long time in anybody's book.'

Damian laid a hand on top of the big man's arm. 'Don't get miserable on me, Jack.'

Jack laughed, rubbed the stubble on his jaw. 'Divorce stories. They're as cheap as old sump oil.'

'I've caused you a lot of trouble coming here, but you won't have to worry about money soon. This is only the start.' Damian dabbed at the bruising on his lip, glanced across at him as if he were waiting for a response.

Jack was staring at a tiny pool of water on the lino. Suddenly he reached out and grabbed the young man's wrist, twisting it roughly.

'What are you doing?' Damian said.

'Synchronising watches. Two o'clock we meet, right?'

Damian's face lit up. All the tenseness went out of his shoulders. 'You know what you have to do then?'

Jack nodded. He still had hold of Damian's wrist and he could feel the young man's pulse racing beneath his fingers.

'The cops'll want to talk to me of course, take down my statement afterwards. But we'll divide the loot up back here.'

'You're a handsome fella,' Jack said. 'I suppose a lot of blokes have told you that.'

Damian smiled. He flicked his blond hair off his face, leaned over and said, 'Kiss me for luck, Jack.'

6

A pack of wild-eyed kids were wolfing down coke and hamburgers on the benches outside Central Court. Strips of dyed cloth dangled from their matted hair. They looked up from their feeding as Jack passed. The caretaker was hosing down the pavement outside the club, his huge Alsatian tethered behind the wheel of a Ford. Jack waved and pushed open the club door. Unemployed Spanish bachelors lounged in the dim light fogging the air with their cigarette smoke. Jose Diaz was cutting up lemons behind the bar.

'Feeling lucky this morning, *tío*?'

Jack took his brandy over to the bank of poker machines and selected the one which looked the fattest. He loaded twenty cent pieces into the slot and settled back, watching the reels roll as he sipped his heart starter. Forty-five bucks later he left the club and walked across the wet black road to the Grand Taverna. He sat in a corner at one of the dark wooden tables and ordered paella for one and a glass of house red to wash it down. Eduardo brought it over with a basket of crisp Italian rolls. He had a big thick moustache waxed at both ends and his eyes were sad.

'I'm going to kill myself! I tell my children this morning. Your father he is going to shoot himself. They don't care if I work my fingers into the ground.'

Jack crunched on a roll.

'Enjoy your lunch,' Eduardo said.

Jack bent over his plate and got down to business. Why did he always get the suicidal waiter? The Proprietor, Pepe, was scratching near the door like a well-fed bantam. He nodded at Jack who nodded back. Funny thing about money. Once you had enough of it like Pepe what was there left to worry about? Only food. Jack lifted his head from his plate, wiped the sticky yellow rice from his lips. Four and a half grand. Enough to pay Vick, fix up the deficit at the Club before the Directors got wise and bank the rest.

'Hey, Eddie!' he called. 'You still keep that piece of lead behind the bar?'

Eduardo came over with it. 'Why you want it for, Jack?'

'I gotta see a guy about a bank withdrawal.'

Eduardo jerked his head at the next table full of sailors. 'Bring it back soon, *por favor. Hoy tendré un dia largísimo.*'

Jack slipped a twenty into Eduardo's palm and glanced up at the clock. '*Muchas gracias, hombre.* I won't be gone long.'

It was ten to two.

He went into the toilet and stuffed the half metre of lead piping down his trouser leg. As soon as this was over he was going to take Toby away someplace. All those drugs they were feeding him – poor little fella. He looked worse every time he saw him. Jack went and stood out in Liverpool Street, adjusting his crotch. A man came out of the club carrying a rolled up newspaper and wearing green shades. The Vietnamese guy. Jack watched him turn down towards Chinatown. He seemed to be in an awful hurry to get somewhere. Jack followed. George Street was filled with American sailors, blacks mostly. Tall lean cats with glasses and short flat hairdos that you could launch an F16 strike from. Several had women hanging off both elbows and were pointing at the shop windows as if they'd never seen such cheap shit before.

A truck backed into a building site and Jack had to wait behind the flags. Another skyscraper was headed for the stars. Pneumatic drills hammered away and the air smelled of piss and cement and brick dust. Jack crossed a ramp, turned left into Goulburn and right at Pitt Street. He had lost sight of the Vietnamese guy amongst the Chinatown faces. He eased the piping up out of his trousers and stashed it under his left arm. Nobody seemed to notice a damned thing here. Good. He preferred it that way. A quick neat job and get away without fuss. He quickened his pace. A car backfired in the street up ahead and then another and another in quick succession – short sharp bursts like a whip cracking. A

woman screamed at the top of her voice and somebody
ran out into the road and there was a screech of brakes.
People dived into buildings and threw themselves down
behind parked cars.

Jack gripped metal and started running towards the
screams. He pushed his way between the terrified shoppers. Two Chinese schoolgirls stood sobbing uncontrol-
lably near the phone box. Heads peered out of shop
doorways.

A man was lying face down outside the Haymarket
Post Office. Dark red blood trickled out of a small hole
beneath his ear. One of his arms was stretched out on the
pavement as if he were grasping at something beyond his
reach. A plaited leather wristband lay severed in the
gutter.

'Jeesus!' Jack said, 'Jeesus!' He bent down, cradled the
warm damp head in his lap and rolled the young man
over very gently. Blood had formed in a sticky dark pool
underneath his jaw and was starting to stream across
the footpath. Where Damian's eyes had once been were
now two black bullet-holes.

Jack eased the head back onto the concrete, stood up
quickly and pulled at the skin on his face.

A crowd was forming around the dead man, their
curiosity grown stronger than their fear. A Samoan
security guard came out of a bank and tried to hold people
back. Then a siren started up from the direction of
Central Station, growing louder and louder until it was a
whirring shrieking noise drowning out every other sound.

Jack leaned against the post office wall staring grimly
into the dancing red lights. He looked at his watch.

It was five past two.

7

He stood by the window and watched the light drain out of the sky. When it was gone and everything around him was black except for a flickering street-light across the road he went over to the shelf above the fridge, reached up and took down the bottle of unopened Scotch. He got out a couple of glasses, ran a thumb round the rims of both of them and filled one to the top. The other glass he set down on the table empty. He drank the full glass, poured out a second hit and drank that too. Dark lines carved themselves deep into his brow. After a while he went over to the phone, picked it up, dialled a number, waited a few moments and said, 'Give me Carlos.'

A voice came on the other end. Jack said in rapid Spanish, 'Can't make it in tonight. Something bad's happened. Yeah, yeah, real bad.' He put the phone down and went across to the table, poured himself another big slug of Black Label and threw it down his throat as though it were tap-water. He sat on the edge of the couch his shoulders bunching at the back, his knuckles showing white against the whisky glass in the cool dark room. When the bottle was almost empty he stood up, grabbed his keys and went out. The laundromat downstairs was leaking blue dye into the storm drain. Jack flagged a cab on the corner and rode it into Taylor Square. He got out at the news-stand, bought a late edition of the Tele-Mirror and scanned the headlines. Nothing – not a damned word. Jack threw the rag into a bin and crossed at the lights. Oxford Street was livening up. He stared into gaunt faces as though he were seeking answers from them. People avoided his eyes. Grey-haired gays as thin as garden rakes were banded together for protection. A pink sign on a hotel door announced: *This is a safe place*. The steroid-fed bouncer outside folded his arms on the footpath. Jack locked eyes with him and the bouncer fingered the pager on his belt.

Heat rose from the bitumen, from the grill plates stuck behind the windows of Thai and Serbian restaurants. The air smelled of cooking meat. Jack went into the Beauchamp Hotel. The dump was packed with Americans. The whole Seventh Fleet appeared to be in town. 'Dewars,' he grunted. 'Double.' The barman lifted his heavy-lidded eyes as if he were going to say something, then thought better of it. Sailors parted to let Jack through. He took his drink over to the window and stood there swaying a little. 'Hey!' a voice twanged. 'You're standing on ma fuckin toe.'

Jack stiffened, turned his head slowly.

A beefy American serviceman with a pale freckly face and a voice like an out-of-tune banjo said, 'You looking for trouble, bud?'

'I ain't looking,' Jack said. 'I'm it.'

The marine leaned a shoulder forward; Jack moved to the side quickly and brought a fist up hard into the pit of his stomach. The marine sat back on his stool sucking air in like a codfish. Feet scuffled on the bar floor. A set of steely dark fingers wrapped themselves around Jack's wrists. Two big black sailors pinned his arms from behind. 'Cool it, man, cool it,' the taller one said. 'What's all this aggro shit for?'

Jack spat on the bar floor.

'Why'd you do that, man? Why'd you hit Dragan?'

'A friend of mine got killed today,' Jack said.

The tall black sailor peered at Jack through wire-framed glasses, nodded at his crewmate who released his grip. 'This fren. What happen to him?'

Jack picked his glass up off the sill and drained it. Dragan was still clutching at his stomach, wheezing through purplish lips. Jack looked down at him and said, 'Murdered.'

'Hey, Virge!' the black guy called to his buddy at the bar. 'Get the man a bev'rage here!' He turned to Jack. 'Police got any idea who kill't him?'

'Dunno,' Jack said. 'I ain't talked to them.'

Virge came over with a tray load of bourbons. Jack took one and threw it down. Faces crowded in around him — myopic young men with shorn crinkly hair and USS Independence stitched on their white tunics. The big black sailor said, 'You move well. You ever fight professional?'

'No.' Jack shook his head. 'I'm a late sleeper.'

The man grinned. Somebody passed Jack a jug and he lifted it to his lips. It was as heavy as an iron bucket. Sailors started clapping as the warm sudsy beer tumbled down his throat and chin. A group of Beauchamp women with bright red lips streamed out of the Ladies toilet and linked arms with the servicemen. Jack steadied himself with a hand on the fun machines. His head was swimming. Next minute a whole mob of them were standing out on Oxford Street yelling into the traffic. The night sky was black and murky. The big Afro-American leaned into Jack's ear, 'Stick around wit us, man, we show you a real sweet time,' and slapped his arm across Jack's back.

Teenage boys were hustling dollars in Taylor Square; an old bag lady was rolled up in a pie-shop doorway. Sailors flexed their muscles, the women under their arms shrieking with laughter from too much cask wine. They went up the stairs of a dark nightclub and stood inside a small draped-off area with blue aluminium lights above a shiny metal bar. A DJ with a bald nicked head flicked a switch and the whole place started to pulse with strobes and music. Jack opened his wallet for the American to get more drinks. His mouth was drier than his boots, his heart beating like a snared bird against his ribcage. He

took his whisky over to a stool in a corner and stared at
the lean bodies slinking across the dance floor, his mouth
getting drier and drier with every drop he took. Soon
even the rap wasn't loud enough to blot it all out.

'Loosen up man. Loosen up,' a voice said.

But all he could do was picture the young man flopped
down in the middle of Pitt Street like some dirty fucking
clothes bag. Damian lying there dead with his eyes shot
out.

Jack stood up so quick that the room tipped. He made
for the stairs concentrating hard on his two feet. A face
jumped out at him from the shadows and his head
exploded with pain. Dragan had a monkey wrench in one
hand. The big black sailor was trying to wrestle it off him
saying, 'Don't rile the natives, man.'

Jack stumbled down the stairs and into the street.
Warm night air rushed at him. Blood was on his hands,
on the collar of his shirt. He tried to prop himself against
the wall, clenching his teeth together like a vice. He was
in the temple of alcohol. Beyond nausea now, beyond
caring. He saw the lights of the city, the blues and greens
and throbbing reds, and staggered towards them.

Three thin youths crept out from under a concrete
ramp and followed him down Oxford Street. They stayed
seven, eight metres back all the way, their eyes lit yellow
by the headlights of the cars. Jack stopped; they stopped.
He turned, pulled out his wallet and emptied it on the
pavement. 'Here. Take it,' he yelled. 'It's yours.'

They watched him closely, but didn't move. He turned
away. When he reached the park he glanced over his
shoulder. The three youths were down on their knees
scooping up notes and coins. Jack pressed two fingers
against the lump on his head; the fingers came away wet.
He had to find somewhere. His legs were gone. A derro
on a wooden bench hissed as he drew close and something
furry skittered up a tree. All the other benches were
taken; furrowed faces glared up out of smelly dark bun-

dles. Jack staggered along the edge of the path. The city hung over Hyde Park like some monstrous shadowy neighbour, its tall sharp buildings knifing the sky. He went down some steps and crossed Elizabeth Street. The honey-combed towers were swollen with light: the dirty bright city, the hard shitty city. He looked up at the ugly tubes of concrete and his legs buckled. His hands shot out and grabbed at a shop window. White-faced mannequins watched expressionless as he fell. His head banged against the plate glass. Damian. Blinking up at the burning office lights. Crawling across the pavement on his hands and knees. Never know how much people mean to you. Never. Rolling up into a ball on the cold marble steps of a shop doorway, Jack passed out.

8

He woke late next morning, one leg pointing towards St James's station, the other leg pointing up Elizabeth Street. Somebody had moved him. A man with a cap and grey side-whiskers held open the door to David Jones, his back stooped from years of bowing. Had to have been him. Jack tried to focus on the Saturday morning shoppers as they stepped around his legs. Disgust was written on their faces. He propped himself up against DJ's window, smearing the glass. A sharp pain stabbed at the back of his eyes. He got to his feet slowly, like a man learning to walk again, steadied himself on the iron railing. A group of schoolgirls went by. Jack could smell their hair. The lights turned green and he shuffled across Elizabeth Street, leaned against the wall of St James's station. The headlines on the news-stand leaped up at him:

MAN SHOT DEAD IN CITY

He grabbed a *Herald* off the pile, ran his eyes over the front page.

A 24-year-old man was gunned down yesterday in broad daylight. Shoppers were forced to scatter at lunchtime as two gunmen opened fire in lower Pitt Street. Homicide detectives have withheld the dead man's name, but have set up a hotline number 008 433659 and appealed for witnesses to come forward.

'A dollar twenty.' The newspaper seller thrust out a grimy claw.

Jack patted his pockets, trying to speed-read the rest of the column:

Pressure continues to build on the State Government to introduce stronger anti-gun legislation in the wake of yet another fatal Sydney shooting.

'Dollar twenty!' The man snatched the *Herald* back.

Jack looked down at the man's dirty bird-like face and tried to shake his head but a pain cramped his forehead. Slowly he walked into the park. The city cast a long shadow over the grass. There was no sunlight here. A fresh young man with wide eyes and ironed jeans stepped out from behind the public toilets and said: 'We've got some coffee and tuna and egg sandwiches in the van.'

Jack followed him across to a rusty Bedford parked in Phillip Street. A big sturdy woman with flabby arms was distributing cups of steaming liquid to a handful of living human wrecks.

Jack took a cup of what looked like mud in both hands, drank it down eagerly, gulping and blinking his eyes. 'I need busfare,' he stammered.

The woman pressed a two dollar coin into his palm. 'Give the bottle away, mister, before it kills you.'

He smiled weakly and got away from there just as soon as the young man brought out a shiny new guitar and started plucking at the strings and calling on his trembling bronchitic audience to join in a singsong. The 372 bus was packed with women bowlers and Jack had to wear their stares all the way to Coogee. He slid down the steps, crossed the road and went round the back of the laundromat. The Greek woman who owned the sandwich bar next door was taking an inordinate interest in his arrival. On the landing he stopped outside his door and took out the key. A cigarette butt was pressed into his geranium pot. He picked it up, examined the filter between his fingers. Vick didn't smoke Benson and Hedges and he didn't know any first grade cricketers either. He turned the lock, stepped inside and listened. The place was quiet. He took the whisky bottle out to the kitchen and emptied the remainder down the sink. Enough of the self-pity. From now on in he had to use his nut. He shaved, showered and changed into his black and whites, burying the bloodied shirt in the bin. A soft scab had formed on his temple and he trimmed the hair around it. He scrambled some eggs roughly in a pan, sat down with them in front of the TV and ran through the channels. Nine was the first to come up with a news break:

'Lunchtime shoppers in Sydney yesterday were horrified by the brutal slaying of a twenty-four-year-old male model. Innocent bystanders ducked for cover as Damian Andrew Frick, 24, of King's Cross, was shot dead near Haymarket in what police believe was a robbery attempt which went terribly wrong.'

Jack pulled at his jaw. Pictures of Chinatown flashed across the screen and a journalist shoved her mike under the nose of some nervous local citizens outside the Oriental House Emporium. Jack removed a sliver of eggshell from between his teeth. It was only a matter of time now before the cops got onto him. The Senator knew his name.

They'd be crawling all over the club soon and those
Homicide boys weren't known for their delicate touch.
The phone rang three, four times. Jack lifted himself out
of his chair and picked it up on the fifth. The line went
dead as soon as he spoke.

He kicked the off switch on the TV and went across to
the window, looked up and down the street. Nothing. A
Mercedes bus steamed past with some old ladies hanging
on to their summer hats. Maybe he should go to the cops.
And tell them what? That he and Damian had become
lovers? That they had been planning to knock off nine
grand together? That the money was to come from Damian's own account which had been 'lent out' to persons
unknown? With a story that loose the cops were bound to
brick him up with a Long Bay holiday. Think, Jack,
think. He grabbed his red tie and knotted it tight around
his throat. He was in this up to his fucking ears. He went
into the bedroom, rummaged in his sock drawer for his
last twenty bucks. Then he went downstairs and hailed a
cab. All the way into the city the driver, a scaly-skinned
Queenslander with thin lips, talked about how the econ-
omy was rooted, how Kerry Packer should become the
new President of the R.O.A. 'Desperate times need desperate measures, matey.'

'There's certainly a lot of desperates around,' Jack
agreed and pocketed his change.

He got out, swung the club door open and passed
through the smoke-filled foyer. The office walls were
carpeted with the same fire-resistant red pile that graced
the floors. Carlos got up out of his seat smelling of
rosewater when he saw Jack. 'Just the man. I want to
show you something.' He steered Jack over to a stack of
local Spanish newspapers. Up close Jack could see talcum
powder sprinkled across the back of Carlos' thick neck.
'Look at this, look at this.' Carlos was sweating with
excitement. On page one was a photo of the assistant
manager gripping the Senator's hand and smiling. '*El*

Senador Callagher y Señor Carlos Perez...' the caption
began. 'What do you think, Jack? *Bueno,* huh?' Carlos
took out a big white handkerchief and dusted his forehead. 'A strong man I think. *'Un hombre con cojónes!* A
man with balls, Jack. *Me entiendes?*'

'Loud and clear,' Jack said.

Carlos lowered himself back into his seat, patted his
stomach in under the desktop and reached for his coffee.
'Everything alright at home?'

'My sister's boy,' Jack said. 'Motorbike accident.'

'The young people these days.' Carlos floated his coffee
in sugar. 'Where are they going so fast?'

Jack looked at him. The buzzer rang out in the foyer.
He lifted himself off the edge of the assistant-manager's
desk and peered through the one-way glass.

A woman was bent over in the foyer examining the
statue of Don Quixote's horse. She had long brown muscly
legs that stretched up to a gathered fifties skirt, a wide
leather belt and a loose creamy top which set off her
broad swimmer's shoulders. Jack watched her straighten.
He wrapped a hand round the metal doorknob, twisted it
firmly and went outside to take a closer look. She was
about thirty-four, thirty-five with faint-lined cheeks and
a nice shaped mouth. She wasn't what he called pretty –
attractive yes, sexy sure, but not pretty. She had a face
that had lived plenty and wasn't hiding one bit of it. She
removed her wrap around sunnies and a pair of hard blue
eyes stared at him from underneath thick dark eyebrows
which looked as if they had never seen tweezers in their
life.

'You finished inspecting me?' Her voice was sharp
enough to cut floor tiles.

'I was just looking.'

'Well I'm not a bookshop,' she said. 'Manager in?'

'He's in,' Jack said, 'but he's digesting his coffee.'

'Maybe you can help me. I'm looking for a doorman
called Jack.'

'Yeah?' Jack said. 'A lot of doormen are called Jack. It's a common name for doormen. Like Eric for electricians.'

The woman fixed him with her dark blue eyes. 'He said you were handsome in a rugged sort of way. Maybe the light's all wrong in here.'

'This is a licensed club,' Jack said. 'We like it dark and smoky. So you got a name?'

'Angela.'

'Do I know you from somewhere? I'm real forgetful with faces.'

'You're not my type, Jack. Enough of the cheap spiel anyhow. We need to talk.'

He ushered her through into the bar, pulled up a pair of chairs at one of the low black tables. A party of pensioners stood around pumping the poker machines with little coin purses scrunched up in front of them.

Angela took out a packet of cigarettes. Benson and Hedges Extra Mild.

Jack said nothing. He liked to be one step ahead.

She slit the cellophane neat with a long fingernail, screwed a cigarette in between her dark red lips and lit it. Then she thrust her elbows down onto the table. 'I want to know what happened, Jack? Who killed him?'

'I got no idea,' he said.

She leaned forward. 'I know all about you. You were fucking my brother right. Now he's dead. I want to know who did it and I want to know why.'

Jack glanced over his shoulder. Jose Diaz had stopped cutting lemons behind the bar. 'Keep your voice down,' Jack said.

'Don't you tell me what to do!' Her big silver earrings jangled against the sides of her neck. 'I've just come from Glebe. From seeing him laid out on a concrete slab. Ever done that, Jack? Ever identified dead family? Well I can tell you one thing: there's nothing in this whole world that's nearer to hell. So if I feel like raising my voice then I will – okay?' She bared her teeth at him and for a crazy moment Jack thought she was going to leap across and sink them into his face. Then she rocked back on the legs of her chair, smiling uneasily.

Jack looked up at the video monitor: a thin young matador from Badajoz was sticking it to some fat old bull. He scraped a knuckle along the line of his jaw and frowned. 'How'd you get onto me?'

'Three nights ago he rang. It was late. Real late. He sounded weird – like he was out of it. He said that if anything bad should happen to him I should see you. He made me write down your address. I was pissed off because it's not much fun talking to someone doing chemicals at three-thirty in the morning. I asked him if he was in some kind of trouble. He just gave this stoned laugh. 'You know me, Ange. Always in trouble.' She picked up a coaster and began to shred it with her nails. 'Well, I do know my brother. I know he always had some scheme going. What was it? What were you two up to?'

Jack raked the bar with his eyes. Jose Diaz was stacking bottles of Corona into the fridge. The lunchtime crowd hadn't come in yet.

'He had this plan. He needed somebody else in. So I said yeah.'

'What sort of plan?'

Jack lifted his shoulders.

'Spill it, Jack.'

He leaned forward and glanced down at her uncrossed legs. They were so smooth those legs he guessed she must've just had them waxed. He caught a strong smell from her scalp and a whiff of perfume as he bent close to her ear. He told her how Damian had lent out his account to persons unknown, he told her the works. When he finished talking she jerked her head away quickly as if there was something wrong with his breath. Her hard blue eyes didn't flicker at all, but he could see her throat swallow.

'So that's why you haven't been to the police yet?'

'How'd you know?'

'Cause when I mentioned your name they seemed very interested.'

Jack gripped the edge of the table. 'You *told* them about *me*?'

Angela pulled at her dark hair. 'It was funny. Afterwards they asked me twice as many questions.'

Jack shut his eyes tight, pressed his forefingers hard up against the bridge of his nose.

'You alright?'

'Headache,' Jack said.

'I don't think they give a damn about Damian. There's two types of people in this town who get second-rate treatment from the law. One is prostitutes and the other is gays. So what hope in hell does Damian have?'

Jack looked at her sharply.

'Yes, Jack. Damian was a rent boy. For someone who's obviously been around, you're surprisingly naive.' She clicked her fingers at the waiter who came over to their table. 'Vodka and lime. No ice.' She turned to Jack. 'What are you drinking?'

'Nothin,' Jack said. 'I gave up.'

'How long ago?'

'A few hours.'

She watched the waiter glide back to the bar. 'So he didn't tell you. I'm not surprised. Damian'd come a long way from the Wall, but he was still selling it.' She mashed her cigarette out in the Don Quixote ashtray.

Jack stared at the dark violet shadows under her eyes. A crucifix hung around her neck and he wondered if it was just there for decoration. Jose Diaz brought her vodka over and she brought it straight to her lips. 'What are you looking at?' she said.

Jose grinned, backed away.

She pulled the hem of her skirt down. 'I want you to help me, Jack, find out who did this to my brother. I can pay you if you like. Damian said you liked money.'

'That right?'

'Yes. He told me a lot of things.'

'All in that one short phone call?'

'You bet.' She twisted her hair in her fingers and a cracked expression came over her face. 'He said that you were a desperate man. He said you'd do anything for a buck.'

Jack said, 'Only thing he ever said bout you was that you were pretty screwed up.'

Angela's hard blue eyes flickered fast; her hand moved as quick as a snake. Jack jerked to one side but he was too slow. The glass caught him on the side of the cheek and shattered on the floor.

She stood up fast. Her lips were curled back over her white uneven teeth. 'You're just another burnt-out low-life,' she said. 'Sydney's crawling with your type!'

It flashed through his mind as he wiped the alcohol from his stinging eyes that he should send her flying right now.

She kicked back her chair. 'Fuck your sleazy club!' Members looked up from their spinning lemons as she stamped across the foyer, arms swinging and fisted the door open. Light flooded in from the street and then it was semi-dark again.

'Man, that is one hot-blooded lady.' Jose Diaz whistled. 'What you say to her, *tío*?'

'Shut up, Jose!' Jack fingered the spot below his eye. 'Go get a broom.'

Carlos emerged from his office, croissant crumbs masking his lips. He frowned at Jack. 'What was all that about?'

'Dunno,' Jack said. 'Never seen her before in my life.'

9

A sea breeze tore at Jack's shirt. He walked along the cliff edge, looking down at the huge slabs of sandstone below. Half a kilometre out to sea some surfers, seal-like in their sleek wet-suits, were waiting for that next big wave. Jack wondered if their mothers knew where they were. He leaned on the rail, gazed out over Wedding Cake Island. He'd read somewhere that gay-related murders accounted for over thirty per cent of homicides in New South Wales. Whoever had killed Damian presumably knew about the nine grand. He had gone over and over it in his head. He was in deep water. And like those boardriders down there would have to be very careful that he wasn't carried in onto the rocks. For the first time since he'd returned to Australia, he wished he was back in Madrid. He couldn't get Damian out of his mind. Those two short nights with him had been more enjoyable than the last two years with Vick, but he'd suspected from the start he was going to pay for them.

He turned away from the dark rippling sea and walked towards home. The sun was going down over the hideous blocks of Coogee flats. Outside the Delphi Delicatessen bunches of yellow chrysanthemums drooped in a plastic bucket. Jack went inside. The Greek woman's shop always smelled so sweet, of figs and nectar and rotting fruit. Her head barely reached above the glass counter; wisps of grey hair hung off her chin like Spanish moss. When she saw him her lined face darkened.

'Hullo, Pythia,' Jack said. 'Got any of your wheat and honey cakes left?'

'I want to speak to you.'

Her eyes warned him it was serious.

'Two men come in here asking questions about you. They go up to your flat. A long time they are gone. I watch them leave.' Tiny hands fluttered from the raggedy black sleeves of her widow's cardigan. 'I can still smell them in my shop. Be careful. These are evil men.'

He took the stairs very carefully, leaning on the wall to avoid the weakened floorboards. He had a bad feeling in his balls about this – like someone had slipped a loop of chicken wire around them. On the landing he paused, hand gripping the bannister. His front door stood wide open and voices were coming out of his bedroom. He inched down the hall, muscles tensed. The voices were loud. He jumped sideways through the bedroom doorway, blood pumping, arms rigid. All the drawers were pulled out of his pineboard dresser and the bedside radio squawked back at him. Jack flicked it off and dropped on to the edge of his bed, let the tightness go out of his neck while his eyes scanned the room. Then he went right through the flat checking everything he owned. The place had been turned over, but nothing was missing. He worked his key into the deadlock in the front door, tested the spring. It hadn't been forced. These guys were either pros – or else worse.

Shoes hit the stairs outside and banged down hard on the landing. Jack threw his weight against the front door just as a large blunt-toed shoe forced its way in between the door-edge and the jamb and a voice growled: 'Open up. Police.'

He stepped back. Two hard-looking men in dark brown suits stood there with their hands reaching inside their jackets.

'No encyclopaedias today thanks, fellers,' Jack said in an unsteady voice.

'Still the same smartarse, Butorov,' snarled the leaner man. He had a flat busted nose, thinning hair and a crooked jaw. When he talked it was like he had a big piece of gristle stuck in his mouth. 'You shouldn'ta come back to town, shithead. That was the second dumbest thing you ever did.'

'This a social call, Lindsay, or you just practising your break and enterin skills?'

'We got some questions for you, Butorov. You wanna talk here or else we go for a little drive together.'

Jack said, 'I ain't going nowhere with you two cork-screws until I see a warrant and some ID.'

The shorter one laughed. 'He'll be wanting to make a fuckin phone call next.' He had big gapped teeth and was wearing Cuban heels. A long white scar ran across the knuckles of one meaty fist.

Jack ignored him. His eyes were fixed on the lean man's crooked jaw. He was thinking if he had the chance to take out anyone, Quarrell was the man to nail first. 'I heard you'd left the force, Lindsay.'

'Well you heard wrong shithead. And it's Detective Sergeant to you.' He prodded Jack hard in the chest with his blunt fingers. A foul smell lingered in the door-way like bad teeth. 'Friday two o'clock. Where were you?'

Jack backed slowly into the hall. 'Grand Taverna, Liverpool Street.'

'Got any witnesses?'

'Pepe Valbuena and Eduardo Lopez.'

'You know Damian Andrew Frick?'

'I did,' Jack said.

'We hear you were cornholing him. That true?'

Jack stopped against the wall, clamped his lips together.

The stocky detective leered into Jack's face. 'He's an arse bandit.'

'You wanna be careful where you stick that dick of yours, Butorov. I hear that dead faggot's blood was so infected with HIV even the morgue boys wouldn't touch him.' His dead-grey eyes watched Jack closely.

'The new broom they put through the force, Quarrell. It must've missed you two rat-tails,' Jack said.

Detective Sergeant Quarrell grabbed Jack by his shirt front and slammed him up against the bedroom doorway. His other hand jumped out from under his jacket and it was packing an ugly lump of steel. He jammed the two inch barrell of his Smith and Wesson .38 Special under Jack's chin, forcing his head back against the architrave. 'I can blow you away now, shithead, and it'd be like squashing a roach. I wouldn't even have to fill out the paperwork.'

His partner clicked his tongue: 'Shoot the cunt, sarge.'

Jack braced himself against the wood, left eye twitching like crazy, the revolver's muzzle digging into his skin, knowing too well that Quarrell was capable of doing it. Knowing he'd done it before. 'An unarmed man shot dead in his own flat,' he said. 'No search warrant. It might've worked in the good old days, Lindsay, but they're long gone.'

'When questioned, the suspect confessed to having arranged his lover's death.' Detective Sergeant Quarrell's voice was slow and flat like he was talking into a tape recorder. 'When told the victim had tested HIV positive, the suspect then grabbed a kitchen knife and threatened the lives of the two investigating officers. In the ensuing struggle the man was shot dead.' Turning towards his partner, 'How does that sound, Bill?'

Detective Brown grinning. 'Yeah, I'd buy it. Part the prick's ears.'

'Well I wouldn't!' Jack was right up on his toes, straining to get away from the man's dog breath, waiting for the bullet to come that would shatter his bones and teeth, separate soul from body. 'Neither would Internal Affairs. They might even dig around in the past.'

Sergeant Quarrell's eyelids dropped a fraction and he yanked his police special out of Jack's face. 'You're a dead man anyway, Butorov. You just don't know it yet. One morning soon you're gonna be crossing that road down-stairs and you ain't gonna see the bus that hits you.' He nodded at Brown who moved to Jack's other side. 'Person-ally I don't give a shit about your little dead hump, but I think you mighta done it anyway. So we're gonna check your story out and then we're gonna pay you another visit. Only next time we won't be so fuckin pleasant.'

Jack smoothed at the dent in his throat with his fingers. 'There's only one thing lower than a bent cop, Quarrell, and that's two of 'em.'

Detective Brown swung a meaty fist which travelled from up high and landed hard and low under his ribs. Jack's mouth opened like he was going to scream, but no sound came out; his eyeballs rolled upwards. Then Detec-tive Quarrell jerked him around by the shoulders and crashed his knee right between Jack's legs. It was a quick, neat job.

Jack dropped to the floor gasping as a black pain exploded in his balls. Vomit rose in the back of his throat. He pressed his forehead down hard against the cool dark lino as waves of nausea flooded his body.

'There's still one good thing about the force they can't take away from you, Billy.' Detective Quarrell adjusted the sleeves of his snuff-coloured suit jacket. 'And that's the job satisfaction.'

The two cops drifted towards the door. Halfway down the hall Quarrell turned and muttered out the side of his buckled face: 'Any complaints, Butorov, take them up with the Ombudsman.'

Detective Brown's laughter lingered in the doorway. Jack could taste grit and dust on the end of his tongue. He stayed down on the floor with his mouth open and hot wires burning holes where his testicles used to be. He had an overwhelming urge to piss but he couldn't make it to the bathroom. A TV was playing theme music through the thin walls: *The Bill*. Boards creaked out on the landing and a dark figure moved in the hall. Quarrell had come back to finish him. For a moment Jack was almost glad of it, he wanted to be rid of the past. For three years he'd tried not to think about that. Now it was out in the open again.

10

'You alright?' A black-haired angel was bending over him. 'What's wrong?'

His lips mouthed the word, 'Balls.'

Angela lifted his elbows like a pair of crumpled bird's wings. 'Keep your head down between your legs.' Pumping his arms. 'Breathe in,' she said. 'Now out. Come on. It'll pass.'

Getting to his feet was like climbing Uluru. He limped into the living room, leaning on her broad bare shoulders. She wore a pair of green culottes and a white sleeveless top. As far as he could tell she wasn't wearing any deodorant either. 'What are you doing here?' he said, surprised at how high-pitched his voice sounded.

Hard blue eyes stared back at him from underneath her dark eyebrows. 'The police do this?'

'Yeah.' Jack sunk down into the sofa, cupping his genitals and breathing real careful. 'They had a few questions for me. Like how to get to Bondi Beach. Routine stuff.'

'I saw them down in the street. That Detective Sergeant. He's the one who interviewed me. He's the officer in charge of the investigation.'

Jack tried to laugh.

'They got something on you?'

'Cops are like elephants. Big feet and long memories.'

He took his hand away, let the air hiss out through his teeth. 'What are you doing in my flat?'

'I wanted to talk.'

'I thought you'd already done that.' His fingers went up to his cheek.

'You shouldn't've said what you did. You don't know anything about me. You're just somebody my brother picked up in the street.'

Jack said, 'So you're not going to apologise then?'

'No,' she said, 'but you are!' Glaring at him with her feet apart like she was going to kick him one herself.

'Okay. I'm sorry. So you're not screwed up.' She was standing in the middle of his living room like some genie in her green culottes. Small freckly nose, familiar lips.

She unzipped a polka dot purse, counted out five hundred dollars in worn fifties and twenties and dropped them into his lap. 'There,' she said.

Jack didn't move. 'The apology's free.'

'That's for the first week. If we find Damian's killer you'll get another five hundred. You and I are going to find out who did this.'

'I'd like to help you,' Jack said. 'But I'm leaving Sydney.'

'You're running away, that it?' She raised an eyebrow.

'I'm not a private eye, I'm a doorman,' Jack said. 'All that stuff you watch on TV with amateur sleuths in trenchcoats beating the cops to the clues, that's all bullshit. Police departments have got million-dollar forensic labs, they've got helicopters, computers. I've got no gun, I haven't even got a fuckin car.'

'I have,' she said. 'I'll pick you up in it tomorrow 8.30 sharp.'

He brushed the money off his knees. 'What can we do? You tell me one thing that we can bring to this that the cops can't.'

'The police are just going through the motions. You know that. They don't care about Damian.'

'It don't matter whether they care or not, it's whether they catch the people who did this.'

She stared at him coolly. 'Your Detective Sergeant Quarrell. He's going to catch them?'

'Dunno,' Jack said. 'But one thing's for certain. If I stick around here Quarrell's going to make a road accident out of me.'

'What'd you do to him?'

'I did nothin, but he's threatened to kill me anyway. He'd do it too.' He pushed himself up onto his feet, shot a hand out to steady himself. 'I hear there's a big demand for bouncers in Buenos Aires.'

She turned away and walked across to the window, looked down onto the street below. For a long while she didn't say anything.

Jack could smell her scent in the small room. He moved towards her and she stiffened.

'There's a car down there,' she said. 'It's not the police, but I think someone's watching this flat.'

Jack leaned over her bare shoulder and squinted into the dark: two men in a Commodore Berlina parked outside the bus shelter. He couldn't make out their faces, but he had a good idea of what they were doing. 'They're not watching us,' he said. 'That park. It's a pick-up place for gays.'

She pulled away from the window, averting her face from his as if she thought it might betray what she was thinking. 'Damian used to come back here?' Her voice sounded different, softer.

'Yeah,' Jack said. 'Twice.'

She lit a cigarette and sat on the arm of the couch. 'When I left home he was only nine years old. Mum'd died two years earlier and I got in with the wrong set, wiped myself out more times than I care to remember. Five, six years ago I dropped out of the scene and watched Damian going down the same path I had.' She blew smoke down at the boards. 'You wouldn't understand, but

I owe my brother. There were a hundred things I should've done.'

Jack said, 'You can't tell people what to do. You've got to let them make their own mistakes.'

She turned her head and fixed him with her blue eyes. 'The police told me there were two witnesses to the shooting. Maybe if we talked to them, we might find out something.'

Jack said, 'What makes you think Homicide are gonna just hand over names and addresses?'

'They don't have to.' She dug around in her purse, fished out a torn-off sheet of paper with typing on one side. 'It was just sitting there on top of the desk.'

Jack said, 'You're serious aren't you?'

A smile wrinkled the corners of her nose, and he wanted to reach out and touch her mouth, run his rough chapped fingers over those full lips.

She said, 'I can't do this alone, Jack.' She slid off the couch and peered behind the stereo. 'You got an ashtray?'

He pointed to the kitchenette where a frypan, two plates and a large black cockroach were soaking in the greasy sink. He waited until he heard her opening and shutting cupboards then counted the notes quickly, folded them and stashed them in his back pocket. His eyes met hers as he straightened up. 'Find it?'

She nodded her head, watching him closely. 'I've got to go now.' Her voice was tight.

He stepped in front of her. 'You can stay here if you like.'

Her eyes flicked at him.

'I'm not talking sex. I don't think I'm capable of that. I just mean if you want – ' He lifted his shoulders, rolled his big hands over.

'No thanks. I've already got somebody and you and me – we're strictly business.'

He watched her walk down his hall. He liked the way she moved. There was a sureness about where she was going. 'By the way,' she said, turning her head. 'I'd do something about your kitchen.'

'Yeah. What do you recommend?'

'Cleaning it for a start.'

'You got to clean kitchens?'

'Funny man.' She pulled the door shut behind her and he heard her steps fade on the stairs, then he went down to the toilet, leaned one hand on the cistern and fumbled in his fly with the other. An engine fired up in the street outside and a car drove off with a squeal of rubber as he watched the water in the bowl turn red. He flushed, closed the lid and removed all his clothes, hung them over the seat and examined himself carefully with his fingers: his balls were swollen and discoloured; a long purple bruise was spread across one kidney. He rubbed at the long puckered scar running down his left breast, reached into the shower recess and turned on the tap. One week is what he'd give her and then she was on her own. It was time to get out.

11

Eight-thirty the next morning she was standing on his doorstep wearing brown Ray-Bans, jeans, a black cotton top and a pair of ox-blood Doc Martens.

'Got the same pair myself,' Jack told her. 'Wear em on the door.'

'Are you ready?' She jangled her car keys at him.

'Hold on.' He took a bite of cheese toast, ran thick fingers through what remained of his hair, and swallowed.

She stared up at the posters lining the hall: *Corrida*

Del Toros, Pamplona; Goya's *The Burial of the Sardine*. 'I meant to ask you,' she said. 'What's the attraction with Spain?'

Jack came out of the bedroom tucking an alligator sports shirt into his new grey linen trousers. 'I lived there for three years.'

'Doing what?'

'Working bars, picking olives, helping rich people practise their English.'

'You speak Spanish?'

'I get by,' Jack said. He turned his key in the deadlock, closed the door behind them and went down the stairs. A butter-cup yellow EH Holden was parked outside the laundromat, sunlight bouncing off the chrome strips and creamy white roof.

'This yours?'

She got in behind the wheel and removed the steering lock.

'It's in good nick.' He slid in beside her. The back seat was taken up with skirts, old coats and dresses. She planted her foot and swung the wheel. Ice-cream wrappers and chip packets swirled around under his feet. 'You should do something about cleaning your car,' he said. He reached for the safety belt as they tore down Alison Road, found the strap had been chewed clean through; he could see the teethmarks. 'Your boyfriend do this?'

Angela ignored him, kept her eyes fixed on the road.

'Where'd you say you lived again?'

'I didn't.'

'That's what I like. An open partnership.'

She turned and stared at him through her Ray-Bans. 'This isn't a partnership, Jack. I'm paying you.'

'So I'm the muscle, that it? You're the brains?'

'Something like that.'

She crossed Anzac Parade and steered left along Dacey Avenue past the links. Jack squinted out his window. The sky was so blue it made everything – factories,

chimneys, Japanese golfers – stand out in sharp relief.
Waterloo wasn't the kind of suburb you ever stopped in;
it was more the place you passed through on the way to
somewhere else. Unless, that is, you were on the Department of Housing waiting list; then you might end up in
one of the thirty-storey concrete towers which shot up
from between the lawns and narrow paths of the huge
housing estate. Angela parked in Phillip Street, locked
her Club Bar onto the steering wheel. A gang of teenagers
bounced past spitting in front of their shoes, baseball
caps pulled down low over their brows. She checked the
slip of paper and walked across the dried-up lawn. Jack
followed. The place looked like a hospital, there were that
many elderly people tottering about. She went in through
the glass doors of one of the fawn-coloured tower blocks
and ran her eyes over the directory in the foyer. 'Resi-
dents are advised that the Dept of Housing will no longer
remove old beds, TVs, robes or refrigerators,' a notice
said.

They rode up in the small lift, Jack wondering how
they'd fit the robes and fridges in here anyway. Angela
slipped off her Ray-Bans and led him down a poorly-lit
corridor which smelled of yesterday's pork chops. She
stopped outside number 1408 and knocked loudly.

'Let me do the talking, Jack, okay?'

'Sure,' Jack said. 'I'll just do the heavy lifting.'

Her eyes flashed at him as a bandaged arm appeared
around the edge of the door and a freckly-faced ginger-
haired woman said, 'Yeah?'

'Mrs McEvoy?'

The woman's mouth tightened like a zip. 'Whaddya
want?'

Angela opened her purse. 'I wondered if we could have
a few words with you, Mrs McEvoy. It's about the murder
you witnessed in Chinatown.'

The woman frowned. 'I told the cops everythin. You
reporters?'

Angela held up her gold driver's licence. 'I'm Angela Frick. The young man who was murdered was my brother.'

'Oh, I'm sorry,' the woman said, but didn't open the door any further.

Angela nodded abruptly. 'Can I ask you some questions, Mrs McEvoy?'

'Celia,' she said. 'I'm not married. Just told the cops that. You know what cops're like, want to know every damned thing.'

A child was crying in the background. Celia rubbed at a red eye with a knuckle, yelled over her shoulder: 'Turn it down, Walter.'

The crying cut out all of a sudden.

Jack stretched on his toes, trying to see behind the door. 'Can we come in and talk?'

'Talk out ere,' the woman said. 'I thought you two was Social Security. They been sniffing around the flats all week.'

Angela said: 'Can you tell me what you saw exactly, Celia?'

'Like I told the police. Your brother was turning into the post office when these two men ran up and tried to take his briefcase off him.'

'What did they look like?'

'Asians they were – black hair, brown eyes.'

'Asia's a pretty big place,' Jack said. 'Were they Thais, Koreans, Cambodians?'

Celia narrowed her eyes at Angela. 'They was Asian that's all.'

Angela said, 'Go on, Celia.'

'They were worked up, real excited, screaming away in their language. Your brother didn't seem to understand what they were saying, but he wouldn't give the briefcase up neither, even when they shot him they had to prise it out of his hand. He was lying on the footpath bleeding when they stuck their guns right in his face, both of them did, and fired point blank.'

Angela stiffened. Jack put an arm around her but she pushed him off. 'Do you remember what were they wearing, their age? Anything?' she asked.

Celia's forehead wrinkled up with thought. 'It was all so quick. They weren't real young. Late thirties. Both of them had tatts.'

'Where?' Jack said.

'All over their arms. The one doing most of the yelling he had gold fillings and a tattoo of this big blue horse with a horn.'

'You mean a unicorn?' Angela's voice was thin.

'That's it.' Celia said. 'I thought it was gonna be another Strathfield Plaza, honest, there were people crouched behind parking meters shitting themselves. But the killers they ran straight past us, down into Chinatown.' She jerked the door open, reached out and grabbed Angela's wrist.

Jack caught a glimpse inside of a whale of a man in a white singlet and shorts lying on a vinyl sofa.

'I'm real sorry about your brother, love.'

Angela nodded, blinking rapidly, then, without a word, turned and walked down the long dim corridor.

Jack hurried after her. 'You alright?'

'I'm fine,' she said. 'I'm fine.' The skin around her eyes and mouth was pulled tight. They rode the lift down in silence, Angela gripping the thin metal rail. Outside in the estate a milk truck with a smashed roof and windscreen was cordoned off with strips of checked police tape. Jack gazed up at the thirty-storey block and then down at the yellow outline painted on the dried-up lawn, wondering what floor whoever it was had jumped from. A bunch of kids in coloured sunnies stood around leaning on their antler-handled bikes. Angela didn't take her eyes off the path all the way back to the car. The front seat was burning hot. Jack laid his big hand on the wheel as she started up.

'Anything I can do?'

'I don't want your sympathy thanks.'

'I'm not giving you any,' Jack said. 'Just asking.'

She rammed the gears into first and took off through the narrow streets of Redfern and Alexandria, the road twisting and turning like it was trying to throw them off. A newspaper flapped against Jack's ankles. He hung onto the dash wondering why he'd got involved with her in the first place. He didn't want to be here. He didn't even like her much. He liked her looks sure, but that wasn't enough reason to hang around. He blinked as the Holden swerved right in front of a petrol tanker then cut a sharp left into Canterbury Road. He said, 'You ever drive at Bathurst?'

She didn't answer. Her mouth was set firm as she steered the EH past the used car yards, video parlours and drive-in food huts. They passed an egg-blue mosque perched on a hill. A group of women wearing black hijabs filed along the pavement in the heat.

'Where the hell are we going?'

She turned her head sharply, a pair of long silver dolphins dangling off her ears. 'The suburbs, Jack. Haven't you ever been out west before?'

'I grew up out here,' Jack said. 'Doesn't mean I wanna go back.'

Angela pulled up outside a fibro house on a big wide block which climbed up to the railway line. Grapes grew down one wall and over the car-port. Tomatoes, corn, and beans competed for space in raised earth beds that smelled of chicken shit. There were peach, nectarine, banana, avocado and half a dozen different types of citrus trees. A screen door at the side had a hole in it big enough for a cat to jump through. Angela knocked on the wooden frame and a white-haired man with a large pickled nose shuffled out onto the verandah holding something shiny in his hand.

'Harold Dark?' Angela asked.

'Thass me.' The man looked them over carefully, like

he was trying to place them in his memory, then slipped his dentures into his mouth. 'What can I do for you?'

Angela told him. She spoke in a loud voice using a lot of hand gestures. Jack didn't say a word, just stood behind her with his arms folded. She said slowly, 'If you could describe the two men you saw, Mr Dark.'

'Can't. Didn't see their faces exactly. Don't see too good, not faces anyrate, but I know they was V'namese.'

'How do you know?'

'I know them.' The old man nodded. 'I know their lingo.'

'You speak Vietnamese?' Jack put in.

'Son,' the man said. 'You been up to Bankstown Square? You're tripping over 'em up there. You want a feed, it's all V'namese. Wanna loaf of bread, same thing. Go in the chemist, buy a pack of Codral, whaddya hear? I grew up in the Bankstown area. Now it's changed like you wouldn't believe. So I don have ter know V'namese, know who they was and I told the cops that too.'

They walked back to the car, sat inside with the windows down, Angela chewing on the curved end of her sunglasses. There were dark bags under her eyes and her short black hair was sticking up. She said, 'You believe him?'

'Who knows,' Jack said.

Angela said, 'You read the paper today?'

Jack shook his head. 'Should I?'

'Read it,' she said. 'Go on.'

He plucked the *Sun-Herald* from under his shoe and flipped through the first few pages. The Government was in deep trouble in the polls again and unemployment was climbing through the roof. Nothing new on that score. A paragraph on page five caught his eye:

Police have issued a description of two men they wish to assist them with their inquiries into Friday's fatal shooting in Haymarket. The two men were described as medium height, well-built and believed to be of Vietnamese origin. A police spokesman said both men were heavily tattooed with one bearing a tattoo of a stallion on his right forearm.

'A stallion?' Jack put the paper down.

'Apparently,' Angela said. 'Apparently some Vietnamese gang have moved into Chinatown and are extorting shops and restaurants. The three bullets they found in Damian came from a .32 pistol. That's the calibre these gangs traditionally use.'

'How do you know all this?' Jack said.

'Those two detectives told me. They went out of their way to. Trouble is it's all too pat. Why would a Vietnamese gang want to shoot my brother?'

'No idea,' Jack said. 'Whoever they were knew he was carrying money. We know that much. Now either the killers knew about it themselves or else they were working for someone who did.'

Angela turned the engine on, sat there pumping the accelerator pedal a moment. 'No,' she said. 'Damian never knew any Vietnamese people.'

Jack pulled at his blunt-shaped jaw. His eyes grew thoughtful. 'I've got something to tell you.'

Angela looked up at him sharply.

'When I was leaving Friday afternoon to meet Damian, this Vietnamese guy comes outta the club and hurries down towards Chinatown just ahead of me. Night before, the same guy's in the club when Damian was there.'

'What are you saying, Jack?'

'I'm saying that maybe we should try and find this guy, talk to him a little. Maybe he knows something, maybe he even saw something.'

'Did he overhear you and Damian?'

'I dunno,' Jack said. 'It's possible. Him and his wife seemed to be working some racket with the pokies. They won a jackpot on a machine that is not known for paying out jackpots. So I kept an eye on him. It was the night Damian came into the club with that senator's party.'

'Bryan Callagher?' she said.

Jack nodded. 'That's the one.'

'He's a friend of dad's.'

'Your father's still alive?' Jack said. 'Damian told me he was dead.'

'He might as well be.' She reached over into the glove box for her cigarettes, fished one out, lit it and inhaled mechanically. 'You smoke?'

'Gave up.'

'Funny thing all the women I know smoke now, none of the men do.' She stuck the point of her elbow out the window, jammed a Doc Marten down on the accelerator and spun the Holden round. Harold Dark and two brown, bare-chested children were standing on the verandah squinting at them as they slid out onto New Canterbury Road. Pennants fluttered from a used car-yard on the corner and a salesman in a mauve suit was collaring Lebanese customers outside the real estate agent's.

Angela pressed her palm against the wheel. 'Okay, let's go find this guy.'

12

The roads into the city were clogged with four-wheel drive vehicles of varying size and wheel-base. Vitaros, Pajeros, Saharas and Jackaroos crawled along Broadway spewing out petrol and diesel fumes as their drivers battled for the bridge after Sunday lunch. Angela turned into Liverpool Street and braked outside the club.

'Stay here,' Jack said. 'Don't want you smashing any more glasses.'

She gave him an icy stare and lifted the middle finger

of her left hand vertically. Jack went across the road and in through the double doors, adjusting his eyes to the smoke and darkness. A bunch of elderly men huddled at a low table sipping Centenario brandy and studying their cards. The Algerian girl in the change box waved Jack over nervously. She whispered through the security grille: 'Committee members ask me if I see you take money from the machines. I say I never see that, I say you don't steal.'

'*Gracias*, Rana.' Jack winked and went up to the bar. Jose Diaz was stocking the Panatella box with long fat Cubanos. He grinned at Jack. 'Hey, *tío*, you're a popular man. Half of Sydney's been in asking about you.'

'Yeah,' Jack said. 'Like who?'

'Like two mean-looking suits. Wanted to know if you was in here last Friday.'

'Say who they were?' Jack said.

'No. But they had to be cops. No one else is that fuckin rude. Also some Asian with a big fat Aussie wife was asking everyone where you were.'

'Vietnamese guy?'

Jose Diaz lifted his eyebrows. 'Who knows, man. Weren't Spanish.'

'Okay, I haven't been in today, alright?' Jack looked at Jose who was grinning madly, then reached into his hip pocket, took out a ten dollar bill and tucked it into the tip jar behind the bar. 'Button your lip, *camarero*.' He elbowed the gents door open and checked out the urinal; an old skinny Spaniard was grumbling to himself in front of the mirror and scratching at his chin with a cut throat razor. Jack shut the door, ran his eyes over the members standing in front of the machines, walked swiftly across the blood red carpet, out through the foyer and into the street.

The moment he stepped outside he saw it. A big black Ford – a Fairmont maybe or a Falcon. It was twenty metres behind the Holden sticking half out into the traffic lane with its motor running. Jack blinked into the light as he stepped off the pavement. The Ford gunned its motor and pulled out with a screech of rubber. He saw it coming, saw it clearly, the big wide tyres slapping the shiny blue road, but it was like his legs were buried in sand, his mind not working properly. The driver's hat was pulled down over his head and he wore wrap-around sunglasses. Angela yelled as Jack started to move, started to get out of the way. He lurched forward as the car swerved to collect him, the motor cooking, sharp metal headlights protruding like the horns of a bull. The front panel struck his leg, lifting his whole body up in the air and hurling him across the bonnet of the Holden where he rolled once, twice, and slumped into the gutter outside the Grand Taverna.

'Jeesus Jack!' Angela flung her door open and leapt out.

'My leg!' he cried. He lay there on his back with an awful pain rushing up his left shin.

Angela dived back into the Holden, searched through the glove box and grabbed hold of something red and shiny.

Jack's eyes widened as she bent over him. Without a word she sliced his new grey trousers open from knee to hem with a Swiss army knife. She peeled back the flaps of material and examined the lump on his shin. 'Can you move your leg?'

Jack grunted a little.

'I don't think the bone's broken,' she said coolly, 'but the shin casing's going to swell up.'

'Quarrell,' Jack said. 'Fucking Quarrell.'

'We should go to the police,' Angela said. 'It's attempted murder.'

Jack laughed. 'You get a description of the driver?'

She shook her head.

'Get the number of the car?'

'I don't think it had one.'

'So what do I tell em?' Jack said. 'I was almost skittled

by a driverless car without any plates?' He pushed himself up onto his feet, and grabbed her roughly by the arm. 'There's a Homicide cop out trying to kill me while I'm pissing around with you playing amateur detective.'

Angela jerked her arm free. 'Let's get one thing straight, Jack.' She held up five fingers. 'I'm paying you five hundred dollars, right. Five hundred dollars!'

'These strides,' Jack said, 'these strides cost me a hundred and five. So you're only paying me three hundred and ninety five.' She walked off and he hobbled after her. 'And this boyfriend of yours – why isn't he helping us?'

Angela stopped and glared at him. 'You finished?'

'No,' Jack said. 'I haven't. Ever since I laid eyes on you I've been jinxed. Look at my leg!'

'What's it got to do with me?'

'Nothing whatsoever. Except without you Quarrell wouldn't know where I lived. Wouldn't even know I was in town.'

'Sooner or later he would have found you. You can't run forever.' She opened the driver's door, got in, dropped her penknife into the glove box and started the motor. Jack limped around to the passenger's side, his trousers flapping at the side. A grimy old man wheeling a trolley made from old bike parts and scrap metal looked across at Jack and smiled like they had something in common.

Holding his leg straight as a pool cue, Jack lowered himself into the front seat. Angela shot out into Liverpool Street without checking the mirror and turned right. The city streets were quiet, the windy concrete plazas deserted. They drove through the business end of town. Tall glassy buildings spearing the clear blue sky. Jack could see the Holden reflected in dozens of insurance office windows and bank fronts. The city was like a big dirty mirror and if you looked hard enough into it you could see your own dark shadow.

Jack shifted his eyes away. 'Take me home.'

Angela's mouth tightened. 'What about this Vietnamese guy?'

'You find him,' Jack said. 'I've had the dick.'

She hit the brakes hard and brought the EH to a halt right in the middle of Castlereagh Street, forcing the olive BMW behind to swerve round them and the exec with the orange bow-tie and gold-rimmed glasses to blast his horn. Angela lifted off her shades. Lines creased her forehead and careered out from the corners of her eyes. A pimple had erupted on the ridge of her chin and she didn't look so tough any longer. Or sexy. Just tired.

Jack reached out a big hand and laid it on her cheek. 'You look done in,' he said. Her skin was pale and her breath smelled a little sour.

'Look.' She turned in her seat. 'I don't believe Damian's death was a simple robbery. His killers knew where he was going to be and what he was doing there. They knew he had money. I also think they had a good idea of what he was planning. Maybe they even knew about you. In fact I wouldn't be surprised if they tried to fix you next.'

'Well, they'll have to get in line,' Jack said, glancing around at the cars behind them. 'There's others waiting.'

'I'm gonna find my brother's killers, Jack. With or without you.'

'Just like the song eh?'

'Yeah,' Angela said, 'just like the song.' She rammed the gear stick into first and sent the Holden flying down Castlereagh. Neither of them said a word until Angela pulled up outside the laundromat in Coogee and Jack eased his leg out of the car like it was a piece of rare Ming china. Before she drove off she said softly, without any emotion in her voice, 'The funeral's set down for tomorrow.'

'I never go to funerals.'

'Just as well,' she said. 'You're not invited.'

13

He held the receiver at arm's length twisting the dirty cord in his fingers and running a broken thumbnail over the tiny voice holes. The phone was hot and sticky in his hand; drops of condensation ringed the mouthpiece. Every ten seconds or so he lifted the receiver up to his lips and said, 'Yeah,' then took it away again. He rubbed the nub of a pencil against his square jawbone while a voice crackled back at him. He closed his eyes, blinked them open and rolled his neck first one way then the other. He brought the receiver up close to his mouth and said, 'Listen, Vick, I can't take him this weekend, okay. I gotta move outta here. I don't want what happened to Nepo happening to me alright.'

The voice crackled in response. He listened for a few moments until there was a pause at the other end and said, 'Tell Toby I'm real sorry. I'll make it up to him.' He hung up, wiped the sweat off his face onto his T-shirt and thumbed through the yellow pages under F. He found the number he was after, dialled it, gave his name and address, and made an arrangement for the owner to call around at three. He kept the prongs of the phone down and the receiver cradled under his chin while he searched in the white pages for the real estate agent's number. Sweat was dripping off the hand piece and down the coils of the cord while he worked the phone. When he finished, he went into the bedroom and got out his bankbook. He locked the front door and hobbled downstairs to the street favouring his left leg.

A wall of grimy heat struck him in the face. There was no breeze at all. He limped up to Coogee Bay Road, past

a tall wheezing woman in a straw hat pushing a pram up
the hill; her baby had a big bald head and wore a tiny
pair of sunglasses. Jack mopped at his brow; his skin
burned and all he could think of was his damned leg. He
crossed the street. The bitumen bubbled and stuck to the
soles of his shoes. At the end of the road lay the shimmering sea. Sunburnt kids sheltered under awnings, their
eyes red and veiny. Jack selected a piece of John Dory in
the window of the fish and chip shop and went in to order.
A pregnant woman was wiping her face on a towel and a
thin Englishman was working the chip vats; a trickle of
sweat ran down his long bony nose. 'Lemon?' the man
said, scooping up wedges from a tray and scattering them
over Jack's fish and chips. Jack bought four VB stubbies
in the Coogee Bay bottle shop and carried them up to the
reserve. He ate his meal in a shady spot near the baths
watching the sea drag in and out while a pair of scarred
seagulls eyed his chips from the railing.

It was a pity about Coogee; he'd miss the beach. He
pulled on his beer and leaned his big jaw in the crook of
his hand. He was crazy to have come back to Sydney in
the first place. Should've stayed over in Avila eating
paella and fried pig's ears. One thing for certain, Quarrell
was going to keep coming after him. Like a mad dog. And
there was only one thing to do with mad dogs. He flicked
a thumb through the pages of his bankbook. He had to
get hold of some ready, and quick. Five hundred she'd
promised if they could identify her brother's killers, but
this driving around the western suburbs asking dumb
questions'd get them nowhere. Whoever Damian had
been ripping that nine grand off had most likely hired a
couple of Saigon cowboys. Jack slid the passbook into the
hip pocket of his Levis and leaned back.

There was nothing they could do for Damian now,
though it was no use telling her that. She was taking on
this whole business like it was some kind of quest, like
she was some modern day Don Quixote without the

laughs. Well, the only quest he believed in was survival –
his and his kid's. He drained his beer, wiped the grease
off his lips and stood up, sending a pack of seagulls flying
out over the rocks. He had the feeling that if he stuck
around her for very long he was going to end up in the
crematorium beside Damian. He walked back along the
edge of the sand in the burning sun. The beach was
empty, apart from a topless girl playing ball with a pair
of alsatians. He went into the Commonwealth Bank and
had a cheque made out to Vick, mailed it off at the post
office and limped home. In the bedroom he got down on
all fours and slid the suitcase out from under his bed,
unlocked it and began stuffing in shirts, trousers, his
well-thumbed passport. The doorbell buzzed. He pushed
himself up onto his feet and moved down the hall. 'Yeah?'

'Les's furniture,' a voice called.

He opened up and looked into a large moon face
presiding over a cut-off biker's T-shirt and dirty overalls
tucked into a pair of big black riding boots.

Jack said: 'You Les?'

The woman grunted, staring into the dimness of his
flat. 'Whatcha got?'

He waved her inside and led her through the narrow
rooms while she ran an appraising eye over his possessions. Jack said: 'There's some real good pieces here.
Double bed's brass, fridge's almost new.'

She gave the bed a solid kick and rattled his dresser.
In the front room she whacked the oak bookcase hard
with the flat of her hand. 'Yep, I'll take the bed,' she said,
'the bookcase, sofa, the dresser, that table over there and
the silky oak chairs. Two suxty for the lot.' Les folded her
arms and her muscles rippled like waves in a pond.

'You a Kiwi eh?' Jack said.

She hoisted the table onto her broad shoulders and
disappeared down the stairs. Jack stripped the mattress
and sheets off the bed, removed all his crime thrillers
from the bookshelves. He watched Les throw a couple of

kitchen chairs under one arm, considering whether he should offer her a hand when the phone rang. He let it ring. Les lingered in the doorway, eyeing him, thumb hooked under the strap of her overalls. 'Aren't you going to answer that?'

'I know who it is,' Jack said. He helped load her Dyna truck downstairs. Up close Les smelled sweaty. She counted out thirteen brand-new twenties, slapped them in his palm. 'Wanna sell yer old records up there?'

'No,' Jack said, 'I'm keeping them.'

'Suit yourself, skip.'

When she was gone he lay on his living-room floor sorting through his blues collection and listening to an old tape of Hound Dog Taylor. He was down to the basics now – a fridge, hi-fi system, a milk crate full of tapes and records, and one hundred and ten paperbacks. The sky was darkening outside his window and a sudden roll of thunder shook the glass. Footsteps clicked on the stairs outside and fingers rapped urgently on the wooden frame.

Jack threw open the door. She had on a long mauve dress, Aboriginal earrings and was clutching a cassette in one hand. Lipstick was smeared across the corner of her lips like someone had kissed her good.

'I knew it was you who rang.'

Angela looked at him. 'I didn't ring.' Lightning forked across the sky and the hall lit up yellow. 'The weather's gone crazy out there,' she said. 'How's the leg?'

'Oh you know,' he said, hobbling into the front room.

Her gaze fell on the shadows of dust where the furniture had been and her top lip darkened. 'So you're moving out?'

'Be a fool if I stayed.'

She strode across to his tape deck, ejected Hound Dog Taylor, poked her own cassette in and jabbed at the play button. 'Don't talk. I want you to listen to this very carefully.'

Soft music faded out and a female voice started speaking in a brisk foreign language. Jack leaned against the wall with his eyes hooded. He opened his mouth but Angela flung a hand up to silence him and reached over and fast-forwarded the tape. 'Now listen again,' she said.

A different language came on this time. He could tell that much. More nasal with a wider variation in tone. He listened for several minutes in complete ignorance, then Angela hit the stop button.

She said: 'That was Cantonese; the first language you heard was Vietnamese. I taped them off 2EA. This morning I took the cassette over to Waterloo and played it to Celia. She is certain that it's the second language the gunmen were speaking when they shot Damian.'

Jack looked at her. 'So?'

'Don't you see Jack!' Angela's dark blue eyes glittered with excitement. 'Don't you see that they weren't Vietnamese after all.'

'Maybe they were Vietnamese who could speak Cantonese. Maybe Celia is not a very good linguist.' He rolled his big shoulders. 'Maybe this is not worth a pinch of old catshit.'

'First the police issue a description of a suspect with a stallion tattoed on his arm; but we know it's a unicorn. Then they say the two men they're looking for are of Vietnamese origin; but they're not, they're Chinese.'

'Congratulations,' Jack said. 'The case is solved.'

All the sparkle went out of Angela's face. She glared at him across the room. 'Don't be such a patronising arsehole. These detectives aren't as dumb as they look. They're deliberately releasing misinformation. Why? I've got no idea. Except getting even with you seems to be more important to this Detective Sergeant Quarrell than investigating my brother's murder.'

'Okay,' Jack said. 'Okay so what if you're right.' He walked over and switched on the light. It was only five o' clock, but the building was growing dark. 'Where does that leave us?'

'For a start, instead of running out to Cabramatta, I think we should scour Chinatown – the bars, restaurants, cafes, the gambling clubs. Damian was shot near Haymarket and we know the killers took off on foot. That tells us something already.' She stopped, peered into the kitchenette at two enormous cockroaches crawling slowly across the sink.

Jack scooped up a paperback from the floor and flattened them both with one hit. He scraped wings and yellow gunk off the cover of *Farewell, My Lovely* and ran it under the hot water. 'Let me get this straight,' he said. 'You want us to go out in an electrical storm looking for some Cantonese speaker with a blue unicorn tattoed on his forearm?'

'No,' she said, 'first we're going for a ride up the Cross.' She stepped around his books and lifted her cassette out of the tape deck. 'Coming?'

Jack leaned against the window, struggling to get his shoes on. Seagulls wheeled above the park outside and thunder rumbled in the distance. He wondered whether he should tell her about the black Berlina parked across the street.

'You read a lot of crime fiction, Jack?'

'Why, you wanna borrow some?' He moved over and laid his hands on her bare shoulders. Her earrings danced madly as she backed away.

'Don't do that.'

'I like your mouth, Angela. I like it a real lot.' He pressed his lips against hers. Her skin smelled faintly of some kind of floral perfume.

She balled her fists at him. 'I told you. I don't want to get involved with you.'

'You are involved with me,' Jack said. He took his hands off, held them up in the air like weights. 'There's somebody else, yeah I know. Well how come I never see

the guy. How come he never makes an appearance?' He
moved down the hall. 'Switch off the lights willya. I'm
trying to save money.'

'Sex and money. That all you ever think about?'

'What else is there?' Jack said, as the door clicked shut
after them.

14

Rain spattered the windscreen. Angela lit a cigarette and
flicked the match out the window with her thumb. Cars
with their lights on were driving too close. She hunched
over the wheel, concentrating on the broken white line.
The Hyatt hotel was misted in dark grey clouds; power
lines jittered in the wind. 'You like the Cross?' she said,
frowning at the broken tail-lights of an RSL cab that cut
in front of them.

'Hate it,' Jack said.

She glanced over at him. 'Wanna tell me about it?'

'There's nothin to tell,' Jack said. 'Some places you'd
rather just forget.'

'This where you met Detective Sergeant Quarrell?'

'No, I met him in Darlo in the Lord Roberts Hotel. I
was tending bar and Quarrell was working in the armed
hold-up squad then. Him and a lot of other lowlife used
to come in.' He stared out the window at a pack of
tattooed young men striding up the hill towards the Coca
Cola sign. 'What are we doing here anyway?'

'The police released Damian's possessions,' she said. 'I
thought we could have a look in his flat.' A key poked out
between her clenched fingers. She crunched the gears
and turned into Bayswater Road. She hung a hard right,

crossed a busy intersection, went right again and came up around the Paddington side of King's Cross, then swung left into a leafy cul-de-sac and nosed the Holden in against a plane tree.

Jack said, 'You seem to know your way around here.'

She turned the engine off and unbuckled her belt. 'We've all got pasts, Jack. I'm the same as you. I don't like to share mine either.'

'This person you're involved with. It's a woman isn't it?'

Her face broke into a grin. 'Keep trying.' She led him up the path to a four-storey block of flats painted buttercup-yellow with green bay windows, ornamental stonework and a lead-framed security door. Rain was starting to fall outside as their shoes clacked across the black and white tiled foyer and she fitted the key neatly into the lock of Flat 2. A narrow passageway led into a small living space. The walls were papered with familiar fifties icons: Jimmy Dean standing in the rain; Marilyn holding down her dress. An eat-in kitchenette ran off to one side with a shelf full of Cordon Bleu cook books, but not enough elbow room to swing a frypan. The bedroom was different. Two huge candles stood guard over a king-sized iron bed bolted into the floor. Black satin sheets were draped over a thick rubber mattress. Wrist cuffs and leg harnesses hung from the four corners of the bed. The room was big and dark and musty.

'Looks like a torture chamber.' Jack pulled open a dresser drawer and a stack of coloured objects tumbled forth: rippled latex penises, multi-headed vibrators, a rectal syringe, studded neck collars and one long pliable bar with bulldog clips on either end. 'What the fuck's this?' He pressed the jagged teeth open and shut.

Angela glanced down. 'S and M.'

'But what do they do with it?'

'Use your imagination.'

In the wardrobe were rows of leather underpants, straps, long knotted cords, even a leather face mask with a large mouthhole stitched in red. 'Know what strikes me most about all this shit?' Jack said. 'There's nothing personal here. No books, no nick-nacks, no photographs. It's like a set for some bent B-grade porn movie.'

'It's an office,' she said. 'A workroom.' She turned away and walked back into the living room, sat with her knees together on the futon. 'I think Damian used to sleep in here.' Her eyes swept over the modest furniture. 'See, there's his clothes. His alarm clock. I think he only used the bedroom for entertaining.'

Jack looked at her, but she wasn't smiling. He picked up the phone, ran his fingers behind the cabinet. 'No address book.' He stood frowning, his hands empty at his side. 'He sure had me fooled. I *believed* he was a model.'

'My brother was very unhappy inside. Had been for a long time.'

'Didn't seem so to me,' Jack said. 'Scared maybe. Unhappy no. In fact I'd say the exact opposite.'

Angela shook her head. 'I think I know him a little better than you. Don't you think?'

'No. I think you knew him when he was nine. I knew him when he was twenty-four. And that's the difference.'

She said, 'You're a hard person to like, Jack, you know that?'

'I'm a realist,' Jack said. 'If I see shit on the floor, I don't say it's Vegemite.'

She stared at him coldly. 'I think you're shocked. I think you can't handle what you've just seen.'

'I'm not shocked,' Jack said. 'I don't like to be lied to that's all.' He could hear the rain out there. He could hear three distinct noises it was making: there was rain blowing against the windows, rain drumming on the road and rain gurgling down a drainpipe. And there was something else too. It sounded like glass smashing.

Angela flew to the window, clawed open the Slim-Lines and peered out. She banged a fist on the lead frame and called out, 'Hey!' then started for the door.

Jack followed her. Rain slashed at his legs in the shiny black street. Two wet shapes were running down the cul-de-sac. One was holding a pinch bar.

Angela unlocked the driver's door. The glove box lay open. She swept big chips of glass off the front seat.

'You get a look at them?' Jack said.

Angela shook her head.

'They take anything?'

'Only my driver's licence, but they'll know where I live.' She slumped against the car in the rain.

Jack reached out to touch her arm when a dark-skinned woman came running out of the flats unfurling an umbrella and called, 'You two alright?'

He squinted at her familiar maroon jacket with the Don Quixote logo stitched across the breast pocket. 'Rana – that you?'

'Jacques?' She waved one hand wildly. 'I see them out my window. I come down. Is the third time this month we have cars broken into.' She moved in close to Jack and held the umbrella over his head.

'You live here?' Jack said, pointing at the block of flats.

'I tell you before I live in the Cross –'

'This is Angela,' Jack interrupted. Angela sat on the hood with her head in her hands. She grunted. 'Angela's brother used to live in Flat 2.'

'Your brother? Was him?'

Angela nodded. Rain was streaming down her nose and chin.

'I feel so sorry for you. I only ever speak to him once or twice. He always friendly.'

Angela sat up. 'Did he get many visitors?'

Rana said, 'Sometimes I hear people down there at night. Once I hear screams coming from his flat. Next day I ask what happen. He say he has nightmares. The other tenants complain. Then I read in the paper. . . *lo siento.*' She put out a hand. 'Come inside. I make you hot shocolate.'

Angela jumped up off the car. 'We've gotta go.' She strode round to the driver's door and hopped in, started the engine up.

Jack squeezed Rana's arm. *'Gracias, amiga.'*

'Carlos wants to see you,' Rana whispered. 'Have big trouble last night at club.'

Angela hit the pedal as Jack got in and the Holden fishtailed out of the cul-de-sac and swung left into Victoria Street. A bunch of feral youths sheltered in the grounds of St Vincent's Hospital, boys mainly. Angela fixed her eyes on the road ahead. 'Your friend doesn't know about you and Damian?'

Jack picked slivers of glass from between his legs. 'No. Rana's a virgin. She thinks hetero sex is bad enough.'

'How do you know she's a virgin?'

'Cause she told me. She said she'd never let a man put his thing in her.'

'And you were trying to I suppose?'

'We're just friends,' Jack said. 'Okay.' He stared at the fine dark hairs running along her arms and as she looked over at him he caught a flash of Damian around her mouth and chin. 'I didn't ask you about the funeral. How was it?'

Angela didn't answer.

'You don't wanna talk about it?'

She gave her head a shake.

'Your father go?'

'He went,' she said brusquely as South Dowling Street widened into Anzac Parade and she stamped the accelerator to the floor. They tore past Moore Park and the road curved dangerously to the left. Rain was driving in through the smashed fly window and Jack hung on to the dash calling out to her to *slow it down.* She finally lifted her foot off the accelerator and looked over with a real crazy grin pasted across her face as if she took delight in scaring the shit out of him. He wondered where she'd learned to drive like this. She drove like a pro racer. Her eyebrows were streaked back in the wind and the left side of the windscreen was a blur of water as a wiper jerked uselessly against the glass. She pulled up outside the laundromat in Coogee and checked her Swatch watch by the light on the dash. 'I've got to get home quick,' she said.

Jack opened his eyes waiting for his heart to start beating at its normal rate of sixty-five a minute. He stared up at the aluminium windows of his flat and frowned to himself.

'You turned off the lights?'

'Yeah,' she said, 'why?'

'Take a look.'

15

They leaned forward in the dark with the engine off and the rain beating on the car roof. Water from the overflowing gutter lapped at their tyres. Angela glanced up and down the empty street and then back to the lit window. 'Who do you think it is?' she said.

'Dunno.' Jack rubbed at his jaw. 'You got a tyre wrench handy?'

'In the boot,' she said. 'I'm coming with you.'

Outside the laundromat a dead fruit bat blocked the drain, its furry body dyed blue. Jack gripped the wrench in his right fist as he led her in through the car-port and up the slippery metal stairs. He stopped on the landing and held a finger to his lips. The rain was pelting down outside. He put his ear to the door and listened. He handed her the key and stepped back while she eased open the lock. Then he burst in down the hall swinging the tyre wrench in front of him and yelling. He kicked his bedroom door open. Clothes were scattered across the room; his suitcase chucked in a corner. Springs and stuffing spilled out of the slashed Slumberland mattress. In the living room, cupboards were pulled off the walls, his books were shredded on the floor and the fridge was lying on its side like a dead polar bear leaking water all over the lino.

'There goes the bond.'

Angela's eyes widened as she picked her way through the wrecked flat. 'What the hell were they looking for?'

Jack bent down next to the smashed turntable. His records in the milk crate had survived. 'They must've found what they wanted,' he said.

'Or else,' Angela looked at him quickly, 'we disturbed them.'

She reached the window a second ahead of Jack and stuck her face out into the teeming rain. The red tail-lights of a car disappeared down Alison Road. 'It's them! I told you they'd come after you.'

'Why didn't they kill us then?'

'Maybe they wanted something, or maybe this is their idea of a warning.'

Jack went into the bedroom and started throwing clothes into his suitcase. He clamped his jaw tight, breathing through his nose.

Angela stood in the doorway, her wet mauve dress clinging to her breasts and thighs. 'Where you going?'

'Somewhere cheap I can hole up. A backpacker's maybe. They must've been beneath the stairs when we came up.'

'I've got a proposition for you, Jack.'

His eyes widened.

She shook her head. 'You can stay at my place for a few days.'

'Sure?'

'But I want you to come with me to Chinatown, okay? We're getting close to solving this now. I can feel it.'

'So can I,' Jack said. He dragged his suitcase through into the front room, stood there with his arms folded, surveying what remained of his life from the last nine months. 'Pity about the fridge. I would've got a few bucks for that. It's a Lemair. They're Russian you know. My old man was Russian.'

Angela went to the window. Rain was hammering on the roof. 'At least you've got your tracks.' She checked her car down in the street, and then her watch. She slid the window shut.

'I'm thirty-six years of age,' Jack said. 'I've got a very sore leg, no fucking prospects, my flat has been trashed and there's an unknown number of people out trying to kill me.' He placed a big hand on the crook of her arm. 'Right now I need to hold someone.'

'Is that what you and Damian did? Hold each other?'

Jack said, 'That was part of it.'

'I always wanted to know what gays do exactly in bed?'

'I'm not gay.'

'Aren't you?'

'Maybe I don't know what I am,' he said. 'Maybe I'll find out with you.' He pressed his lips tight against hers and her mouth opened like a flower. He felt her cold arms go round his neck and the firm padded mound of her loins push hard against his. He felt the strength that she possessed in her broad shoulders and the softness of her breasts and tongue. He felt her eyes watching him closely as she bit down sharply on his lower lip then pulled her mouth away like she was removing the sticker from a piece of fruit.

'We have to go.' She bent down, heaved up the pink milk crate with his records and tapes, and walked off with it down the hall.

Jack licked at the blood on his lip and grabbed hold of his suitcase. He left the front door sticking open and galloped after her down the iron stairs. Water rose up from the gutters and rushed at their feet. The big fig tree in the park creaked and swayed like a hanged man in the wind.

Angela pumped the pedal with her foot. Drops of water flew off her hair as she spun the Holden around. The back wheels began to skid in the wet but she corrected the drift with ease. There were no two ways about it. She was good. She changed down smoothly as they hit the corner and headed west.

'Tell me about your father.'

'Why?'

'Why not?' She smiled.

Jack said, 'My father came out here in '47 with a whole bunch of Poles, Lats and East Russians. He was from Novgorod and my mother was from Nowra. We lived in Eden. He worked the fishing boats up and down the coast and he used to drink. He used to drink spirits – gin, vodka, but mainly whisky. He used to drink til he couldn't stand, then he'd drink some more til he couldn't sit. That was just weeknights.'

'What was his name?'

'Ivan, Ivan Butorov. But my mother called him Vanyusha.' Jack turned and looked out past her nose towards town. Sydney Tower was sticking up through the mist like a giant syringe.

'So that's why you work in the liquor industry?'

'Basically, I've had a lot to do with alcohol all my life. When I was ten my mother came into my room at dawn, packed my port and we took a bus and then the train up to Sydney. I never saw the old man again. He never rang or tried to get in contact. Later on we found out he'd hooked himself another family. Me and my mother started out in Homebush, then moved to Stanmore.' Jack lifted his shoulders. 'She died when I was in Spain.' He poked at the hole in the window with his fingers and said, 'Now it's your turn.'

Angela's knuckles were bunched on top of the wheel like chalk marks on black rock. The wipers flicked in front of her face but the rain kept coming. 'You've probably heard of my father?' She stared straight ahead. 'Frank Frick?'

Jack snorted like a horse. 'No shit.' Frank Frick was one of those Australian success stories that the newspapers were always keen on. A property developer and ex-Olympic rower, Frank Frick had forced his way into the top fifty richest men in Australia. He'd made a lot of dough in the mid eighties, but was very careful not to overstretch his capital. When the stockmarket crash came and the other big boys were sinking like leaky boats, Frank Frick had survived and diversified. Frick Developments had put up several of the tallest steel and glass towers in Sydney, and even in the nineties with fifteen per cent of office space going vacant, the name Frick still glowed on the giant cranes that gathered like dinosaurs round the city's dustbowls. 'Yeah,' Jack nodded his head slowly. 'I've heard of him.' He loosened his grip on the severed seat belt and said, 'So you're Frank Frick's daughter?'

'Don't hold it against me.'

'I won't, I may want to marry you though. How much is your old man worth – one hundred, two hundred mill?'

'I don't know.' Angela shrugged. 'Dad re-married soon after mum died. He's got three more children now. Neither Damian nor I've had much to do with him for years.'

'All that dough,' Jack said. 'Was me I'd be over his place every afternoon helping him count it.' He planted his jaw in the palm of his hand while his brow furrowed. He stared at the sun-cracked dash then across at her dark serious face and started grinning to himself as if he'd just pulled off five golden Incas. 'So why didn't you tell me all this before? I might've been more co-operative.'

She wiped at the windscreen with the blade of her hand. 'Don't get any ideas, Jack. You'll only be disappointed.' They whizzed past a paper factory and she turned left down a narrow inner-city street. Melaleucas shaded a row of small Federation terraces as the road dipped.

'Erskineville?' Jack said.

She nodded and parked at the end of the street in front of a single-storey cottage. Its spiked iron fence held back some straggly plumbago and an overgrown frangipani tree. Rain glistened on the pointed leaves and the perfume from its yellow-hearted flowers sweetened the air. Angela pushed the iron gate open, stormed up the two small steps and banged on the screen door. A figure stirred behind the glass panels and she called out, 'It's me, honey.'

A girl of about twenty came out in a short skirt, steel-capped Blundstones and a blue working man's singlet. Three silver rings were inserted in the left side of her nose and her hair was redder than a fire truck.

Angela said, 'Some creeps broke into my car and stole my license. I was worried they might come back here.'

The girl's face grew serious. Jack watched her hand stroke Angela's bared upper arm. The girl disappeared indoors and came back a moment later with a beat-up red shoulder bag and rolling a cigarette. She whispered something in Angela's ear which made Angela laugh, then the two females embraced in the doorway and kissed on the mouth. As the girl brushed past Jack on the path she gave him a tart smile.

Jack went up the steps saying, 'Listen. I don't want to put you two *ladies* out here.' But Angela had already gone inside.

The house smelled damp as if rain had got in between the brickwork. A long corridor led Jack down to a small living area. Other rooms with their doors closed ran off to the right. He could hear floorboards creaking in one of them. He stood in the living room eyeing the Sony TV and VCR. A teal blue couch and matching armchairs ate up the floor space. There were two Aboriginal bark paintings on one wall and opposite, a Marilyn Monroe poster, identical to the one in Damian's flat. He glanced up at it and a shadow moved behind him.

He turned quickly.

A child as thin as a pencil stood in the hallway. She had long blond hair and her eyes were big and blue and curious. She regarded him in silence while her small hands fiddled with the edge of her skirt.

Jack's mouth opened.

Angela appeared behind her in the doorway and said, 'This is Clea.' She placed her hand on the child's shoulder. 'Clea, this is Jack. Jack's going to be staying with us for a couple of days.'

Clea looked at Jack and Jack looked at Clea and for a moment nobody spoke. The child's wide eyes were fixed on the older man's suitcase.

'Is Jack going to be sleeping in your bed, Mum?'

'No.' Angela shook her head firmly. 'Jack's going to be sleeping here on the couch. Aren't you, Jack?'

'But Mum, there's no blankets for him.'

'Don't need em, Clea,' Jack said. 'I always sleep in my clothes.' He followed Angela down the hall and helped her drag her heavy wardrobe and a hatstand against the front door.

16

Bright flickering lights and high-pitched voices pulled Jack out of a deep dark dream. He adjusted his eyes to the colours on the TV. The curtains were drawn. Clea was perched on the arm of his couch in spotted quoll pyjamas, a remote control in one hand and a slice of unbuttered toast in the other. She said, 'Do you like Alvin and the Chipmunks, Jack?'

Jack blinked at the blaring 24-inch screen. 'Never miss em.'

'It's my favourite program too.' She pressed the volume button up a decibel. 'Do you have a family?'

'I did have.' He rubbed his hips and worked some feeling back into his pins.

Clea looked at him, frowning. 'Where are they?'

'I lost them,' Jack said.

'Are you divorced?'

'Sure am. Your mummy divorced?'

'I don't have a father.'

'You're the only kid then?' Jack said.

'Only child,' Clea corrected him. 'I'm not a goat.'

'No, guess not.' Jack grabbed his trousers from the floor, rolled off the couch and bobbed down behind the chair to pull them on.

Clea said, 'I thought you slept in all your clothes?'

'Not my trousers,' Jack said. 'Don't want them crumpled.'

'I can iron them for you if you want.' Clea chomped heartily on her toast. 'I iron all my own clothes.'

'No thanks sweetheart.' He lifted up his case and lugged it through into the kitchen. Masonite had been laid down over the uneven floorboards. The tiny backyard was stacked with planks of wood and sheets of iron. He dug out a T-shirt, shorts and some old runners from his case and changed in the bathroom. Paint tins were piled underneath the lip of the bathtub and a pair of ladders leaned against the wall. The house was in a frozen state of semi-renovation.

He left Clea glued to the TV set, went down the hall and shouldered away the furniture from the front door. It was still early and the sun was shining over Coogee way. In the grounds of the nearby State school he stretched his limbs and completed fifty leg squats and the same number of push-ups. His bones creaked like the timber in an old house. He had the feeling that something bad was going to come down and he wanted to be ready for it when it did. The only reason Angela'd invited him home was she'd felt it too. Somebody had sent that crew over to rip his place apart. He wondered who, and what it was they were looking for. He spread his legs in front of the school wall and fired short, sharp combinations, twisting his shoulders, bringing his big fists up centimetres short of the brickwork. He was tired of being kicked around; it was time to kick back. A train clacked along the Bankstown line and Jack pushed off through the empty streets of Erskineville, feet pounding the pavement. He knew this part of town like an old lover – Enmore, Newtown. He passed the Police Boys Club where he'd gone as a young hood. The rain had cleared, the sky was grey and a wind was pushing leaves about. He ran on, along King Street and down through the back streets of south Newtown, past the workers' cottages with their iron lace and grimy windowsills. He liked to sweat, to feel it oozing out of him like this. It felt more than good. He entered her street from the south as three short swarthy youths with flattened noses and hooded tracksuits jogged towards him. They flicked their fists in front of them, rolling their heads, feinting and ducking as they came on. Jack nodded at the tall emu-legged trainer running alongside, a man who'd been around the area for years.

Angela stood in her doorway wearing King Gee overalls. A power drill whined and smoked in her hand. She prised off the old snib latch and fitted a new deadlock with a special bit attached to the Makita. Jack watched her work. Her long black eyelashes flickered. She was one of the few people he'd met who looked better in the mornings. She smiled at the wet T-shirt plastered to his chest. 'I wouldn't overdo it if I were you, Jack.'

'You reckon?' He went down to the bathroom, showered and shaved and pulled on an old pair of jeans and a fresh

T-shirt. He found an iron pan in the kitchen, fried up some potatoes, garlic and finely chopped onions, hunted out six eggs, beat them in a bowl and added the mix to the pan. Clea sat cross-legged in front of the Sony switching channels. He rattled a spoon in the doorway.

'Want some breakfast, little goat?'

Clea jumped up. 'Can you make cakes?'

'I only do eggs,' Jack said. 'And toast.' He set three places at the table and sprinkled flakes of parsley over the tortilla while Clea called her mother.

'What the hell are you doing?' Angela wiped her hands down the sides of her overalls.

'It's called cooking,' Jack said.

'Where'd you learn this?'

'Spain.' He watched mother and daughter pull up two stools together. They had the same dark blue eyes, though Clea's were more alert and lively than her mother's, and she had her uncle's blond hair.

The child said, 'Did you ever go to a bullfight, Jack?'

'I used to go lots. Sit in the shade on one of the little cushions they hire out, take some red wine. *La corrida de toros*. Yeah, it was good.'

Angela regarded him closely. 'What did you like most about it? The colour, the spectacle?'

'It was the blood. See it come oozing out of those big bulls' necks.'

'Yuk,' Clea went.

Jack grinned at her. 'I just liked the ritual I guess.' He reached over for the knife and hewed off a hunk of bread.

'Guess what, Mum, guess what? Jack's divorced.'

Angela ignored her. 'Why'd you go to Spain for anyway?'

He glanced over at Clea who was humming to herself while she mopped her plate with a crust of bread.

Angela stopped, turned to her daughter. 'Go and get dressed now, darl.'

Clea climbed down off her stool. 'That was yummy,

Jack.' Her plate was licked clean. She went down to her room, her sandals clicking on the masonite.

'Was it because of Detective Quarrell?'

'She's very grown up,' Jack said. 'Who's the father?'

'There's no father.' Angela's voice hardened. 'There was a man who donated his sperm one night, but I've been mother and father to her since she was born.' She picked up the bread knife and ran the edge of her thumb along the sharp point.

Jack said, 'I've been thinking. Maybe you should go to the cops, tell them what you've got so far. Let them take over.'

'I've got no evidence. You know that.'

He leaned towards her. There were gold studs in her ears and her lips were full and ripe for the picking. He laid a big thick finger across both them and said, 'Sure you want to go through with this? It could get dangerous.'

'Don't worry about me,' she said. 'I can handle myself.'

'I'm not worried about you.' He jerked his head towards the doorway. 'It's the kid.'

Angela gripped the bread knife very tightly in her fist and thrust it up in front of his nose. 'If anyone tries to harm my daughter I'll kill them.' She said it calmly, but with total conviction.

'I believe you,' Jack said. 'Now will you put down the knife. I'd like to keep my eyeballs.'

She got up from the table and went out of the room. He sat there with his elbows propped on either side of the frypan. If things got outta hand he might have to leave quicker than he expected. It was a pity – all that dough she was connected to. If only he had a big enough stake, then he could go places, start afresh. It always puzzled him when people said if they had their lives to live all over again they wouldn't change one bit. Well, if he could start from scratch he'd change everything.

'Talking to yourself now, Jack?'

'Was I?' He looked up, saw her standing in the doorway.

She'd ditched the overalls and was wearing jeans and a sleeveless black top with Reebok written over it. A Nikkon camera dangled off her right shoulder.

'You'll have to watch that.' A smile broke at the corners of her mouth.

He couldn't figure her. She was on and off like a fucking tap. She chucked something on the table in front of him. A Commonwealth bankbook.

'Take a look,' she said.

He grabbed at it. The name Damian Andrew Frick was typed inside. And there, entered in the first week of February, was a deposit for 9,500 dollars; then, two days later, the 9,000 was withdrawn. He flicked through the tiny pages. The same pattern stretched back month after month: 9,500 in, 9,000 out. His eyes paused at the current balance of $5,642.36, thinking hard.

Angela said, 'Damian left everything to Clea.'

As if she could read his mind. He swallowed, pushed his empty plate into the middle of the table and said, 'Last night I lost my bond and my fridge because of your brother. I need money and I need it bad. I got debts,' he muttered, 'big ones.'

She nodded staring at him intently.

'I'd like to be a saint, Angela, but this is the real world. Without money you might as well be an empty chip packet.'

She turned and walked off down the hall. He followed her into a small lavender room with a toy panda reclining on the bed. Clea in a green dress, white socks and matching shoes was drawing skyscrapers at her desk. Her mother took her hand without saying a word.

In the car Clea said, 'I want to sit with Jack, Mum.'

'You're easily bought aren't you,' her mother said.

Clea climbed over into the back as Angela executed a U-turn and sped up Erskineville Road, striking all the potholes. 'Say something in Spanish, Jack.'

'*Buenos dias, señorita. Métetelo en el culo.*'

'What's that mean?'

'G'day, miss. Up your bum.'

Clea's eyes sparkled. She looked at Jack and then out the window, her pale skinny legs dangling off the edge of the seat. Angela scowled at the pair of them as she reversed the Holden into a no parking zone in King Street.

'That's our shop,' Clea said. Candles, imitation jewellery and a hat rack stood in a window. Jack could see boxes of secondhand dresses through an open door and an Avengers poster stuck high up on a wall. A sign above the entrance read, ALL GEAR ON SALE. Angela got out and came round to the back door, grabbed her daughter by the arm and took her inside. After a moment the girl with the three rings in her nose came out onto the footpath with Angela. She was wearing the same faded blue singlet as last night and some kind of decorated felt hat. Angela waved at Clea and said something to the girl who nodded. Jack watched them closely. When Angela got back in the car he said, 'The punkess – she your employee?'

'Helen's my best friend. You know what a best friend is?'

'Yeah,' Jack said, 'I had one once myself.'

17

Chinatown had grown rapidly over the last few years. Once confined to a few dark alleyways around Dixon Street, it now stretched in a large triangle from Central Station across to Darling Harbour and back up Liverpool Street. In the Haymarket it spilled east as far as Castlereagh. The old centre had been spruced up with new paving stones and Chinese lanterns flying coloured ribbons overhead. A pair of sleepy lions guarded an archway. Tourist stuff, Jack knew, but it worked. It was harder to get a park here than anyplace in town. Angela drove around for twenty minutes before she found a spot. Delivery vans blocked the backstreets and cement trucks rumbled past bound for the new high-rise tower that was going up. She fixed her Club Bar onto the steering wheel and locked the doors. She had to be careful, she said, hers was the only antique car in the street. The Nikkon slung over a shoulder, she walked ahead peering into restaurant lobbies. The plaza was crowded. Waiters darted in and out of glass doors like busy magpies. Thin-faced workers in cheap runners were pushing trolleys round the sides of buildings, unloading meat and sacks of vegetables off trucks. In the club Jack had heard that the 45,000 Chinese students Hawke had let in were still working for four bucks an hour. Nobody he saw was fat. Lean figures jammed the doorway of the Lucky Food Store. An old chainsmoker shuffled up a side street in his Kung Fu shoes. Everywhere there was movement.

Jack said, 'What are we looking for exactly?'

'You know as well as I do,' Angela replied. 'A man with a unicorn tattoo.'

'Doesn't this seem a little ridiculous to you?'

She turned and faced him with her feet apart. 'Either you help me or you don't.'

'Okay,' Jack said, 'okay.' He concentrated on her features as she poked her head into Yum Cha doorways. He liked her nose. He liked the way she walked. He had a bug about her. They went inside takeaway stores, Ginseng Centres, an optometrist's with Chinese characters on the eye chart. They combed Chinatown from top to bottom. On the other side of Pitt Street there were fewer tourists and the alleyways smelled of star-anise and boiled vegetables. An old disused theatre was boarded up, a big grimy building. The pavement was stained and greasy. Cockroaches ran about with purpose and brownish water dripped from rusted guttering. Storerooms were stacked with tins of lard and Sal Fry.

In the window of the Woo Ling Barbecue Shop, glazed ducks hung from hooks, their feet trussed with wire. A butcher in a plastic apron inside was splitting duck bones, bringing the meat cleaver down again and again onto a big wooden block, skilfully missing his fingers. On the man's hairless right forearm Jack caught a flash of blue.

He stood outside the barbecue shop with his eyes fixed on the neatest bit of needlework he'd seen in a long while: a big blue unicorn. He turned and waved at Angela across the street as a broad-shouldered man barrelled past, went in the doorway at the side of the shop entrance and climbed the stairs. Jack stepped back onto the road. The second and third floor windows were barred. The door at the side had a welded steel frame and another man sat on the edge of a table in the shadows.

'What is it?' Angela's breath felt hot against his ear. He watched her stare at the outstretched arm of the man chopping bird bones in the window. He watched her eyes and the line of her jaw set tight. She unslung her camera and unclipped its case. The butcher started scraping entrails into a plastic tray. He had a stringy black moustache and cheeks more pitted than the dartboard at the club. Jack followed Angela inside. She leaned on the chipped tiled wall at the rear of the narrow shop and removed her lens cap. The pockfaced butcher glared at her as she lifted the camera up to her eye.

'No photo, no photo here!'

Angela ignored him, bending low to snap him twice.

The butcher lunged across the counter. 'You want trouble?' He grabbed at her camera strap, gelatine and strips of duck flesh flying off his fingers. Jack sprang forward and shoved him in the chest. The man blinked with surprise as he stumbled back, knocking a tray of steamy guts over the floor. He grabbed his huge meat cleaver and jumped the counter.

'Hey,' Jack said. 'Drop the chopper.'

'Gwei-Lo!' The butcher hacked at the air in front of Jack's big nose. Jack's feet slipped in a slimy puddle of gizzards and he hit the deck. A mirror shattered centimetres above his head. He rolled over once, twice in the sawdust and jumped to his feet as the butcher charged at him, sharp black eyes like razor cuts in a pitted bony face. The cleaver whooshed past Jack's ear and he shot a hand up to check if his lug was still hanging there. This guy was trying to kill him: the realisation hit Jack like a smack in the mouth. He bobbed, ducked, stepped to the side and poked a right at a moving cheekbone. The man screeched like a wild cat, swiping at Jack's head. Duck bones crunched underfoot as Jack tripped and fell against the counter, saw the blue unicorn dance in front of his eyes, the blade of the cleaver raised overhead. He flung up an arm to protect his skull. The man screamed, a piercing scream, and his tongue seemed to swell large in his mouth. The cleaver dropped to the floor and both his hands went up to grapple with the meathook sticking out the back of his neck.

Angela stood over the butcher lying in the sawdust. Her breathing was high pitched, furious. Her dark blue eyes blazed as she snatched up the meat cleaver. Jack leapt up and knocked it from her hand. He felt her shoulders trembling with anger as he held her tight, the sharp smell of her hair in his face, her fists beating against his rib cage.

A lightbulb jerked on its cord overhead. Footsteps thudded down the stairs at the side. 'Let's get outta here,' Jack said. They ran out of the shop into Campbell Street. Young, well-built males in sawn off T-shirts yelling in Cantonese were pouring out of the neighbouring doorway like wasps from a nest.

Angela slung the camera off her shoulder, ripped at the

lens cap as they backed across the road towards the old rundown theatre. She said, 'See what I see?'

He nodded. All three men coming after them had unicorns tattooed on their forearms. Jack knew they were fighters – Wing Shun, Hapkido – he'd seen that look plenty of times in the academies he'd passed through. They closed in from either side. Up on the soles of their feet, holding their straightened fingers down away from their bodies like knives. No fear at all in their faces. Ready.

Jack pushed Angela away. 'Run,' he said. 'I'll try and hold them off.' He had five, six minutes of fight in him before he'd run out of petrol. There was only one way to go – full bore. His hands swept up to guard his face. Chin tucked low, he charged, jabbing his big fists. A round-house kick caught him high on the shoulder; he blocked another, sidestepped. A squat man with his head completely shaved whirled towards him, flicking his feet up into Jack's face. A third or fourth Dan he knew from the snap of those kicks. The man flashed a mouth full of gold-capped teeth. Jack backed against the wall.

Angela was standing on the road, clicking her camera.

'Get outta here!' Jack roared. A scissor kick almost tore off his head. A kung fu shoe hit him smack in the chest and he felt his heart buckle. Then they were on him. A foot whacked him in the ribs, another struck his face. Blood gushed from his nose. The man with the shaved head closed in. The edges of his hands calloused, his knuckles worn smooth as ivory. He spun in mid-air and hit Jack in the ribs with a turning kick so hard that Jack's legs folded underneath him like a beach umbrella.

Tyres screeched on the road; a cab door flung open. Jack saw the gap and dived into the back seat as a hand grabbed at his ankle. He booted at the face behind it, rolled over onto his belly as Angela yelled, 'Go, Go!' and the cab shot off down Campbell Street, door flapping in the wind, Jack's feet dangling out and half a dozen shoppers standing on the pavement staring.

The cabbie lifted his eyes as Jack pulled the door shut, flopped against the seat, holding his nose back. 'He's not bleedin on me upholstery?'

'Shut up and drive,' Angela barked.

Jack looked up at the boning knife she held to the side of the driver's neck. It was more than thirty centimetres long with a narrow black handle.

'Okay, miss. Take it easy. Where we going?'

'Redfern,' she said, digging the steel point in under his fleshy chin. 'Do as I say and you won't get hurt.' Angling her head towards Jack: 'You alright?'

'Yeah.' He shut his eyes. His chest felt like he'd been stomped by a family of mules.

'I thought you could fight.'

'So did I,' Jack said. 'We're gonna need help.'

The road dipped and curved to the right. A Koori mural ran along the wall outside the station. Angela scratched in her pockets, yelling, 'Stop here!' She chucked twenty dollars over into the front seat. 'That's for the ride. If you're smart you won't hang around, buster, just keep on going.' She whipped the knife away from the driver's throat and jumped out after Jack. The cabbie seemed to think about it for a moment and then the cab lurched forward, the man's hand reaching for the radio. Angela and Jack bolted through the turnstiles and flew down the stairs to the Bankstown platform. Five minutes later they emerged from Erskineville station, turned right and cut through the school grounds. They crossed the road quickly and went down the laneway at the back of her street. At the bottom they checked her place out from both sides before they went up the front steps, Jack clutching his ribs. There was no sign of intruders. Nobody in the street. The front door clicked shut behind them and they leaned against the wall, elbows touching, chests heaving. Angela kicked off her shoes and stood there in the hallway. She slipped the camera off her shoulders, dropped the butcher's knife onto the telephone table and peeled off her top. Underneath she wore a black camisole with lace edging.

Jack stared at the tufts of wet black hair poking out from under her arms. 'You saved my life,' he said. 'I thought I was gonna be turned into rissoles.'

She smiled at him, her eyes big and dark in the dimness of the hall. When he kissed her he felt her eyelashes brush against his. He ran a big sore hand up under her camisole, touched her hot sticky skin. With his other hand he pulled at the zipper on her jeans and slid his fingers inside. He said, 'I want you so bad it hurts.'

She laughed. Her lips were red and her head was tilted to the side. Beads of sweat rolled down her cheek. 'On the floor,' she said. She tugged at his belt, pulling him down onto the red Persian runner that bisected the polished floorboards. He kissed her. Long deep kisses which made her stretch her legs and arch her neck. They struggled to get out of their clothes. The pain in his ribs vanished as she eased him inside her and he buried his face in her breasts. A deep murmur rose in the back of her throat. He heard her whisper as he cried out. They lay coupled on the floor afterwards while the light faded and their faces grew dark, listening to the rattle of the trains in the distance.

18

The city rolled past his window, big and busy in the night. Darkness swallowed the carriage then the dingy lights flickered on again and he could see slash marks in the State Rail seats like someone had gone crazy with a knife. He poked a finger into a deep hole next to him, thinking of Damian lying dead in the middle of Pitt Street. He was out of his league here. Too old for the kung fu shit. Ten years ago he might've given it a whirl but now – he pressed two fingers against the curve of his ribs and sucked in air – now he was far too slow.

Standing half-dressed with her in her tiny Erskineville backyard afterwards. 'I want to thank you, for your help today,' she'd said, like they'd been shelling peas.

'Don't thank me,' he said. 'You saved my bacon.'

She shrugged her broad shoulders. 'It's finished now. I'm taking these photos over to Celia first thing in the morning, get her to identify the killers and then I'm going straight to the police.' She nodded her head as if she'd given the matter a lot of consideration.

'Good,' Jack said. 'One thing. I can't help wondering whether you killed that guy with the meat hook.'

'No, it only went in half an inch or so.'

''Cause I don't want Homicide charging us with murder.'

'It was self-defence, Jack. He was trying to kill you.'

'Try telling Detective Quarrell that.'

'Quarrell's not the only policeman in New South Wales. This time I'm going over his head.' She stared rigidly at him as she undid her black and red Japanese robe. 'Would you do me one last favour?'

His eyes swept to the long white scar running from her thick pubic hair up to her belly button. He had the feeling he wasn't going to like what she was about to request. 'What sort of favour?'

'I have to collect Clea from the shop and I want to develop this film tonight.' She pushed the battered toilet door open. 'My car. It's probably got a dozen tickets by now.'

He looked at her wide-eyed as she squatted on the wooden seat, hearing the sound of her piss hit the bowl. 'You want me to go back there alone?'

'Tomorrow I can pay you that five hundred dollars. It's all over, Jack. We've got what we need. And I know you want to get out of Sydney.'

The tunnel roared outside and the toughened windows clattered in their frames. Brakes squealed as the train shuddered into Museum station. He was glad it was over. Time to get on with his own life, time to move. His footsteps echoed through the damp underground walkway. He wondered who she'd thought about when they'd made love. Wondered if it was him. A wino was sprawled across the exit. Jack stepped over his legs and out into the night air. He crossed the road, walked down Liverpool Street following the oil drips from the Monorail. Gangs of movie-goers had gathered on the corner of George Street to watch two paramedics resuscitate a teenager. The kid was out of it, his mouth loose and rubbery. Spectators chewed popcorn while an ambulance-woman stuck a needle into the boy's arm. Jack caught the lights, patting the bulge in his pocket. He'd pick her car up afterwards, but he had something else to do first. Limping, he went into the club. The stale smell of beer rose from the red carpet and cigar smoke stung his eyes. Poker machines hummed in the background like a chartered accountant's dream. He found Carlos in the office reading a Spanish paper, a photo of a gutted Mercedes and three bullet-riddled corpses on the front page.

Carlos looked up slowly, folded the *El Pais* neatly in half. 'You know, Jack. There's only two people in this world I don't like.'

'That all?' Jack said. He could think of five, six, easy.

'The Arab people and the Israeli people.' Carlos dropped the paper into a wastebin. His shiny black hair was sleeked back and his white collar bit into the folds of his neck. 'You ever see anyone take money from this safe?'

Jack shook his head.

'The Directors call in the police today.' Carlos kept his eyes focused on Jack. 'Five thousand dollars is gone missing.'

'Five thousand!' Jack pulled on his chin, trying to figure who had skimmed off the other three and a half. He said, 'You don't know who to trust anymore, do you?'

'Then Wednesday night I put Antonio on the disco door to replace you. What happens? Some men cause trouble for him. Antonio is very stupid; he doesn't press the buzzer, no, he jumps on them. First I lose one doorman, now I lose a second doorman. Antonio is in the hospital with five broken ribs and a fractured skull. Now we have no doormen.'

'These men,' Jack said slowly. 'Who were they?'

'Gangsters from Chinatown. I don't know what's going on down there. But I think it's bad. Seventeen years I been with this club and we never have trouble with the Chinese people before.'

Jack watched the assistant manager shift behind his desk and he had the feeling that he knew more than he was letting on. 'I'm leaving town next week. Going away for a spell.'

'This is all very sudden, Jack. We're gonna miss you. Is not easy to find good doormen now in Sydney.'

'No wonder,' Jack said. 'Place's getting more dangerous every day.'

In the bar he ordered a double brandy and pawed at a bowl of black olives, popping them one by one into his mouth while worry lines ploughed across his brow. He spat the pips into the tray that looped around the bar underneath his feet and ordered another double. He drank that leaning an elbow on the rail. Rana was not in the change box and there was a new Galician waiter behind the counter. Jack borrowed a pen from him and started working out some rough figures on the back of a beer coaster. Including what he was owed from the club and the five hundred she'd promised him he had fifteen hundred all up. Not a lot to start a new life with. It always came back to money in the end. Wherever you turned. He passed a row of backs lined along the pokies and went out into the street. It was quieter here. Cars purled past. Jack crossed the road looking over his shoulders carefully, ears alert for the sound of footsteps. He turned into Sussex Street, saw an Asian guy coming towards him and tensed instinctively before he caught himself. Just because he got a kicking in Chinatown didn't mean he was going to write off every bloke he met with black hair and brown eyes. He'd have to watch that. The man drew closer and Jack recognised the Vietnamese from the club. Pham grinned at Jack like they were old friends.

'Hey, three men bin in the club lookin for you.'

'Yeah, I heard,' Jack said. 'These guys. They have unicorn tatts on their arms?'

Pham nodded. 'I hear them talkin bout you. Say they gone hur you bad, maybe kill you. Sun Sai Gei very dangerous people.'

'Who?' Jack studied the tattooed crane flying up the side of Pham's neck.

'Blue Unicorn gang. They street soldier for Sun Sai Gei. Everybody know that. You ever hear 14K, Big Circle?'

'Triads?' Jack said.

'Sun Sai Gei they number one now. Before was 14K. But they grow fat, lazy. Have big war all round here, force many restauran close down.' Pham glanced over his left shoulder at the passing lights of a car.

'How do you know all this?' Jack said.

Steam rose from a plastic container Pham was juggling in one hand. He said, 'When I arrive Australia first job I get in Chinatown. Work casino over restauran.' He jerked his head towards Dixon St. 'Learn Cantonese, little bit Mandarin. My boss he Sun Sai Gei. When I go Long Bay they tell me not to worry. Pay policeman, big one. Fix everythin. When I get out I meet good woman. Get marry. No more white powder job. My wife – she pregnant now.'

'Congratulations,' Jack said.

'That natural.' Pham shrugged his shoulders. 'These people very bad. Sun Sai Gei the worse all. Be careful, they kill you easy.'

Jack reached out and gripped Pham by the elbow of his new leather jacket. 'Why you telling me this?'

'That nigh in the club. When I win fi Inca, you know somethin wron, but pay me the money.' Pham grinned under the streetlight. 'Now I help you back. Got many fren in Cabramatta.' He pressed the steamy takeaway to his chest and his dark brown eyes swept Jack a look of complicity. 'Very cheap fren. Good figher. You unnerstan?'

Jack nodded slowly, staring off down the one-way street towards where he was headed.

The Holden was sitting with two yellow envelopes tucked under its wipers. No car in front. No car behind. Jack walked straight past it, running his eyes over the back seat. On the other side of the street he stopped in the shadows, checked the windows above the shop front opposite. Three men in black suits staggered by – lawyers or funeral attendants, it was hard to tell which – arms draped over each other's shoulders. They didn't see Jack flattened against the brickwork. He pulled the keys out of his pocket, shifted his weight onto the soles of his shoes and strode across the road, arms swinging, stuck the key in the driver's door, got in, punched the lock down and removed the Club Bar. The engine started first hit and the Holden jumped forward with a little squeal. He swung the wheel heading south through Ultimo. When he had put a fair distance between himself and Chinatown he wound his window down and wiped the sweat from his eyes. Triads. That's all he fucking needed. He pushed the accelerator to the floor. Cleveland Street flew past and the twin towers of TNT rose in front of him. The EH's steering was stiff and awkward and he appreciated her driving skills even more. He passed a streetsweeper in Regent Street and tailgated a van going up Henderson Road. He overtook it blindly, ran a red light at the top of the hill, spun left and turned right down her tree-studded street. At the end of the road he braked and jumped out of the car. Her front door was open and lights were on all over the place.

He ran up the steps and peered in through the screen door. It was locked. 'Angela!' he called. He wrapped his big hands around the handle and wrenched. Wood splintered as the hinges sheared off. He tore down her hallway. Not the kid, he was thinking, don't let it be the kid. When he reached the kitchen he stopped. A draught was blowing in through the open back door. He went out into the yard slowly, cautiously. Voices were coming from the shed behind the toilet. He leaned a shoulder against the door, took two steps back and charged. The door crashed inwards.

'Christ,' Angela said. 'What on earth are you doing?' She was pegging wet photographs on a nylon line in the small makeshift darkroom. Beside her in pyjamas Clea was helping.

Jack stood there with his big empty hands in front of him. 'You alright, little goat?' He scooped Clea up by the armpits, held her high in the air.

'What's got into you, Jack? Put her down.'

Jack lowered the startled child onto the bare concrete floor. 'I had a feeling,' he blurted, 'a bad feeling – '

'Well don't have any more of them,' Angela remarked a few minutes later when she saw her screen door lying on the porch. 'I can't afford the repairs.'

Jack's face tightened. 'If you think this is over with, you're dead wrong.'

19

A shadow passed across the doorway. Footsteps scurried along the edge of the room and the bed gave a little groan. Jack sat up staring into Clea's wide blue eyes. Her legs under her cotton skirt reminded him of paddle pop sticks. 'Why's Jack sleeping in with you, Mum?'

Angela stirred and rolled over onto her side. 'Jack was cold out on the couch last night, honey. He needed to get warm.'

Clea went to climb in under the sheets too.

'No,' her mother snapped. She pushed her daughter back and jumped out of bed herself, snatched her robe and threw it on.

Clea said, 'You broke our door, Jack. Now the flies'll get in. You'll have to pay for that.' Angela grabbed her daughter's hand and led her from the bedroom. 'I did some, I did some drawings, Mum,' the child was saying.

Jack rolled the rubber off his cock. He lay there listening to the South Sydney council workers shouting obscenities out in the street. A jackhammer started up and he slipped out of bed and went to the window, looked out. Angela came back in and shut the door, walked over to the bedside table and grabbed a couple of tissues. 'Come on, Jack,' she said. 'Get dressed.'

Jack stood there watching her pull on fresh pink undies, a pair of black tap dancing shoes, a multi-coloured skirt and a blue silk top. He said, 'I don't know why, but I get the distinct feeling you want to get rid of me.'

'I want to get away early and I want to lock up.' She stared at the shiny scar running across his rib cage. 'What happened there?'

He traced the scar tissue with a fingertip. 'Shark attack.'

She rolled her eyes, tossed him his clothes and stood over him while he dressed. 'You want to buy your plane ticket don't you?'

'What plane ticket?'

'Buenos Aires. Aren't you going to Buenos Aires?'

Jack said, 'I'm thinking more of Bundanoon at the moment.'

In the kitchen he picked up the loose photos lying on the table, sifted through some blurred close-ups of the Blue Unicorn gang while she attended to her daughter. These guys were pros. They weren't to be trifled with. He removed a snap of himself on the receiving end of a Triad boot and dropped it in a bin. Didn't want the cops seeing that. When she came through he said, 'You can't just walk away from this crew. I think we need help.'

'Look.' She planted her feet apart. 'I told you. We've found my brother's murderers. Now I'm taking these photos over to Waterloo and then I'm going to point the police in the right direction.'

Jack waited for her hands to settle. 'Go ahead. I don't think I'll come with you. I've got other things to do.'

'You can't stay here.'

'Why not?' Jack said.

'Because this is my house.'

'You worried I'll go through your drawers or something?'

'Yes, I am.'

'What sort of bastard do you take me for?'

20

Five minutes later Jack walked into her bedroom and
started on the cheap pine dresser. He lifted the drawers
out onto the bed and rifled through her skirts, jumpers,
bangles, even the crafted jewellery boxes crammed with
her earrings. He didn't know what he was looking for,
but he'd sure know when he found it. She had some nice
clothes in here, some black silk panties which felt light
and soft in his big rough hands. He uncovered a pack of
Veet creme depilatoire, turned it over: *New Veet from
France with its striking feminine floral fragrance*. Lot of
F's, Jack thought. For such a hot-tempered woman she
was incredibly neat: every garment she owned was folded;
he'd have to be extra careful. At the bottom of the deepest
drawer he struck gold – a long water pipe. He lifted it up
to his nose and sniffed. A faint sickly smell clung to the
bowl. Opiates. He laid the pipe back under the balls of
coloured socks. What else was she hiding? He turned the
bedroom inside out. He searched in the pockets of her
coats. It was *her*, that's what he was after. Ever since
they'd met she'd been switching the tables on him. And
all the time he remained good ole Jack – thick as two
planks. Well if this was Easter he wasn't going to be the
bunny. He pulled out all the drawers of her desk, a big
wooden thing, sifted through accounts and folders full of
sales receipts, a couple of loose polaroids. His eyes rested
on a fit-looking man in his late fifties, bare-chested,
punching a bag strung up in a backyard. Old man Frick.
Jack had seen him plenty of times on TV. He picked out
a big gold-rimmed album and leafed through its stiff grey
pages. Inside were dozens of photos of a teenage Damian.

All different sizes and qualities. Many of them she must've blown up herself: Damian lying on a leopard skin, Damian getting out of the bath, Damian standing against some dark drapes with his cock sticking up like a boomerang.

Jack stared at the last photo for a good while, then ripped the snap out of the album and slipped it into his shirt pocket. His eyes went to the bedroom window. He wanted to talk to someone. Someone he trusted. That eliminated almost everybody he knew in Sydney. He grabbed the white pages in the hall, ran his fingers down the Macs, found the number and dialled. When he heard the smoke-affected voice on the other end, he hung up and a smile pushed at the corners of his mouth. He'd give his old friend McCredie a big surprise.

In the kitchen he set a chair against the back door, slipped outside, reached in and pulled the chair under the handle. He walked through the yard and hoisted himself up onto the branches of a flowering pink eucalypt and dropped over the sheet iron fence into the lane. Tempe wasn't far from here, but he hailed a cab anyway. It had been a long time since he'd seen McCredie and he was looking forward to it.

Of all the bouncers Jack had worked with Killer McCredie was the best. He wasn't a great boxer, nor did he have a string of black belts to his name, but he could go like nobody else. He'd got his start working the Cross in the early seventies, the Pink Pussycat, the Venus Room – punching on with Maoris, Finks, Commancheros. Like a lot of career bouncers, Killer had been iron-barred, stabbed with broken beer glasses, knifed, slashed with bike chains, but he'd never lost his love for his work. To watch him out on the street was awesome. He'd taught Jack everything about working a door. How to handle the kids on whizz or a pack of bleary-eyed front rowers, how to use whatever weapon was at hand. It was Killer in the first place who had persuaded Jack to branch out from

behind the bar to behind the door. And Jack still held
that against him.

Killer's place was a brown blistered weatherboard
house squeezed in between a paint factory at one end of
the street and a huge motor wreckers at the other. It had
a full-pitched roof, a two metre cyclone wire fence running
around the perimeter of the property and dead banana
trees sticking up out front. As Jack climbed out of the
cab, a Qantas 747 flew so low overhead that the whole
block was cast in shadow. Pieces of an old Triumph were
parked in the car-port like a puzzle that had been too
hard to solve. Jack threaded his way between the rusted
bike parts and a blue tarp, and rang the bell. Dogs barked
at the back of the house and heavy steps thumped down
the hall. The door opened and McCredie, who was built
like a battered cement mixer with iron-grey hair yanked
back into a short pony tail, stood there, a cigarette
burning off the edge of his lip.

Jack said, 'Long time, mate.'

Killer fixed him with his good eye. 'Jack Butorov.' He
spat the cigarette butt out onto the wooden porch and
rubbed at a tattooed arm. The air all around tasted of
aviation fuel. 'So what've you been doin with yourself,
Boot?'

'Working,' Jack said. 'Eating, shitting, watching
television.'

'I heard you was in Africa or someplace.'

'Spain,' Jack said.

'Same bloody thing.' Killer brought a big gnarled hand
up to his scalp and scratched. 'Well don stand there like
a freckled duck. Come in.' He led Jack down a dark-
brown hall into a dark-brown loungeroom that smelled
warm and musty like a cave. A TV was blaring in a
corner. Jack turned his head just as a big dark blur
rushed at him and knocked him backwards. Feet grabbed
his shoulders and he was looking into the jaws of a fully-
grown Doberman.

'Down Stalin, down boy!' Killer tugged at the dog's spiked collar, the veins in his big arms swelling under the strain.

'Get it off me,' Jack cried. 'Christ!'

Killer grinned as he pulled the Doberman away and dragged it out into the bare cement yard where two other black mastiffs lay panting. Jack slumped on the edge of the couch, wiping dog drool off his chin. He looked up and saw a thin, tired-eyed woman in a nurse's uniform watching him from the kitchen doorway. 'My God,' she said, shaking her head, 'Jack Butorov. It must be five years.' She stared at him intensely. 'Time's cruel, Jack. Very cruel.'

Jack ran a hand quickly over his thinning hair. 'You're looking well, Marilyn.'

'Don't lie to me, you bastard.' She kept her eyes pinned on him. 'How's Vick?'

Jack said nothing. A plane flew overhead and every window and door in the house rattled. Marilyn looked to Jack and Jack looked to Marilyn and then her husband came back in and dropped like a load of bricks into his big vinyl armchair. His lips were curled back into what could've been a smile. 'Almost shit himself.' He reached for his Camel Plains, lit one and blew two streams of thick blue smoke out his nostrils and over his barrelled chest. 'Jus like old times eh, hon.' He looked across at his wife.

'I've made a pot of tea,' Marilyn said quickly. 'If you'd like some, Jack?'

Jack said that he would. Marilyn hastened from the room and came back a few moments later with a tray. 'Try one of these oatmeal biscuits,' she said, touching his arm. 'All natural ingredients. Kelvin made them himself.'

'White sugar is a poison,' Killer said. Marilyn sat beside Jack on the couch fidgeting with her cup while they watched a woman give blood on the TV. They dunked their biscuits in their hot tea. When the station break came on, Marilyn got up, kissed her husband on top of the head and whispered something into the mangled lump of cartilage that remained of his left ear. Killer grunted at her, but didn't move. 'Nice to see you again Jack,' she said, leaving the room. 'Give my love to Vick.'

'Sure,' Jack said.

Killer fixed Jack with his bad eye, waited until the front door had shut properly and then said in a low growl, 'So whaddya want, Butorov?'

'Quarrell knows I'm back. Tried to do me in Liverpool Street.'

Killer said, 'I warned you he'd come after you. Look what he done to Nepo.'

'I know what he done to Nepo,' Jack said. 'Don't you think I don't?'

'So you shouldn'ta come back,' Killer said. 'Simple as that.'

'I had to,' Jack said. 'I ran out of dough and I ran out of visas. Anyway I got another problem right now. Triads. There's a bunch of Triads been lookin for me.'

Killer placed his cup down on the table. He leaned forward in his black chair and pushed his rugged jaw out. 'So how'd you get mixed up with the rice-eaters?'

Jack told him. He began with the night in Oxford Street and went on from there, leaving out all the sexual bits.

Killer listened with one eye on *Days of our Lives*, picking at his teeth with a decking nail. His big face was lined and marked like an old ironbark. When Jack'd finished, Killer said, 'Your little mate must've got in over his head, tried to mess with the big boys and they plugged him.' Killer's eyes met Jack's; the right eye looked like somebody had stuck a sharp instrument into the pupil. 'Smack I'd bet. The chinks run the show. If you want any of the hard stuff you gotta do business with them. Right now there's some kind of war boiling over in Chinatown. Bloke in the know told me his construction boys can't pour the concrete fast enough. I'll give you some advice, Butorov. Don't fuck with these blokes. If you're holding some gear of theirs let em have it. Walk away while you still got your legs.'

'I got nothin of theirs,' Jack said. 'Not a gram.'

'Sounds to me like you got somethin they want bad.' A 747 rumbled low over Tempe sounding like a B52 about to drop its load. Jack watched Killer's lips moving, but he couldn't hear any of the words. The picture on the TV jumped about and the whole house shook on its blocks.

Killer lifted himself out of his chair and padded down the hallway. He came back a few moments later unwrapping an oilskin from around a .44 Magnum revolver. He gripped the gun securely with his thumb resting on the hammer, the barrel poking Jack's way. 'I got a prezzy for you.'

Jack stiffened.

'Don' worry, if I'd wanted to kill yer, I woulda done it long ago.' Killer slapped the big black cannon into Jack's palm. 'Here. Take it. You're gonna fuckin need this.'

Jack stood up. Dogs howled out in the yard and one of them slammed its weight against the back door. Jack stared into the marred face of his old friend, weighing the giant Magnum carefully in his hand. 'I appreciate this, but I'd like to try and do it without the gun.'

'Suit yourself,' Killer said, 'but don come crying to me if they stick you in a cigar box.' He took his revolver back and wrapped it gently in its oilcloth. 'You know where I'll be if you change your mind.'

Jack looked down at the faded spiders on the webbing of Killer's hands. 'Thanks, Kel,' he said. 'I owe you.'

Killer lit a Camel and blew the smoke out. 'Know somethin?' He walked Jack down the hall. 'Twenty years up the Cross and I've never seen the town lookin so bad. In the old days there were hard men – remember Johnny Cheika, Leon, Tony the Greek? Now there's just rats with guns – speedballs who think life's a Hollywood movie, they think if they get blown away they'll come back in the next picture.' Killer undid the three deadlocks on the door. 'Watch your back out there, pal.'

Jack pumped his friend's hand. The jet fumes outside gave him an almost instant lift. He was out on the footpath when he turned, saw the big grey-haired bouncer standing barefoot on his wooden porch. 'Hey,' Killer called, 'I always said you were one hell of a lucky bloke.'

21

Climbing over the sheet iron fence was a lot more difficult from the other side. The branches of the eucalypt groaned under Jack's ninety-five K's and the purple bougainvillea scratched at his face. He slid down the tree trunk and landed with a bump in a herb bed. At the back door he applied his shoulder and heard the chair scrape across the kitchen floor. He listened for footsteps, then slipped inside and checked all the rooms, even the kid's. Nobody. He reached above the fridge and smelled the sweet sherry bottle first, stuck it back on the shelf and grabbed the other one. He poured himself a big tawny McWilliams port in an ETA peanut butter glass. He drank that sitting at the kitchen table then licked his lips and poured himself another. Creases angled across his forehead. Every now and then he rubbed at his stubbled jaw, elbows resting on a wooden chopping block. Killer was right. He had something they wanted, but what?

He stood up rather quickly, skirted the edge of the table and strode into Angela's bedroom. His suitcase lay at the foot of the bed and he tipped it out onto the floor, rooted through his shirts, strides, dirty socks; there was nothing here that would interest St Vincent de Pauls in a lean year, let alone a bunch of well-heeled gangsters. Slowly he got to his feet, slapped a big hand across his dome. How dumb could he get? It was a wonder he could still feed himself. He went through the house trying to find where she had put it. In the loungeroom he saw it sticking out behind the couch. He lifted the pink milk crate up onto his lap and flicked through his dusty old LPs: Otis, Aretha, Big Mama Thornton, Etta James, some badly scratched Yardbirds. He removed the records one at a time and shook their covers out onto the couch. A black bit of plastic shot out of a John Lee Hooker album. It looked a little like an old 45 single, but Jack knew what it was. A computer disc. He turned it over in his big hands: Damian. He should've twigged the night they pulled his place apart that he'd planted something there. It was easy to say so now, but when you're in the midst of it all, it's hard to see your way through the checkout.

He went back into the kitchen and finished off her port, fiddling with the disc in front of him. So that's why Damian'd been so keen to come back to Coogee. Jack had conjured up that night a lot since: lying beside the young man in the sweltering heat, with desire belting through his mind.

There are times when you have to take the big decisions – and this was one of them. He could walk away from this now or he could try and hook himself some serious bucks. Question was how much were they willing to pay to get their disc back? He needed to take a squiz inside it first and that meant getting his hands on a PC. Trouble was he knew as much about computers as he knew about Zoroastrianism. The front door slammed; shoes tapped quietly down the hall. He pushed the floppy disc behind the fruit bowl and looked up at those big dark blue eyes in the doorway.

Angela lifted a bottle up by its neck. 'I bought some wine to celebrate.'

Jack said, 'I could do with a drink.'

She pulled up a chair, removed her shoes and stuck her feet up on the table. They were small pink feet, but nicely arched. She massaged them with her fingers while he hunted up a corkscrew. 'Aaah,' she said, 'that feels good.' Her eyes were shining and her hair was messed like she'd been in the tunnel.

'Cheers.' Jack clinked glasses and threw back his head.

'You're supposed to sip it, Jack.'

'Yeah?' He splashed more Browns Chardonnay into their glasses and leaned back. 'Okay, I'm waiting.'

Angela nodded quickly, slid her feet off the table. 'I went out to Waterloo. It was them alright. Celia ID'd one of the two gunmen.'

Jack said, 'Which one? You got the photos there?'

'No, I dropped them into the police.'

'You didn't give them to Quarrell did you?'

'You're just like Clea you know that – one question at a time. No, I didn't give them to Detective Quarrell, because he wasn't there. I saw an Inspector Fenton instead.'

Jack wiped at his mouth with the back of his hand. 'Where's Quarrell got to?'

'Detective Quarrell's on extended sick leave. That's the reason there's been a delay with this investigation.'

'How long's he been on sick leave?'

'I dunno,' Angela said. 'Forget about him for one second if you can. I haven't finished telling you the rest of the story.'

'Okay,' Jack said, but his eyes grew restless.

Angela pulled her chair in. 'Inspector Fenton wanted to know how I got hold of these photos. I told him that I'd hired a private detective. I also said that I was going to the papers with the story if they didn't arrest Damian's killers in the next twenty-four hours.'

Jack reached for the bottle. 'What'd he say?'

'He assured me that an arrest was imminent, just as

soon as they checked with their witnesses. He asked me how I'd come into possession of Mrs McEvoy's address in the first place. I said Detective Quarrell gave it to me.'

'Neat,' Jack said. 'Who'd she ID?'

'The squat one with the gold teeth. The one that was giving you a kicking in the street.'

'Him?' Jack passed a hand over his ribs. 'A real little cruiserweight. What about the second guy?'

'Celia thought it was the one from the duck shop.' Angela stared at Jack, circling her glass on the table.

Jack shook the bottle. 'We drunk this already?'

Angela nodded. 'You sure did.'

'Got anything else tucked away?'

She reached into her small black purse and pulled out a wad of notes. She counted off ten fifties and laid them in a tiny stack on the table in front of his big restless hands. 'There. That's what I owe you.'

Jack eyed the dough. 'I wish I didn't have to take this. I never used to think about money. Money was never the main priority with me.' He bundled the notes off the table carefully and folded them into his pocket.

Angela stood up, went over to the stove and lit the top plate with a spark gun. She poured some hot water into the kettle and set it down on the flame. As she was taking out a carton of milk she bumped the fridge door hard against the back of his chair.

'Something wrong?'

She didn't answer.

'I've been doing a lot of thinking about Damian,' he said. 'Why do you reckon they killed him?'

'You tell me. I thought it was because of the scheme you two had cooked up.'

'So did I,' Jack said slowly, 'at first. Then I found this.' He reached over behind the oranges and grabbed the floppy disc. 'Damian hid it in my records. This is what they were looking for when they pulled my place apart. Maybe this is why they killed him too.'

Angela's mouth hardened. She looked down at the cheap plastic disc as a train clattered by a few streets away and then the kettle began to whistle. She stood there, quite still, while steam poured from its spout and the whistling grew louder and louder.

Jack got up and turned the gas off. He said, 'You know anyone with a computer?'

22

Light was fading across the red sky as she drove fast up Erskineville Road, her seahorse earrings swinging in her lobes. Jack rubbed at his jaw with his fingers, hoping he wasn't going to regret showing her. Maybe he should've waited until after he'd had a look inside it himself. Trains were shooting up and down the Bankstown line, sparks flying off the wires. Outside The Rose of Australia hotel three men were drinking schooners on the footpath, their grizzled dogs tied up to a pole. Narrow streets led down into narrow dead-ends.

'I think Damian knew they were after him,' Jack said. 'I've got the feeling this disc is the answer, that maybe this was his insurance. One thing always bothered me about his murder – how did they know in advance he was going to knock that nine grand off. They couldn't have. No way.'

Angela's eyes were fixed on the road ahead. 'Unless Damian told somebody.'

'Why would he? No, this is what they were after all along.' Jack stared out the window at the Police Boys Club, the disc gripped between his big safe fingers. 'I've never used a computer before. What sort's she got?'

'An Apple Mac. She's a writer.'

'I thought there was something I didn't like about her.'

The Holden bumped over King Street and flew down a very narrow lane barely missing the parked cars mounted on the pavement. On the Camperdown side of Memorial Park she pulled up outside a small two-bedroom semi with textured walls and a pale yellow tiled porch that wouldn't have looked out of place in a public urinal. Jack followed Angela down the path at the side. She rapped on the screen door and Helen came out wearing an African hat, a black sleeveless vest with a purple skirt and lace-up kick boots.

'Clea!' she called. 'Your mum's here.' She looked at Jack coolly, and held out her cheek to Angela.

'I need a favour, Hel,' Angela said, squeezing the younger woman's bare arm. 'Can you check something on the Mac?'

They went down the empty hall into the front room. Clea got out from underneath a yellow blanket in front of the TV, ran over to her mother and hugged her. She grinned at Jack. 'Hullo, pigeon legs,' he said. The child started skipping and jumping about like a firecracker as Helen led the three of them into an adjoining room where boxes and books were stacked on the floor. The only bit of furniture going was a big wooden desk with an LC III, monitor and an old printer set up on it. Helen switched the machine on, fiddling with the three silver rings in her nose while she booted up. Jack handed the disc over, and a moment later she said to Angela, 'You're in luck, Ange.'

The screen came alive. A row of names and two rows of figures spilled out from underneath a single heading – SFF.

Jack leaned over Helen's shoulder to read the dates, amounts and numbers, some of which had asterisks next to them. The text scrolled past his eyes. Page after page of it. Behind him Clea was skipping about on the bare wooden floor like she'd been fed jumping beans. 'Stop that honey will ya,' Jack said.

Angela turned to him. 'Don't you tell my daughter what to do.'

'Look, I'm trying to concentrate here.'

'Wait a minute.' Angela's hand clamped onto Helen's shoulder. 'Back up.'

The cursor moved up the screen and stopped, flashing, beside an entry which read: 12/12 – *F. Frick Pty Ltd* – 200,000.

'Your father.' Jack stared at the screen. 'You think they're dollars?'

'Well, they're not pineapples,' Angela said. She tapped the monitor with a fingernail. 'See. This must be some kind of record of accounts.'

'Yeah.' Jack saw alright. He saw that most of the entries had two sets of figures next to them – a smaller set on the left-hand side and a much larger one in the right-hand column. His mind was racing ahead. He began to smell money. Big money. It had an odour all of its own. Jack turned to the younger woman, 'Can you print it out?'

Helen tried to drag the icon over with the mouse. 'That's funny,' she said.

'What is?'

'It won't copy onto the hard disc.' She narrowed her eyes at him. 'Where'd you get this disc from?'

Angela walked over to the window which looked out onto a broken down fence. 'It's Damian's.'

'I'd say he pinched it,' Jack said, wondering what the hell it had to do with the Triads anyway. Why did they want it?

Helen got up from her desk, went over and put an arm around Angela's broad shoulders, then started whispering into her ear.

Jack watched them, thinking how was he going to work this? An opportunity was staring him right in the eyeballs if he could just crack it. SFF, what did that mean? 'Not now hon,' he said as Clea skipped over next to him and touched the mouse with her tiny fingers.

'Guess what, Jack? I know how to use this.'

The kid rolled the text on. The initials TC kept reappearing on the screen beside different amounts. Large amounts. Sixteen or seventeen of them. Jack toted the sums up quickly: three million, four hundred and eighty nine bucks in the right-hand column; twenty five grand in the left-hand column. TC, Jack was going, Tom Cruise, Tracy Chapman. He could hear Angela saying, 'I'm going to see Dad, see what this is about.' Then Helen said, 'I want to come with you.'

Jack said, 'Mightn't it be better if you minded C-l-e-a.'

Helen glared at him and Clea went, 'I can spell too, J-a-c-k.'

Jack pulled up one of the boxes and studied the last three pages of the document. The amounts were smaller here – $40,000 and $50,000 lots – and these were subtracted from the larger columns on the right-hand side. Pay-outs of some kind. He tried to memorise a pair of names – Max Cham, Des Roberts. He said quietly to Helen who was still giving him the bad eye. 'You got anything strong to drink round here?'

Angela gestured to Clea. 'Go and help Hel, darl.'

'Want my opinion?' Jack said when he and Angela were alone. 'This is something big.'

Angela shook her head. 'Not another one of your feelings, Jack.'

'Look at the facts. Damian was killed by a street gang who act as enforcers for a Sydney Triad. Okay, so what are Triads best known for – drugs and extortion, right? So why do they want this disc? That's what you gotta ask yourself. Maybe this is a list of firms round town who owe them money. Maybe they've got some hold on these people and Damian found out, tried to put the squeeze on –'

'Maybe, maybe,' she said. 'That's an awful lot of maybes you're sprinkling about.'

'These figures,' Jack said, 'what do they add up to –
five, six million in total? And half of that from this one
TC. Now where I come from that ain't pinball money.'

Angela worked at her bottom lip. 'What I'd like to know
is – why are you so interested now? I thought you wanted
to get away from here.' She went over to the Mac, pressed
two keys on the board and pulled the disc out from the
machine.

'I'll take that,' Jack said.

She stared at him coolly, her thick eyebrows arched.
'You think there's money to be made out of this don't
you?'

'Damian left it with me. He wanted me to find it for a
reason.'

The phone rang in the hall. Jack went to the doorway
as Helen came out of the kitchen and picked up the
receiver. She listened for a second and then slammed the
phone down hard. 'Bastard.'

'Who was that?'

'Some creep.'

Jack went down to the front room, killed the lights and
parted the cheap African curtains. He took a quick look
up and down the narrow street. Helen came up behind
him with a tall glass of something. In the dark he could
smell garlic on her. Keep the wolves away. He threw the
vodka down; it burned all the way and was good. 'Thanks,'
he said and grabbed her wrist. 'You and Angela are pretty
close aren't you?'

Helen nodded slowly in the dark, sharp green eyes
alert.

'I think she's in great danger. I think we all are.' He
poked the floppy disc under her nose. 'We need you to
print up a copy. Can you do that?'

She shook her head. 'Not tonight.'

'Why not?'

A faint line of dark hair ran along her top lip. 'The
printer's broken down. I can get it fixed tomorrow and

bring the copy over first thing.' She reached out and plucked the disc from his hand.

'Not so fast, Red.'

'You'll have to trust me now won't you?' She narrowed her eyes and her voice dropped to a whisper. 'Two women, that's your fantasy, isn't it?'

Jack watched her tuck the disc into the waistband of her skirt. 'You don't bring that disc back by noon,' he said, 'I'll be on your doorstep looking for you.'

'Men are so phallocentric. It sticks out a mile.'

In the backroom Angela said, 'Who was on the phone, Hel?' Clea's face was buried in her mother's lap, her bony legs dangled above the floor.

'Didn't give a name,' Helen said.

The veins stood out on Angela's forehead as she lifted the sleeping child up in her arms and carried her down the hall. 'You drive, Jack.'

Across the park below the churchyard wall, shadows moved about underneath the trees. Helen checked both sides of the street and gave him a strange smile. He went straight across to the passenger's door and opened it. When Angela and Clea were safely inside he went round and got in behind the wheel.

Angela said, 'You think it was them who rang?'

Jack said nothing. He wondered whether he was mad to leave the disc with the punkess. He didn't know if he could trust her. Didn't know what she was talking about, fallowcentric. The car lurched forward. Clea, sprawled in the back seat, was making faint little bubble sounds, her small chest rising and falling. Jack thought of his own son and what a fucked-up job he'd done as a father.

'Where you going?' Angela said.

Jack tried to steer his way through the maze of New-town back-streets, driving around in circles until finally he swung right onto King Street and the sweet smell of Thai curries rushed at him through the window. Neon strips glowed above the pavement. A man in a shiny brown suit was standing outside the Shakespeare Hotel tearing into a hot dog, his hard lean face lit yellow by a street lamp.

'Look out!' Angela went.

Jack saw the police wagon in front and slammed on the brakes. The Holden stalled. Detective Quarrell was watching them from the pavement, chewing slowly and methodically on a mouthful of sausage. Jack twisted the key in the ignition. 'C'mon, c'mon.' His eyes met Quarrell's and he knew – knew it for sure. Quarrell was in on this. The engine fired and Jack jammed the gears into first, took off fast.

'Watch the road!' Angela clutched her daughter to her breast as he cut across the oncoming lane and turned down towards Erskineville.

'What's he doing here? I thought you said he was on sick leave.'

Angela said, 'Maybe he's just come to Newtown to eat.'

'Nobody comes to King Street to eat a hot dog. I think he's gonna try and kill us.'

'Jack.' Shaking her head at him. 'Don't you think you're being a little paranoid?'

'What do you mean paranoid? You think I'm paranoid? I think Quarrell's working for the Triad. I think he knows about the disc.' He swung right and cruised down her street, peering into all the windows of the parked cars. A thin blanket of grey-black smoke drifted slowly over the suburb from the Waterloo incinerator. Jack parked on the other side of the road from her house and killed the lights. He wiped at his mouth on the back of his hand and said, 'I need a drink.'

Angela looked across at him. 'You drink too much. Anybody ever tell you that?'

'Yeah, plenty of times. But I never listened.'

It was quiet inside the house and even after they'd bolted all the doors and Angela had got Clea down and had gone off to bed herself, Jack stayed on in the front room with a big glass of sherry in his hand, staring at the floor.

Thinking.

23

First thing she said to him next morning was, 'You've been going through my drawers.'

Jack looked up from the nest of blankets he'd made on the couch. A grey dead-looking light filtered underneath the blinds. 'Uh?'

'I said, you've been going through my things.' Standing over him in her Japanese robe, the muscles on her pale tired face pulled tight.

'I was looking for a needle. . .' Her eyes flashed at him and he added quickly, 'to sew my strides.' He rolled off the couch and planted both feet on the masonite. 'You rung your father?'

She kept staring at him, head skewed to one side as if she were unsure whether to believe him. 'Don't you ever go through my things again. Ever.'

'What time we heading off?' Jack said.

'You fucking hear me, Jack?'

'Loud and clear, yep. No problems with the hearing.' He padded out to the bathroom and splashed cold water over his big creased mug. He shaved the brambles off and sprinkled on a little of the eau de Cologne which he kept in his face bag for special occasions. Wasn't every day he got to meet a multi-millionaire. Important to make a good impression. There were voices at the other end of the house. He stuck his head out the bathroom door just as Helen burst into the kitchen, eyes glistening.

'That disc,' she said, 'its got some sort of copy protection device on it. I had a lot of problems printing this.' She thrust a sheaf of papers at him. 'Sorry it's so faint.'

Jack took the printed matter and grabbed her by the shoulders. He hugged her plump body until she winced. 'Good work,' he said. 'I knew we could depend on you.'

'I don't fuck guys,' she said. 'I thought you should know that.'

'Glad you told me,' Jack said. 'Have you got my disc there?'

'So you can forget all about a threesome.' She handed it over.

Jack slipped the disc down into the elastic of his boxers. He flicked through the forty pages of double-spaced print, names and amounts in black and white. He wanted to punch the air.

Angela came through in a smart black skirt and purple jumper and said to Helen. 'Clea doesn't want to go to school today. She says you're helping her with her project.'

'Clea's writing a novel,' Helen said. 'She's up to page four already.'

Jack pulled on some pants in the living room, brushed the dandruff from his best blue coat and followed Angela down the hall. Clea bounced along at her mother's side. 'Can I stay with Helen, mum. Can I?' Angela lifted her child up and squeezed her ribs until she giggled. 'We're just going to the bank, hon.'

Jack said to Helen on the front step. 'Don't answer the door, right.'

Helen said, 'That's my decision.'

In the car he heard Annie Lennox singing *Why* from the house. Shadows stretched along the pavement from the spiked iron railings. 'Why didn't you tell Clea we're going to see her grandad?'

'Because I don't want my daughter having anything to

do with him.' Angela spun the car around, knuckles riding the top of the wheel, mouth set firm.

'Your childhood that bad was it?' He looked at her closely as they sped through Redfern, the dark mulberry – almost black – lipstick she was wearing, the thick kohl around her blue eyes, and it struck him that Angela'd gone to a lot of trouble to look good for her daddy, a man she didn't seem to want her daughter near.

On Crown Street Jack said, 'I'm looking forward to meeting your father. A rich man like him. Must be such a blast waking up each morning thinking, what am I gonna takeover today?'

'You might be disappointed,' Angela said. Huge glass towers flanked the expressway with hundreds of eyes looking out.

'I don't think so.' Jack fingered the wad of papers lying on his knees. He had the disc in his pocket. Whatever happened now he intended making the most of this opportunity.

'When I was a kid all Dad ever talked about was getting rich and finally he got his wish, but it didn't do Mum any good. Or Damian or me for that matter.' Angela swiped at the air with a hand. 'Money doesn't always buy happiness you know.'

'I'm not after happiness,' Jack said. 'I'll settle for a big lump of cash and a harbour view.'

24

Mosman was the kind of suburb where the sun shone just that little brighter, everything was clean and glassy in the shopping centres, and the properties were big, leafy affairs bordered with solid sandstone walls. Chief Executives and corporate lawyers shared prime real estate with the other primates and assorted faunae from Taronga Zoo.

Jack shook his head at the tall, elegant houses flying by. It was hard to believe a normal person could turn their back on all this. The road dropped and curved in front of them and then Angela hung left into a quiet side street with brushbox trees growing along the nature strip. She pulled up outside a wrought-iron security gate and checked her make-up in the mirror.

'This it?' Jack said. A two-metre high stone fence ran the entire length of the street. At one time there must've been three or four house blocks standing here. You had to admire rich people. What they could do.

Angela leaned over as if she were about to say something to him and then shook her head at the last moment. She got out instead and pressed the intercom on the security gate, said a few words into it and the gate swung open. They drove up a long gravelled drive to a sandstone and cedar mansion surrounded by palm trees. The place was old, but as big and as gaudy as a Barcelona church. It had a slate roof and dormer windows peering out at odd angles. Three gleaming white Mercs with personalised number plates – FRICK 1, FRICK 2, FRICK 3 – were parked in a presidential V near the double garage. Angela nosed the Holden in behind the last of them and got out.

Gravel crunched underfoot as she led him round the back of the house to a large courtyard area. Cockatoos screeched from a cage set high up in the trees. In the backyard an Olympic-sized swimming pool was wedged between two tennis courts – one synthetic, the other grass. There was a games room next to the house with a leather punching bag hanging from a beam. Jack stood on the edge of the paving stones staring at the sharp bamboo shoots growing alongside the security walls and ran his tongue thoughtfully round the back of his teeth.

A dark-haired woman came out of the house. Tall, slim and a good ten years younger than both of them. A smile lit up her fine pretty features. 'Angela,' she cried. She wrapped a thin girl's arm around Angela's waist.

'Chalita. How is he today?'

'He knows you're here,' the girl said. 'He's expecting you.'

Angela jerked her head at Jack for him to follow her up the steps and they passed through some lead-framed doors into a high-ceilinged kitchen and then down a hall. Rooms ran off on either side. Angela led him into one of them. A grandfather clock stood next to a bronze Art Deco statue and a deer's head was mounted on the wall beside some Aboriginal bark paintings. There was a piano in one corner with a blue styrofoam model of an apartment tower sitting on top of it next to a photograph of Bob Hawke, Angela's father and a bunch of fishing mates out on a boat.

A noise in the doorway made Jack turn. He almost dropped his papers in shock as an old man shuffled into the room. A plastic mask was clipped on over his nose and two prongs looped around and disappeared up his nostrils. Long green tubing coiled around the back of his head and trailed off down the hall behind him like he was some deep-sea diver.

'This is a friend of mine, Dad.' Angela guided her father over to a Louis XV chair.

The old man moved his thin lips about like a fish.

Jack tried to smile, but Mr Frick didn't even seem to notice he was there. A sandy-coloured toupee sat uneasily on top of his head as if any minute it was going to fly off.

'Dad,' Angela said, 'Dad, Jack's found this list. We think it's to do with Damian's death. One of the names on it is yours. We need to know who you paid $200,000 to on December 12 last year?'

'SFF.' Jack held up the page in front of Angela's father's watery red eyes. 'Those initials ring a bell with you, Mr Frick?'

The old man bent his head and wheezed. 'Can't recall.'

'This is very important, Mr Frick. See the date here and the figure next to your name. Two hundred thou.'

'Angela.' There was a thick gurgling sound in his chest like a broken cistern. 'This big lump. Is he with the police?'

Jack said, 'I was a good friend of your son's.'

'My son was a drug addict and a male prostitute, so what does that make you?'

'Mr Frick.' Jack stared at the shrunken old man. 'Angela and I suspect that whoever you paid that money to had Damian murdered.'

'My son and I parted company a long time ago. Have you got a son, fella?'

'Yes,' Jack said. 'I have.'

'And you're a bloody good father, I suppose?'

'No,' Jack said. 'I'm not.'

This seemed to please the old man for his tongue flicked at the corners of his bluish lips. 'See that tower.' He waved at the blue styrofoam model on the piano. 'Seven hundred and fifty units, an international shopping centre and parking for six hundred cars. The largest apartment complex ever built in Australia and it's being held up by a bunch of useless bureaucrats from the FIRB –'

'Who?' Jack said.

'The Foreign Investment Board, you big dope.' The old man clenched a scaly fist. 'This government's got to do something if they want investment. That's why I gave them the money – get things done or else get out of the bloody way.'

'Who did you give it to exactly, Mr Frick?'

'Bryan of course.'

'Senator Callagher?'

'He wouldn't hurt a hair on Damian's head. Bryan was

good to that boy. Always tried to do right by him. Picked him out of the gutter and gave him a job as a favour to me.' He clutched at his daughter's hand, but she pulled it away. 'Damian loved his mother you see. So we all did, didn't we Gee? Nothing'll bring her back to us. I think Damian'll be happier now he's with her.'

Angela stood up. 'Dad,' she said, shaking her head, 'sometimes you make me vomit.'

'Where you going, Gee?' he wheezed. 'You just got here.'

Angela wore the same dark expression that Jack had seen that day at the Woo Ling Barbecue Shop. She backed slowly towards the doorway, bent down and kinked a length of the green tubing around her fingers, her eyes fixed on her father all the while. Jack watched as she brought the tubing up to her mouth and bit into it sharply with her teeth.

'Chalita,' her father panted. 'Chalita!'

'Shit,' Jack said, grabbing hold of Angela and prising the tubing out of her mouth. There were three puncture holes in the plastic from which oxygen was leaking fast. He pushed her out into the hall and ran back to the old man who was gasping for air. Jack yanked open the drawer of a side table and rifled through it. He found a yellow roll of electrician's tape and peeled a strip off. The old man's breathing sounded like someone working at a metal pipe with a blunt hacksaw; his lips had turned purple. Jack wound the tape quickly around the holes in the tubing as Chalita ran into the room.

Jack said, 'I just saved your life, Mr Frick. The name's Butorov by the way. That's B-u-t-o-r-o-v.' He nodded at them both, gathered up his papers and went out of the room and down the hall. Three girls were playing with blocks on the kitchen floor. Dark-haired with little green dresses on, they looked more like dolls than children. Angela was watching them through the glass doors as Jack took her arm. He led her out and around the side of the house. 'What the hell you do that for?'

She didn't say anything.

The security gates swung open and a CIG truck drove up the drive. Angela got in behind the wheel of the Holden and started the motor as two men rolled a long metal cylinder down off the back of the truck and onto a trolley.

On Military Road Angela lit a cigarette, took a deep long drag from it and let the smoke escape from her lips. 'Want to know how my mother died?' she said, finally.

Jack nodded; he had the feeling he was going to find out anyway.

'She doused herself with petrol and set herself alight.'

Jack gazed out the window at some kids on rollerblades. There was nothing he could say.

'It was Damian who found her after school.' Angela reached for her sunglasses, slipped them on. She looked straight down the freeway towards the bridge, both hands wrapped tight around the wheel. 'So what do you think?' she said. 'You think it was Bryan Callagher who had my brother murdered?'

'I don't know yet,' Jack said. 'All we've got here is what seems to be a list of political contributors to the government's re-election fund. There's gotta be more to it than this.'

Angela said, 'If it was him I promise you he's going to pay for it.'

Jack studied the papers on his lap, trying to fit all the pieces together. They crested a ridge and the city rose in front of their eyes. A big thick forest of towers and then they were driving into it.

25

A steel sculpture shaped like a giant shish kebab was stuck in the middle of Martin Place. A chill wind blew through the square. Jack scratched about in the payphone. He found Callagher, Bryan (Senator) in the book and dialled the number, his mind racing ahead of his fingers. Trying to recall if Federal Parliament was still in session. 'Senator Callagher please,' Jack said. The woman who answered was some kind of guard dog. She wanted to know who he was and what it was in relation to. He said, 'Just tell the Minister I have some important political documents of his.' The woman insisted on knowing Jack's name. 'Damian Frick,' he said. She fed him some Vivaldi while he waited, then a voice cut through the cellos.

'Callagher speaking.'

Jack could feel impatience in the tone. 'Senator, I don't know if you remember me – Jack Butorov. I was a friend of Damian Frick's.'

There was a pause. 'Yes?'

'I've got something I believe belongs to you. A computer disc.'

Silence at the other end.

'And I wondered if you'd like it returned. I'm in the city right now, I could drop it in.'

'You have this disc with you?' His tone was cold.

'I have a copy I can bring.' Jack listened to the Senator's brief, curt instructions, hung up, walked across to Macquarie Street and poked his head in Angela's car window. The papers were spread out over her knees and he could smell her skin. 'We're in luck. Callagher'll see me in half an hour.'

'Just you, Jack?'

'I think it's best if I see him alone. He's more likely to talk to a male.'

She chewed on her Ray-Bans, narrowing her eyes at him. He could tell she didn't buy it completely, but she didn't say anything.

They drove to the Senator's office, a modern low-rise building at the harbour end of Phillip Street. Pneumatic drills hammered away across the road and a pair of girders swung dangerously overhead. Angela grabbed him by the belt as he climbed out. 'You're not planning anything on your own, are you, Jack?'

He rolled his big paws over. 'You don't trust me?'

She said, 'I've never met a man yet I can trust.'

'Except for your brother,' Jack said. He grabbed the wad of papers, tucked them under his arm and crossed Phillip Street, feeling those blue eyes of hers sticking into his back. The brass plaque in the foyer read, Senator The Hon Bryan Callagher – Enquiries 11th Floor. The moment Jack stepped out on the top floor he was met by a tank-sized woman with orange hair and green eye-shadow. He recognised her voice from the phone. 'I've got an appointment,' he said. The woman stood right up close to his face and her breath smelt of peppermints. Jack told her his name and she walked over to a phone on the desk, punched the buttons and spoke quickly into the receiver. She came back and inserted a strip of plastic in a slot inside the lift. They rode down to the ninth and passed through an armour-plated glass partition to a plush reception room. 'Sit,' she said as if he were a cocker spaniel. He sank into a leather chair large enough to get lost in and gazed at the floor. It was made of polished marble and shone like liquid. He started to get thirsty just looking at it.

A secretary came over and indicated with a smile that

he should follow her. Her blonde hair was cut into a tulip shape and her clothes and skin were so perfect he wanted to spit. She glided across the floor and through some double doors into a large shiny room fitted with designer chairs and an oak desk with nothing on it except three black phones.

The light was what struck him first. The Senator's hair was outlined with a halo of bright red light. Jack stared. He heard the secretary's Thai silk dress rustle against her body as she glided past him and then the door shut with a faint echo. The Senator gestured at a wire-backed chair in front of him, but Jack was still blinking at the sparks of electricity, some kind of static force radiating from the Senator's head and hair. The moment he sat down he realised what it was – the play of light from the window behind. There was a smell in the room, powerful and pervasive, a body heat like that given off by the big cats at Taronga Zoo.

Jack dropped the papers onto the desk. 'I believe this is yours, Senator. A list of political donations for your government's election campaign.'

The Senator leaned across the table in his double-breasted Italian suit and thumbed quickly through the pages. He peered over the half-moon glasses perched on the tip of his nose. 'Where'd you get this?' His voice was menacing. 'This is private and confidential.'

'Damian left it with me for safekeeping.' Jack tapped the sheets with his fingers. 'You mind if we speak bluntly here?'

The Senator smiled icily. He had grown fatter since Jack had last seen him and his jowls were longer and fleshier. He glanced down at his Rolex. 'You've got five minutes.'

'Know what I think, Senator. I think Damian was trying to make a little bit of extra pocket money because of what's in this document.'

The Senator's thick eyebrows knitted together. 'You've

got a wonderful imagination there, Jack. That should be
rewarded.'

'I think so too,' Jack said. 'Twenty-five thousand is the
figure I had in mind.'

The Senator laughed grimly. 'I was thinking more of
five to ten in the Bay.' He reached for the phone on the
left and lifted the receiver. There was a brightness in his
cat-green eyes like a switch had been turned on.

Jack said quickly, 'That disc's in a very secure place
right now Senator, but I can't guarantee its safety for
much longer. One of your contributors – TC – is that
Tony Chiu? I think I met him at your party. He's down
here for three million.' He watched the Senator closely,
but the Senator didn't even blink.

'So?'

'So that's a lot of money,' Jack said, 'for one man to
donate to an election fund.'

Mr Chiu is vice-president of the Chinatown Chamber
of Commerce. He's a leading businessman. A millionaire
many times over.'

'Of course he is,' Jack said, 'but if that disc ever fell
into the wrong hands. Well, you know what those reptiles
of the press are like. Always looking to dig up dirt on
successful people.'

The Senator held the receiver snugly against his ear
like it was an extension of his jawbone, the mouthpiece
just touching his jutting upper lip. He pressed a button
with his thumb.

Jack could feel static in the room. His fingers tightened
around the steel rim of his chair. He said quickly: 'A lot
of journalists try and connect things, Senator – like a
murdered young homosexual with a junior cabinet minister in an election year.'

The Senator dropped the phone onto the cradle, leaned
across his big oak desk and said in a low snarl, 'You've
got balls trying this on, but you'd better be fucking careful
someone doesn't chop them right off.'

Jack wiped flecks of spit off his cheeks with his sleeve. He was sweating under his collar and down between his legs. The phone rang. He couldn't tell which of the three was ringing, but the Senator snatched up the receiver on the right without even looking, said into it, 'Yeah,' his eyes fixed hard on Jack while he listened. 'Tell Lee to go ahead.' The Senator crunched the phone down. His hair which stuck out everywhere else on his head was flattened around his telephone ear.

There was silence in the long room. The Senator pulled at the knot of his yellow tie. Without a phone in his hand he didn't appear so threatening. 'Listen, Jack,' he said. 'You're on the wrong platform. Every single donation in our Special Fighting Fund is accounted for and strictly legit. You have my word on that.'

'A lot of people seem eager to get their hands on that disc, Senator. My flat has already been turned over once. So I figure it must be real important.'

The Senator leaned forward in his seat and Jack could smell the heat of him. 'Where are you staying now?'

'With friends,' Jack said.

'Well, leave this with me.' The Senator patted the papers. 'I'm sure we can come to some satisfactory pecuniary arrangement.' He got up slowly from his chair. 'I give you my word, I had nothing to do with that boy's death. As much as I respect old Frank Frick, he was a tyrant. I felt sorry for Damian. The whole family are a sad story. The mother committed suicide and the daughter spent time in a psychiatric unit.'

Jack stood up quickly.

The Senator limped round the long desk towards the door. 'Drugs,' he said, shaking his head. 'The police believe Damian's murder was drug-related. Leave your number with my secretary, Jack. I'll get back to you on this.'

Jack nodded and walked straight out the door, past the Cossack with the green eye-shadow and into the foyer.

Going down in the lift he realised he had muffed it. Come on too strong too early. Now he was walking away with nothing except a vague promise of recompense. He crossed the road, fingering the disc in his pocket. Better to try the papers next. Maybe the opposition too. See what they'd offer him. First of all he had to get another copy made, a good one. Mail it off somewhere safe. McCredie, he could send it to McCredie. His eyes swept along Phillip Street, checking out the line of cars. Angela was sitting behind the wheel of the Holden chewing the chipped red paint from her nails. A dogman swung low across the sky hanging off the hook of a giant crane. Jack slid into the front seat beside her and laid a big sweaty palm over her knee.

'So what happened?' Her voice was edgy. The skin on her forehead was bunched so tight that her eyebrows met in a single dark line.

'Nothing,' Jack said. 'It's his, or the government's at least. Some special fighting fund for this election campaign. But it appears to be perfectly legal.'

'What about Damian?' she said. 'What did Callagher say about Damian?'

'He gave me his word he had nothing to do with Damian's death.'

'You think he was lying?'

'I think he knows more than he's letting on. . . shit.' He stared at her suddenly.

'What is it?' she said.

'Callagher asked me where I was staying *now*. I never said I'd moved.'

Angela wrenched on the gears and hit the accelerator. The Holden fishtailed out into Phillip Street and then they were flying through the city, bank clerks and secretaries skittering to get out of their way.

Jack grabbed at the strap above the door and hung on to it with both hands.

2 6

Erskineville was quiet. Angela spun the car around the corner of Ashmore Street and braked in front of her house. They jumped out, Jack noting the Merc Sports on the other side of the street. Erko wasn't the place for Mercs. Angela pushed through the iron gate, grabbed her keys out of her purse and opened the front door. There was no sound at all from inside. 'Clea,' she called. 'Helen!'

A foul ugly smell drifted down the hall. Tobacco – strong tobacco. He felt Angela's spine harden and he gripped her arm. With his lips he mimed what he wanted her to do. She moved down the hall ahead of him, trying to hide the emotion in her throat, 'Sweetheart – you there, honey?'

Jack followed, crouched and ready to spring. He was counting on one small detail – that whoever was inside hadn't heard both of them come in. He could smell the cigar smoke now – more like old tyres burning. They passed through the living room and Angela's hand went straight to her mouth. She gave a cry as she was jerked through the kitchen doorway and a man in a kangaroo mask stepped out and stuck a gun right in Jack's face.

Jack stared at the finely haired muzzle, erect ears and wet black nose. The mask was a brilliant replica – some kind of latex job done with genuine animal hair and long black eyelashes. The gunman shoved Jack hard up against the wall. Another man in a kangaroo mask had hold of Angela around the neck and she was struggling to break free. At the far end of the kitchen a third man wearing a kangaroo mask was sitting calmly by the stove with a dirty-smelling weed wedged in his mouth, a gun in one hand and Clea clasped tight in his lap. The child started crying very loudly.

Angela went crazy. She clawed and spat at the man who had hold of her. She screamed and she kicked. He whacked her once hard behind the ear with the butt of his pistol and she slid onto the floor and lay there in a heap. Jack went to step forward and the muzzle of a .32 automatic was thrust hard against the end of his nose. He didn't argue. There was nothing you could say to a shooter up the snout; .32 automatics weren't good listeners at the best of times. 'Okay, okay.' He raised his hands. 'You've made your point.'

The man beside the stove was a good deal shorter than the other two, but he seemed to be the boss. He waved a gun in Jack's direction. 'Give me the disc now.'

'Disc?' Jack said. 'What disc?' And felt the tip of his nose bend back until it was almost touching his forehead. 'Ah,' he went.

'Three minutes you have. Then I kill the woman and the child.' The man had one hand up under Clea's skirt holding her firm.

'It's not here,' Jack said. 'You think I'd be dumb enough to carry that disc on me?'

'Two minutes,' the man said. He took the weed out of his mouth and crushed it under the heel of his shoe. He laid his gun down on the floor and picked up a Makita 10mm hammer drill from near his feet. It was still plugged in.

'An hour,' Jack said. 'I can get it for you within the hour.'

'One minute.' The man switched the Makita on and drilled a hole the size of a ten cent piece in the table top just in front of Clea's trembling knees.

Jack's eyes hardened. All three men were packing .32s; that was the same calibre Damian had been killed with. Somehow he had to stall them. He watched the second masked man jam the muzzle of his automatic hard into the nape of Angela's neck and he realised – *no, they'd kill her alright*. The gunman's finger closed round the trigger. He looked to his boss who was studying his watch.

'Mummy,' Clea cried.

The third man lifted his hand like a traffic cop. 'Shoot the woman.'

'No,' Jack yelled. 'No, I'll give it to you. Let the kid go.' He dug into his shirt pocket and pulled out the disc. Clea broke free, ran over and slung her arms around her mother slumped on the floor. Even then Jack hung onto the disc right up until it was snatched from his fingers.

The third man examined a marking on the plastic. 'Copy?' He poked his mask into Jack's face. 'You make copy?'

'No,' Jack said, 'I don't know how to make copy. Why do you want this?'

The third man nodded sharply at the other two.

'I won't tell anyone.' Out the corner of his eye Jack saw it coming: the raised pistol butt and something else – a blurred tattoo on the swinging arm. He tried to duck just as a pain exploded in the side of his head. He hit the floor knees first. His fingers spread out on the masonite like they were waiting for a manicure and he saw stars, but they weren't from any movies. Bright coloured lights were dancing in front of his lids. He pushed himself slowly up off the floor. The back door was wide open and he started to head for it, but his legs had other ideas. The kitchen table came up to say hi and Jack fell over it, crashed into the sink. Clea was making little whimpering noises over her unconscious mother as he gripped the taps, hauled himself up onto his feet. He staggered out into the yard just in time to see the last man hopping over the back fence. There was a screech of tyres in the lane and the white flat top of a van pulled away. Jack steadied himself against the banana trees. Wasps were buzzing in his ear. He shook his head, but it didn't do any good; he could still hear them. He stumbled towards the toilet door, wrenched it open and found Helen trussed and gagged on the edge of the seat. When he pulled the pantyhose out of her mouth she started crying.

'I didn't let them in, I swear.' She took a big suck of air. 'They broke in through the back.'

Blood was trickling down the side of his big blunt jaw. He wiped at it with the back of his fist, swept her out of the way and retched into the bowl.

27

An intern wearing Eartha Kitt glasses and a clean white coat held a hand up in front of Jack's nose and said, 'How many fingers?'

'Seven.'

'I think we'd better take some X-rays, Mr Butorov. You're fortunate that you possess such a hard head.'

'You're not too bad looking yourself,' Jack said.

She shepherded him down the corridor to a small dark room where a twitchy man strapped him into a machine and zapped his dome five times from different angles. The man had a musk lolly rolling around the back of his teeth, but he didn't offer Jack one, just told him to go wait outside until they called him. Jack went through into the Casualty waiting room of Royal Prince Alfred Hospital, Camperdown. It was important that he keep track of his bearings. He sat in a three seater between Clea and Helen and shrugged off their questions. Sure he felt sore, but he wasn't going to make a song and dance about it. He was more cut up about losing that disc. There was big money wrapped up in that piece of plastic. He was certain of it. If they were prepared to kill a woman and a kid, then it had to be worth plenty. He should have made another copy. Christ, he should've made ten copies! How could he be so fucking dumb. The opportunity of a lifetime staring him in the front teeth and he'd dropped the ball. A young man in a wheelchair with a blanket spread over his legs was staring up at the air-conditioning pipes. Maybe a dozen other people were sitting around looking terminally bored. Clea leapt out of her seat when her mother came through the doorway with her head bandaged on one side. Her face was pale and the corners of her mouth set hard. She hugged her daughter and then Helen.

'How you feeling?' Jack said when Angela got round to him. For a moment he thought she was going to lash out at somebody. Her hands were trembling so much and her face was knotted with emotion.

'They threatened my child, Jack! They threatened Clea.' Everyone in the waiting room looked up then, as if the TV had been switched on.

'I know,' Jack said quietly, 'I was there.'

'It was the same ones that killed Damian.'

'Yes,' he said. 'It was.' He put an arm around her shoulder and held her close to him. She was shaking right through. Jack ignored the stares they were getting as they walked to the door. Out in the ambulance bay Helen whispered, 'You forgot your X-rays.'

'My scone ain't cracked,' Jack said. He shook his head as if to prove his point and then had to hold onto the pedestrian rail as his vision blurred.

'You alright, Jack?' Clea grabbed at his sleeve.

'I'm fine, pumpkin.' He picked her up. He had forgotten all about Clea. Forgotten she was there. He put her down again as a white Ford Falcon GL pulled up in front of them and the window wound down. A pair of very big men were crammed into the front seats like two King Parrots in a budgie's cage. 'Which one of youse's Angela Frick?'

'That's me,' Angela replied.

'Newtown Detectives.' He flashed his ID in her face. 'We'd like to ask you some questions back at the station. Ambulance guys reported a serious assault at your residence.'

'You're a bit bloody late aren't you?'

'It won't take long, Miss. If you'd all just like to get into the car.' His scalp shone pink through his close-cropped hair.

Angela's eyes flicked to Jack's. Jack started to walk off in the other direction when the other detective said, 'Wait a minute, pal,' getting out of the Ford fast for a big man. 'Where you going?'

'Home,' Jack said. 'I got a bad migraine.'

'Get in the car,' the detective said. He jerked at it with his thumb.

Jack didn't budge.

'If you wouldn't mind,' the detective smiled coldly, 'sir.'

Jack got in after Angela and Clea and then Helen squeezed in beside them. It was a tight fit and there weren't enough seat belts to go round, but the police didn't seem to mind. They put on the siren in King Street, because the traffic was a little heavy; Clea seemed to get a kick out of it anyway.

Newtown Police Station was an ugly looking three-storey concrete joint next to the pink courthouse in Australia Street. There were the usual posters of prohibited substances stuck up in a glass case and a couple of tired trannies standing around in purple miniskirts. A policewoman came out and took charge of Clea while the two detectives led Helen, Angela and Jack upstairs to an untidy room with aluminium windows. An older man came in and glared at all three of them. He had a big leathery face with puffed eyes and smelled of onions. He looked like he might've been a pug in his day. 'I'm Senior Sergeant Hooper,' he said. 'What's the story here?'

'Three men broke into my house,' Angela went. 'They

threatened my daughter.' She stared at the three cops as if she wanted them to do something right now.

'It's true.' Helen nodded. 'They came in over the back fence. They tied me up and gagged me.'

'They had guns,' Angela said. 'They were going to shoot us.'

'Hold on, hold on,' the Sergeant said. 'One at a time. Can you describe these men?'

'They were wearing masks,' Angela said. 'Kangaroo masks. They almost fractured my skull.'

'These men,' Sergeant Hooper said, 'they take anything?'

Jack nodded. 'A computer disc.'

'Nothing else?'

'I know who they are,' Jack said. 'Chinese muscle. They work for a Triad operating out of Chinatown.'

The two other detectives were leaning their buttocks against the edge of their desks and stroking their impassive jaws. Sergeant Hooper said, 'But you didn't see their faces at all?'

'No,' Jack said, 'but I saw the tattoo on the guy that slugged me. A blue unicorn. That's the name this gang go by – the Blue Unicorns.'

'These are the same people,' Angela said, 'who killed my brother. Damian Frick. He was shot dead in Haymarket.'

One of the detectives drawled, 'Remember that, Fred? Made a splash two, three months ago.'

'Four and a half weeks,' Angela said. 'And you still haven't put them away.' She pressed two fingers up to her temple. 'Those killers are walking around scot-free. What's wrong with you people? You should have done something by now. You have the photographs, everything.'

Hooper stared at her. 'What photographs?'

'Ring Inspector Fenton at South West Region Homicide,' she said, her voice rising in pitch. 'Go on. Ring him

– he'll tell you.' The skin on her forehead was bunched up tight and she was blinking hard at the three detectives. Helen stepped forward and put an arm around Angela's shoulder. She stroked her neck.

Jack saw the glance that shot between the two junior men. The sergeant picked up the phone and dialled. 'Newtown Detectives, sir. I've got an Angela Frick here. Seems there was a break-in and assault at her premises.' He cupped his hand round the earpiece and his eyes narrowed to pencil points while he listened.

One of the detectives reached into his desk drawer and took out a pack of spearmint gum. He offered it around. Angela and Helen shook their heads. The detective shrugged, peeled off a stick for himself and one for his partner. Sergeant Hooper was saying into the blower, 'Photographs, sir. She mentioned some photographs.'

'It's alright, Angela.' Jack reached out a hand. 'It's over with now.'

Hooper hung up. He looked across at Angela and then to Helen and finally to Jack. He gave his head a big slow shake. 'Fraid your photos drew a blank.'

'What do you mean?' Angela went.

'The witness denies they were the men she saw.'

'No.' Angela shook her head firmly. 'No, that's not true.' She turned to Jack. 'Celia was definite. She told me so herself.'

Jack said, 'Quarrell's got to her.'

The two detectives stopped chewing; their gaze fixed hard on Jack's mug. Silence fell in the room. Then Sergeant Hooper leaned over and poked the stub of his finger in front of Jack's nose. He said, 'You referring to Detective Sergeant Quarrell?'

'That's right,' Jack said, meeting his stare head-on. 'You fellas'd know him wouldn't you?'

The two detectives looked at each other and then at their sergeant. 'Cup of coffee, sarge?'

'I'll help you Shad,' his partner put in. They went

out the door together. Two hundred kilos of law enforcement. Hooper was still staring at Jack, his big lined face
looking like a leather football that had been left out in
the yard for years. He said, 'I've seen you before haven't
I?'

Jack didn't answer.

'Want to know something?' Hooper said. 'Twenty-five
years I been in this game.' He looked to Helen. 'Got two
kids bout your age. Got a ten-year-old Toyota Corona and
a house in Mortdale. But I've never been on the squeeze.
I got no truck with that type of copper. This disc they
lifted.' He fixed his eyes on Jack. 'What's so important
about it?'

'It belongs to a well-known politician,' Angela chipped
in. 'We believe there's a connection with it and my
brother's murder.'

Hooper tugged on the lobe of a big gristled ear. 'The
gang that bust into your home – you telling me they're
working for this politician?'

'It's a possibility,' Jack said.

'But you've got no proof of course?'

'My brother was killed, Sergeant,' Angela said. 'Two
hours ago I was bashed and my six-year-old daughter
had a gun stuck to her head. This isn't something I made
up.'

'Look, Miss Frick,' Hooper went. 'We'll investigate the
assault charge sure, but you have to understand that
without a positive ID of these characters we haven't got
a lot to go on here.' He reached across the desk for a
yellow Post-it pad and scribbled something down. 'In the
meantime give this number a ring. Ask for Superintendent Lamb. He's heading a special task force right now
and he's an expert on these gangs. Mick's a straight
arrow. Used to play for the Bluebags.' He tilted his head
as if he were trying to recall something else.

The door opened and the two pumped-up detectives
came through with plastic cups of coffee, Mars bars and

packets of Lites chips gripped between fingers the size of frangipani stalks.

Hooper said to them, 'You can run these people home now, Shadbolt.'

'Now, sarge?'

'That's right,' Hooper said. When his men were halfway out the door he called out to Jack, 'Newtown Police Boys' Club – 75, 76 wasn't it?'

Jack turned, saw Hooper watching him.

'You and that skinny kid used to come in. Real classy little welterweight, what was his name?'

'Nepo,' Jack said, 'Nepo Kemp.'

Hooper stroked his jaw thoughtfully. 'The old memory box eh – still ticking.'

They picked Clea up downstairs and walked round with her to the squad car. It was getting dark out. The time of evening when the chimney tops and TV aerials come into focus. Newtown was different at night; you couldn't see the grime so much and the peanutty smell from a score of Thai and Indonesian kitchens made the air more palatable. In the back seat Angela leaned over and whispered, 'If you want to back out now's the time to say so.'

Rain was starting to spit down and Jack looked out the window at the workers emerging from Newtown station with their arms swishing and their heads bowed like they were under sniper fire. He fingered the lump on the side of his head and closed his eyes.

28

Angela was packing a Namco case in the living room. She threw in a blue sleeping bag and two bath towels and marched down to her daughter's bedroom. She came back, arms loaded with neat little piles of dresses, socks, underwear. Clea tugged at her mother's dress saying, 'Where we going Mum? Where we going?' Angela quickly folded a small ribbed jumper in on top and pressed the case shut, then she went down the hall with Helen. Jack could hear the two women conferring in muted voices and then a number being dialled. Clea climbed up onto the arm of his chair. 'Guess what, Jack? We're going away.' She had copied her mother's serious expression, but it was someone else that she reminded him of. He tousled her long blond hair, trying to catch who Angela was talking to. 'Don't mess me up,' Clea said, 'I'm all neat.' He took his hand away. 'Sorry, Miss Minnie.' He heard the receiver clunk and then two sets of footsteps down the hall. Angela came through and knelt in front of Clea. She placed her hands squarely on her daughter's tiny shoulders and looked her in the eyes.

'You and Helen are going to take a holiday together.'

'You're not coming, Mum?'

'Later, hon. I've got something to do here first.'

Helen said, 'We're going to stay near the beach. You and me, Clea. There's pelicans up there. We can feed them fish.'

Clea looked to her mother and her whole face crumpled like tissue paper. 'You have to be a big girl,' Angela said. She wrapped her arms around her daughter's ribs and squeezed her tight. For several minutes they remained locked together with Jack staring down at his feet and the only sound in the house the whirr of the Kelvinator from the kitchen. Then a horn bipped twice in the street. Helen picked up the suitcase and went down the hall. Jack followed. A cab was double-parked outside and when the driver saw them he sprung the boot lid open. Jack stood back against the wrought-iron fence while Angela bundled her sobbing daughter into the back seat. He watched the two women kiss through the car window. Angela stayed out on the pavement waving at the taillights of the cab while Jack walked back inside. He sat on the teal blue couch and lit one of her B&H. It was seven years since he'd had a cigarette, but what the hell. People always said the first eight were the hardest. The nicotine grabbed at the back of his throat and he felt the pain in his head ease. He blew the smoke out as he gazed up at a corner of the ceiling where the paint was peeling off like dead skin. When he looked down again she was standing there in the doorway with her eyes as red as her nails.

'They're not going to get away with this, Jack. I'm telling you.' She blew her nose and balled the tissue up in her fist. Tiny drops of water shone in her short black hair.

'Where's Helen taking her?'

'Her parents have a shack up at Seal Rocks. Clea'll be safe up there.'

'Right.' Jack nodded.

She sat down at the other end of the couch and frowned at a damp patch on the far wall. She said, 'One thing I don't understand – all those donations on the disc. Isn't that information publicly available after the election?'

'If it's disclosed sure,' Jack said, 'but say the donors for some reason don't want their names revealed. Or that Callagher's juggling the books.'

'So if that disc fell into the wrong hands he might do anything to get it back, even have my brother killed?'

'It's possible,' Jack said. 'On the other hand Damian's death could have nothing to do with this. According to Callagher, the cops think it was drug-related. That seems to fit better with the Triad connection. I know Damian was snorting, but was he using as well?'

'He wasn't cranking,' Angela said. 'He liked to chase the dragon sometimes, but he wouldn't use a pin.'

Jack's eyes fixed on her. The rain outside had started up again and he could hear it rushing at the window behind his back. He said, 'You seem to know a lot about it.'

Angela touched the gauze bandage on her temple. Her face was white as paper. 'Let's not go into the past tonight. I told you before. That part of my life's finished with. When Clea was born everything changed for me.'

'She's a top kid, yeah.' Jack reached a big hand across the cushion and fastened it around Angela's long fingers. Her mouth was tilted towards him and he leaned over and kissed it. Her lips tasted sweet. He kissed her again and felt her resistance loosen. 'You've got a lovely mouth, Angela. Anyone ever tell you that?'

Her big dark pupils stared back at him.

'When this is over with, we should go away someplace.' He put his hand on her thigh but she stopped him when he got to the waistband of her tights.

'What do you really want, Jack?' she said.

'I want money,' he said. 'I want to be someone import- ant. You ever feel inside of you that something's not right?'

'How do you mean?'

'Like some part's gone missing you know. Well I do. I feel my life's like a movie and I'm watching it go past but I'm not even in it. I want to get back inside of the picture.'

'What about your wife?' she said. 'You ever think about her?'

'Not much. Vick left me. I don't blame her for that. I

would have left me too. I've done a lot of rotten things in my time but I've never killed anybody.'

Angela stood up quickly. Her hands were at the sides of her skirt. She studied him closely for a moment. 'But you're still gonna help me though?'

'I think it's too late to pull out of this now even if I wanted.'

She lifted up her skirt and peeled off her black tights. He saw the red stripe of blood in the middle of her panties. 'Won't be a tic,' she said and opened the back door with a whoosh of cold air. A purple bougainvillea was jerking its thorns against the paling fence. The wind blew down the side of the house and the door banged. Rain slanted inwards and began to form a puddle on the kitchen floor. Angela came running back inside. She bolted the door behind her and shook the water from her hair. Jack followed her down to her bedroom. They undressed on either side of the bed and slipped under the cotton sheets. She took his hand and cupped it over her right breast as he tucked his knees into the back of her legs. They lay there, warming up together, with the damp smell of her hair in his face and the rain striking the iron roof like it wanted to get in.

29

An hour later, when he was certain that she was asleep, Jack slipped out of bed, grabbed his clothes and tiptoed out to the kitchen. He lifted her keys out of her black leather purse on the table and dressed hurriedly. He went down the hall, hunted through the phone book and dialled. A man answered; Jack recognised the voice. Rain was gurgling down a drainpipe outside and he hoped the noise was loud enough to prevent him being heard in the bedroom. 'It's Jack Butorov.' He pressed his mouth against the tiny holes in the phone. 'I wonder if I could see you tonight. Yes I know it's late, but this is real important.'

Jack hung up, stood there in the dark hall listening. He took a couple of steps and pushed her bedroom door open gently. She was lying there with her head angled across the pillow, the fresh white bandage like a lump of plaster on the side of her head and her long dark eyelashes remming softly. She could have been playing possum, but he didn't think so. He pulled the door to, crept down the hall and clicked the front door shut behind him.

Standing there on the porch for a second, watching bits of plastic and a dead currawong wash down the gutters. In the Holden he let the clutch in and coasted as far as Ashmore Street before he switched the engine on. The roads were black and greasy in the rain and the back tyres skidded around corners. Taxis whooshed by like bats in the night. Jack squinted between the busy wipers at the blinking coloured lights of the city, the electric blues and reds. SANYO. NEC. JETABOUT. Going over the bridge he stared up at the giant steel girders and wondered if what he was doing now was such a good idea. Sometimes you had to clutch at any chance. He'd stopped believing a long time ago that life was fair. Things didn't turn out right unless you made them. With one hand he flipped open the glove box and reached in for her street directory.

Jack parked in front of a red and black striped Magna outside the wrought-iron security gate and walked back along the side of the two-metre high stone wall. He could smell peanut sauce. He pressed the button on the inter-com and gave his name. There was some lettering on the

side of the Magna next to a picture of a big black cat
wielding a flashlight. The two security guards in the front
seat were eating noodles out of plastic containers and
they didn't take their eyes off Jack for a second.

Jack nodded at them as he squeezed the EH past and
drove up the gravelled drive. The huge sandstone house
was lit up like a Christmas tree; lights burned in all the
leadlight windows. He got out of the car and walked up
the paved path, staring up at two video cameras installed
under the eaves on the roof. In all his life Jack had never
been to a bigger house than this one. A woman came out
of the front door. She wore a yellow uniform with white
sandshoes and she had a little dark moustache. 'Mr
Frick's expecting me,' Jack said.

The woman led him down the hall and into a study.
Another woman in an identical uniform was folding a
plastic sheet in the next room. Old Man Frick was rugged
up in a black wing chair with a thin tube running from
his nostrils back behind his head and down along the
carpet to a green oxygen cylinder in the corner of the
room. Beside him, holding a little dark-haired girl to her
breast stood the young woman Jack had seen before. She
looked at Jack like he was going to pinch the medication
bottles off the marble mantlepiece.

'It's alright, Chalita. Mr Beetleoff's come to tell me
something.'

'Butorov,' Jack said.

Chalita walked straight past him, with her head turned
away and went out the door.

Old man Frick gripped the arms of his chair with his
dry bony hands. 'Well, spit it out, son.'

It was hot and stuffy in the study and Jack could see
the thick blue cords in the old man's neck expand and
contract with each laboured breath.

'They bashed your daughter,' Jack said. 'They stuck a
gun in her face and threatened to kill her.'

'Who did?'

'Triads,' Jack said. 'They slugged me and swiped my disc. I think Bryan Callagher's behind it.'

'Rubbish! You're talking through your arse.'

'I thought you'd be concerned, Mr Frick. Don't you care about your daughter?'

Old man Frick held up his right wrist. 'See that!' A long jagged scar ran diagonally across the radial artery. 'Just after her mother died, she attacked me with a kitchen knife.' He hawked and spat into a yellow hankie. 'I made a lot of mistakes with my first family, son, and I regret that deeply. But to build up a company as big as Frick Developments wasn't fucking easy. Sixteen hours a day I've worked since the age of fifteen.'

Jack said, 'Was it worth it?'

The old man nodded his head firmly and his watery eyes gleamed.

'I saved your life, Mr Frick. I think you owe me.'

Old man Frick laughed. 'And how much do I owe you, son?'

'Five thousand is a nice little figure.'

The old man tapped the tubing looped under his strawberry nose. 'C.A.L they call this. Lungs don't draw enough air now, but I can live for quite a while without the plumbing. You overestimate your good deed, son, but I'll tell you what I'm going to do. I'm going to write you out a cheque on one condition.'

'Yeah?' Jack shifted his feet on the thick carpet.

'That you don't ever come near this house again. I've got a new family now and I don't want to be bothered any longer with the old. Pass me that pen.

Jack grabbed a gold fountain pen off the edge of a fat grey textbook entitled Concrete Constructions. The skin on the old man's hands felt dry and flaky to the touch and his breathing was like another presence in the room.

'You know where the future is for Frick Developments, son?' He pulled a chequebook out of the top drawer of his carved desk. 'Townhouse apartments, high-density housing. Bryan Callagher and I – we share the same vision for this country.' The old man sucked in a mouthful of air. 'A hundred million people living here. That's what we need.' He pushed the freshly inked cheque across the desktop and a smile worked its way across his pinched blue lips.

Jack snatched the cheque up in both hands. For a moment he didn't get the joke and then he checked the figure again. 'There seems to be a pair of zeros missing here, Mr Frick.'

'That's right, son.' The old man reached under the desk and a buzzer sounded in the hall. 'Now get the hell out of my house!'

Driving back under the curved spine of the bridge, rain nudging the wipers and dark-brown clouds pressing down on the concrete towers, Jack imagined he could hear the city breathing, sucking the salt air in like some giant grey bellows. He dug around in the pocket of his trousers, brought out the cheque and a two dollar coin which he flipped into the basket on the automatic tollgate. He held the cheque up to the light of the speedometer. Fifty bucks. He scrunched the cheque into a ball and shoved it into his shirt pocket, hoping the tight old bastard would choke on a chicken bone. At the very least he should've got five hundred out of him. He needed it for Toby, needed it bad. In Harris Street, he accelerated through three orange lights, then sat on the red tail-lights of a Jag XJ6 as far as Erskineville Road, swung the Holden left then right and coasted down the quiet, tree-lined street in second gear. All the lights were extinguished in the little terrace windows. He parked outside her place and walked up the front steps, tried three keys in the lock before he found one that fitted and manoeuvred the door open gently. He crept down the hallway, wondering what he was going to say if she was awake. Outside her door he stopped, removed all his clothes, including his socks and tiptoed in, dumped everything over the back of a chair and slid as quietly as a bush rat under the sheets beside her. Her body was hot, her skin smelled of oils. He laid a hand on her hip and she recoiled at the touch of his cold fingers, murmured in a thick sleepy voice, 'Where've you been?'

'Nowhere,' he said, 'just the toilet.'

30

It was eight a.m. when he awoke to the sound of a 747 coming in low from the west. Windows rattled. Jack patted the empty space beside him with his palm. Her side of the bed was warm and he could still smell her skin under the sheets. He rolled out and hit the floor on the balls of his feet. He slung open the curtains and peered out through the misted glass. The side fence was stained from the rain and clouds hung low in the sky. Erskineville had once been a swamp and today you could feel that. When he turned around she was standing there by the bed. She had on a blue corduroy jacket zipped up to her throat, Levis jeans and an old pair of Reeboks. She looked like she meant business. 'Get your duds on,' she said. The smell of fresh bread wafted from her brown paper bag. He went down the hall ahead of her and tidied up in the bathroom. There was a swelling above his left ear and the skin around his eye was the colour of boiled beetroot. The pain was so bad he wanted to vomit.

'How's your head?' he asked her in the kitchen.

She shrugged her shoulders as if there were nothing to complain about. That worried him: it was like she was storing it all up inside.

He ate a fresh wholemeal roll with cheese and a sugar banana. He didn't drink coffee as a rule, but he took the cup she had prepared for he had the feeling that today was a special day and he was going to do a lot of things that weren't usual. There was a photo of the Prime Minister on the front page of the *Herald* and Jack could tell from the coal bags under his eyes that he wasn't doing so hot in the polls. Who are we? and Where are we going? They were the big questions. He poked at the hole drilled into the table top and looked across at Angela. 'You got a plan, or we just flying blind?'

'First we go see Celia,' she said. 'I want to hear what she has to say.'

The Holden was parked across the road behind a black Mazda RX7. Three boxers in Tooheys Blue T-shirts were leaning on the Mazda's doors. Their tall thin trainer waved at Angela as she slid behind the wheel of the Holden, put it into gear and took off like a bullet. The three boxers grinned. Jack watched her hang right and tear down Henderson Road scowling to herself over the wheel. The concrete towers of Redfern and Waterloo housing estates rose above the rooftops of the terraces. She parked on the Redfern side and they walked across the clipped lawn. There was nobody much about, just a few hundred pigeons and a rusting ship anchor. It was even quieter in the foyer. They rode the lift up and walked down the corridor to Room 1408. Angela gave the doorbell a good long press. There were noises inside like furniture being shifted about. Then the door opened. The moment Celia saw them both she started violently and tried to slam the door in their faces. Jack thrust his size 11 Doc Marten in the way; the hollow door wobbled on its hinges.

Angela said, 'We just need to talk to you for a moment, Celia.'

'I don't have to talk to you,' Celia said from around the door. 'You're not the cops.'

'Just answer me one thing. Why did you change your mind about the photos?'

'I made a mistake, that's all.'

'But you were so certain before,' Angela went. 'You swore they were the men who shot my brother.'

'No!' Celia shook her head, 'no, it wasn't them. Now you get out of here. Go on,' she said. 'I've got a very sick husband to look after.'

Jack could hear soul music playing softly in the flat, a velvety voice singing, 'If there's a rock n roll heaven.' He jammed his shoe further in the doorway. 'Did Detective Quarrell threaten you or offer you an enticement?' He liked the sound of that word.

Celia's small green eyes flickered with fear. Then the door jerked open all the way and an enormous man in faded pyjamas was standing there right behind her. He must've weighed 150 k's at least. 'You heard her,' he said. He had a little squeaky voice like a kid's. 'Shove off.' He kicked at Jack's leg with his slippered foot and Jack stepped back into the corridor. The man tried to come at him, but he was so large he couldn't fit frontways through his door.

'Okay,' Angela said, 'okay, we're going now. But you've got to realise, we'll be back, Celia. You're our only witness.'

Heading down in the lift Jack said, 'You see her face when I mentioned Quarrell's name?'

They sat in the car together with the engine running. Angela pressed her forehead against the wheel for a minute. She shut her eyes and then opened them. She put the car into gear and looked straight ahead.

'Where to now?' Jack said. But he knew there was only one place left.

31

Railway Square was alive with people. They steamed out of the tunnel and spilled across the pavements. Wave after wave of them. They dashed inside the glass-fronted buildings while the city glittered in the bright morning light. Angela swung the wheel and pulled the Holden into a no standing zone in a dirty rundown alleyway off Hay Street. She cut the engine and they sat there a hundred metres away from the Woo Ling Barbecue Shop. The steel security door at the side was shut, but Jack could see heads moving about on the second and third floors. 'Now what?' he said.

Angela wound her window down. Sirens screamed in the distance. She kept her eyes fixed on that steel door. 'Now we wait,' she said.

Jack studied the tiny wrinkles at the side of her ear.

'What makes you so certain it was Quarrell who got to Celia?'

'I know the man,' Jack said. 'I know how he works. He's attracted to power and money like a fly is to shit.' He turned his head as a white Toyota Hiace braked in front of the Woo Ling Barbecue Shop and two men got out. One was tall and heavy; the other a short fuse of dynamite with a shaved head.

'That's him,' Angela said, 'the one Celia ID'd.'

Jack shifted in his seat. He remembered the guy alright – almost busted half his ribs. He watched both men walk over to the steel door. The taller one was carrying a soft-sided sports bag with *Tigers* written on the side. From the way he tipped to the right Jack could tell that bag was extra heavy. The shaven-headed man was talking into a mobile phone. The steel door opened electronically and then clunked shut behind them.

'Place's like a fortress,' Jack said. 'We couldn't get in there if we tried.'

'I don't want to get in,' she said. 'I want to take that bastard off the streets.'

'You mean kill him?'

'No, kidnap him. Take him somewhere and make him confess.'

'Look.' Jack gave his head a shake. 'That guy's a pro. He's as hard as nails. He wouldn't talk if you stuck a blowtorch under both his feet and turned it on high.'

Angela gripped the top of the wheel in her fingers. 'He's got to pay for what he did.'

Jack rubbed at his jaw. He didn't like the way she was staring at him waiting for an answer. 'How you gonna snatch him eh? He's not gonna just come waltzing home with us.'

His eyes went to the steel door as it swung open and six men came out, three of them toting soft-sided sports bags. For a split-second Jack thought they had spotted the Holden in the alley, but they just stood with their sleeves rolled up and their Unicorn tattoos showing, looking up and down the busy street. Two of them crossed the road – one with a bag, the other without – and got into a red Toyota 4WD Runner and headed west. Another two climbed into a blue BMW 525 in front of the Hiace and sped off towards the eastern suburbs. The last two got into a light green Porsche Carrera with Queensland plates, spun it around and headed for the bridge. The shaven-headed man stood in the doorway talking into his mobile phone. When the three vehicles were finally out of sight he handed the phone to his well-built assistant, took a chunky cigar from out of his khaki shirt pocket and lit it.

Angela jabbed her elbow into Jack's side. 'See that!'

Jack's fingers played with the cold metal doorhandle.

He could hear the city rumbling away like a man with a bad bellyache. He watched the squat sharp-faced killer suck pleasurably on the end of his swollen cigar, while his eyes roamed across the grimy facades and down into the alleyway. Then the man said something to his body-guard and both of them strode over to the Hiace, got in and turned the van around.

Angela had the Holden in gear and the motor running in less than two seconds. She pulled out without even bothering to check her mirror.

'I think he saw us,' Jack said. 'Hang back a little.'

She was breathing hard through her nose and her knuckles showed white as she turned the wheel. The Holden slid into Campbell Street. Jack saw the Hiace double-parked outside the Hong Kong Bank with its hazard lights flashing. He watched Damian's killer go into the bank holding his mobile phone up to his ear, his bodyguard carrying a soft leather briefcase. Angela dropped the Holden in behind a yellow Sydney City Council truck and slipped the stick into neutral.

Jack's eyes were locked onto the bank's glass doors, his fingers just touching a hairline crack on the dash. And he was thinking how much he owed this little rib-kicker. He owed him for thrusting that gun in the child's face and for the sapping he'd taken back at her house, but most of all he owed him for shooting out the eyes of his young friend. He owed him plenty. He reached over and gripped Angela's arm. 'Okay,' he said. 'Let's do it.'

Her mouth softened at the edges. She leaned over and brushed her lips against his. He could smell Sunsilk shampoo in her hair. She didn't say anything to him then, but he could tell by her eyes that she was pleased. The doors of the Hong Kong Bank parted and Damian's killer came out with his bodyguard holding his briefcase, got into his van and took off towards the heart of Chinatown.

Angela followed. She turned right into Hay and left

into Thomas. She passed the Choy Lee Fut Martial Arts Federation. Cement trucks rumbled down the narrow street, old people hopping to get out of their way. The air was filled with dust and the hammering and drilling from a construction site; yellow helmeted workers clambered spiderlike across the scaffolding. The Hiace swung left at the top of the street and disappeared into the bowels of a big blue concrete and glass tower which looked like some boy architect's idea of a rocketship. Angela braked outside the parking entrance just as the boom arm lowered. 'Stay here,' Jack said. He leapt out of the Holden, bounded up the steps of the scraper and went into the foyer. He ran his eyes over the small gold lettering on the information board until he found what he was looking for – *T Chiu Pty Ltd Importers/ Exporters Flr 9*. Jack went outside and stood on the top step, stroking his big jaw with his thumb and forefinger. Angela was parked on the corner of Quay and Thomas. Twenty metres behind her two Asian men were sitting in the front seat of a black Commodore Berlina. Jack went down the steps, and got into the Holden. He said, 'Don't look now, but we've got a tail.'

Angela slipped it into first. She said, 'They've been with us since the bank.' She planted her foot and the back wheels spun. The Holden shot forward and she swung the wheel left and then left again. Jack was staring into the side mirror at the black Berlina looming up behind them. He hung onto the door strap as the Holden slid out into George Street and they were heading towards the city. Angela trying to work her way over into the right lane through a thick stream of Mercedes buses.

'He's still with us,' Jack said. He put his foot up on the dash as they hit the lights on Hay Street. They hit them fast and they hit them turning red. The Holden skidded around the corner and the back end began to drift. Jack saw a concrete pole shooting towards his door. But Angela didn't brake. She just pressed down on the accelerator and for a second the Holden seemed to be in two minds as to where it was going. Then it straightened.

Jack looked in the mirror as they shot up Hay Street. There was nothing behind. He said, 'You give lessons?'

'Hold your line in the corners, Jack. That's the secret of racing.'

Most people he knew only steered, but Angela drove. He said, 'I think you lost them anyway.' He picked her bandage up off the seat and gently pressed it over the nasty lump on her temple. He was thinking how this woman was something special.

'Find anything back there?' she said. Her eyes were fixed on the road.

'Only that Chiu's got an office on the ninth floor. Which means there's a link running from this gang to Tony Chiu right through to Callagher. All we gotta do now is prove it.'

'That's why we need a confession,' Angela said, 'to break the chain.'

'So what have we got?' Jack counted off his big blunt fingers. 'We know that Tony Chiu's been donating large sums to the government's election fund and we know that Damian was killed because of that disc.'

'Why didn't they kill us too, when they had the chance?'

'Killing four people involves a lot more mess and investigation than killing just one. Besides,' Jack said, 'they've got it back now. All of this is only our word against theirs. One thing you can be certain of is come election day Callagher won't be disclosing all of those funds to the Electoral Commission.'

'But what's in it for Tony Chiu? What does he get out of this?'

'Dunno,' he said. 'But I think we should have another talk to Senator Callagher.'

Angela turned left into Central and sped up the ramp towards the country trains entrance. Jack got out and walked over to a bank of blue phones. A Tangara glided into the station from the city loop, as smooth and as shiny as a snake in its new skin. Jack dialled the Senator's number. He put his fingers over the moist mouthpiece and asked if he could speak to Mr Callagher urgently. The woman said that she was sorry, but the Senator was in Canberra. She said, 'Can I have your name and number please?'

The black Berlina swept around the corner and braked just behind the EH. Two men got out. They were big men. One of them sidled up to Angela's window, his hand reaching in towards the bulge under his suit jacket.

Jack dropped the receiver and ran towards them, yelling and waving his arms to attract attention.

The man pulled his hand out of his coat pocket, flashed a badge in the air. 'Federal Police,' he said. 'Stop right there.'

Jack came to a halt, leaned a fist on the bonnet of the Holden, his heart thumping against his rib cage, staring into the eyes of the biggest Eurasian cop he had ever seen. The man had a hard tough face set on a thick bull neck and a black moustache which seemed to stream out of his nostrils, but it was his hands that impressed Jack the most. The knuckles had been broken and badly re-set; the fingers were gnarled and twisted. He stuck one of the over-sized mitts in Jack's direction and said,

'I'm Detective Superintendent Mun Bun Lamb. But you can call me Mick.'

32

Security was drum tight at the Australian Federal Police building in Goulburn Street. It needed to be. The murder of Assistant Commissioner Winchester in 1989 outside his Canberra home had brought a total upgrading of security procedures. To even get into the lift Jack and Angela had to pass through plate-glass doors which were operated by Federal officers seated behind bullet-proof windows. They rode up in the lift wearing visitor's badges clipped to the front of their clothes. Superintendent Mick Lam – (No B, he'd told Jack in the car) – shepherded them down a corridor and in through a security door which he operated with a metal strip. White computer modules lined the desks around the windows of what was obviously a briefing room. The plush pile and clean modern lines of the furniture were more in keeping with an architect's office than a cop shop. Mick Lam gestured Jack and Angela towards two chairs and waved over the other police officer who hadn't said a word so far.

'This is Chief Inspector Yu Kam-Cheung of the Triads Bureau of the Royal Hong Kong Police,' Lam said. 'Inspector Yu's been seconded to our Special Operations Unit.'

Yu nodded curtly at them both, but didn't say anything. He wore his hair slightly long for a police officer, but looked remarkably fit. On his right arm a pale-pink skin graft stretched from his wrist to his elbow.

'We believe you two might be able to assist us in our investigations.' Lam's dark button eyes swept over Jack and Angela. He pressed the controls in front of him and the TV screen on the wall flickered into life. Lam said, 'Stop me if you recognise anyone.'

The tape had obviously been shot from cramped quarters outside the Woo Ling Barbecue Shop. A procession of slightly out-of-focus male faces filed out of the doorway and stood on the pavement with their arms folded.

Angela jumped up from her chair. 'That's him,' she said, pointing at the screen. 'That man there. He murdered my brother.'

Lam froze the tape. A short, shaven-headed man was smiling at his bodyguard and displaying a mouth full of gold teeth. 'Lee Fang,' Lam said. 'He's the 426 for the Sun Sai Gei Triad.'

Jack lifted his eyebrows.

'Fang's in charge of enforcement. We also believe he's directly involved in drug importation, extortion, illegal immigration and murder – the total package.'

'Then why haven't you arrested him?' Angela piped up. 'If you know all this stuff. Why's he still free?'

'Because we've nothing that will stand up in court, Ms Frick. Please.' Lam held up a big gnarled hand. 'Can we continue?'

The tape rolled. More than a dozen men were gathered outside the barbecue shop when a white Merc SL 600 slowed and pulled up on the far side of the street. Fang went over to the passenger's door. The camera zoomed in until Fang and the man he was talking to filled the screen.

Jack stared at the well-dressed face – the black glasses, the short hair parted rigidly to the right. He looked like one of those economists that are pictured in the financial pages of the *Herald*. Jack recognised him immediately.

'Tony Chiu.'

Mick Lam nodded his smooth round head. 'Chiu's the 489 of the Sun Sai Gei or dragonhead. He's a trained accountant amongst other things, but don't let the eye-wear fool you. The man's as ruthless as Pol Pot and as camera shy. Ninety per cent of the heroin coming into Australia is now controlled by the two Triad syndicates. It's a billion dollar business. And Chiu runs the Sun Sai Gei like any other large corporate structure – he has his managers, sales reps, distributors, gophers. Chiu's a very clever fella and what he craves most of all is anonymity. He's never been charged with any offence here or in his native Hong Kong. In fact he's never even been interviewed.'

Yu said something quickly to Lam in Cantonese and

Lam nodded. Jack wondered whether the inspector understood English.

Lam continued in his broad New South Wales accent: 'In the past three months a number of prominent businessmen have gone missing in Chinatown. We suspect they were murdered on Chiu's orders.'

'What's this all about?' Angela said. 'What's this got to do with my brother?'

Detective Superintendent Lam pulled at his thick black moustache. His eyebrows bent closer together. 'Your brother, Ms Frick, was money-laundering. Small time stuff. Lending out his account so it could be used to wash the proceeds of crime. It's a common practice in Hong Kong and one growing in popularity here, but it's highly unusual for the societies to use a non-Chinese.'

'How do you know about Damian?'

'Because we've had the Sun Sai Gei under surveillance for three months now. We believe your brother was killed as a warning to others. We think he was planning to rip them off.'

Jack remembered the black Berlina parked outside his flat in Coogee. He said, 'No, that's not the main reason Damian was murdered.'

Lam and Yu frowned at him.

'You tell em, Angela,' Jack said. 'Go on.'

Angela stood up slowly and walked over to the window. Jack didn't take his eyes off her for a moment. He watched her nails run along the sharp corner of the table as she began telling the two detectives in a very low voice, telling them everything that had happened since that first night back at his flat. He watched her lips move, her small pale hands tightening at her side. When she finished talking she sat down in the ergonomic chair, crossed her legs and looked over at him with those dark blue eyes. He didn't need words to know there was something between them now, something solid that he could feel in this cool air-conditioned office.

Detective Superintendent Lam switched off the TV and the screen crackled. Thick folds of skin wrinkled the back of his big bull neck. He pulled the tape out of the machine. 'You two are very fortunate to be alive. Lee Fang likes to kill people.' He took an Alpine out of a pack in his coat pocket and screwed it into a brass cigarette holder. He lifted his big hand at Yu and spoke rapidly in Cantonese.

Yu nodded. He was younger than Lam and gave Jack the impression of a spring that had been tightly wound. His eyes kept sweeping from Jack to Angela as if deciding which face to rest on. There was a long silence and then Yu said, 'Major Hong Kong money has started moving into Australia.'

Jack stared at the Inspector. He had the kind of voice radio announcers in Australia used up until the early seventies: it was as British as the BBC.

Yu said, 'The Triads are preparing for their departure from the colony. Vancouver and Sydney are their two preferred destinations because the RICO Statute has made it too hard for them to get into the U.S.' He scratched at the puckered skin graft on his arm. 'A joint task force has been set up between the RHKP and the AFP to investigate the massive transfer of Triad assets. We are talking billions of dollars.' He fixed his eyes directly on Angela. 'If what you say is true, then someone high up in your Federal Goverment would be the ideal contact for the Hong Kong societies to develop.'

'It *is* true,' Angela said. 'We saw the figures. Didn't we, Jack?'

Jack nodded. 'Three million bucks donated by Tony Chiu to Callagher's secret election fund.'

'I'll have to take this upstairs.' Lam's voice was broad and nasal compared to the Inspector's. 'See the AC.'

'There's a New South Wales detective too,' Jack said. 'Lindsay Quarrell. I think he's mixed up in it somehow.'

'We know all about Detective Sergeant Quarrell. We've had our eye on him for quite some time.'

'What about my brother?' Angela put in.

There were dark bags under Superintendent Lam's eyes. 'I sympathise with your loss. Believe me, Ms Frick, I do. And I can assure you we'll be doing everything in our power to bring these killers to justice.'

'You police always say that,' she said.

Lam's face hardened. 'I apologise for not being original.' He mashed his Alpine out in a small oak tray on the desk and slipped the brass holder back into his inside pocket. 'Look, I'm not trying to give you the short shrift here, but the Sun Sai Gei are a very hard nut to crack. They make the Calabrians seem like schoolkids. We have to move carefully if we're gonna nail them.'

'The Sun Sai Gei,' Yu said, 'are a totally professional criminal organisation. They have none of the old attachments to tradition like the 14K and the Sun Yee On. In less then three years they have become the most powerful Triad society in eastern Australia.'

'Sun sigh gay,' Jack said, trying to emulate the Inspector's rounded vowels. 'What's that mean?'

Yu's eyes gleamed, but his expression didn't change. 'In Cantonese it means New Century. The Sun Sai Gei believe that the next century will be theirs.' He nodded sternly. 'The Chinese century. The Triads are moving their money offshore; at the same time they are working closely with corrupt communist officials in Guangdong province. They will use whoever they can.'

Jack looked over to Angela, but she didn't appear to be listening to them. She was just sitting in her chair, staring at a red mark on the floor, with her hands folded on her knees.

Yu said, 'We have a saying in my country: open the door too wide and the dirt blows in.'

Lam bent his big frame down in front of Angela. 'Give me a few days to run with this, Ms Frick, and I'll get back to you.'

Angela stood up. She smiled at the two senior police.

She was very polite. But even a blind man could sense there was something weighing on her mind.

Detective Superintendent Lam stuck out a hand the size of a steam shovel. There were little black whiskers on his cheekbones he'd missed with the razor. 'Take care of yourselves. We're going to need you two as witnesses.'

They went out the door and down the lift. They passed through the bullet-proof barrier and handed their identity badges to the overweight officer behind the plate-glass window. It was blowing up a gale outside and a pair of young Federal policemen were standing in the foyer looking kind of agitated as if they didn't want to go outside.

Angela and Jack stepped out of the AFP fortress and leaned into the wind. 'Okay,' she said, 'we'll do this on our own.'

33

She drove towards the sea. Ugly red units ran past their windows. A girl at a bus stop was clutching her pleated skirt. Papers swirled across the street and spidery grevilleas bent their silky heads over wire fences. At the end of the road the sea sparkled blue and clear like some private pool. She parked facing Clovelly Bay and cut the engine. She fixed her eyes on the sharp line of the horizon. A flock of seagulls – more than a hundred of them – wheeled over the car park. Waves crashed on the shore, sending up huge sheets of spray. Jack could taste salt in the air. He opened the cardboard box on the seat between them; the Holden filled with the smell of melted cheese and tomato. He pulled off a thick wedge of spinach pizza and passed it to her. They ate with their windows open, listening to the sea bang onto the rocks. He liked the way he could sit like this with her, without feeling the need to speak, just letting the wind blow his thoughts about. He wiped a string of mozzarella from his chin. A bird shot past their windscreen like a bullet; it had a little pointy head and it was in a terrible rush to get somewhere. Angela put down her slice of untouched pizza, looked across at him.

'Tell me about you and Detective Quarrell.'

'I already did.'

'You told me about a fight, but it's more than that.'

'I don't like to go into the past,' Jack said. 'You never know if you're gonna come back out.'

'Just the story,' she said, 'without the bullshit.'

'When I'm finished eating.'

She opened the driver's door suddenly and stepped out into the wind. For a moment she seemed to be blown back. Jack followed her with his eyes as she skirted the rocks and then her dark hair disappeared down behind the baths. He finished the last two slices of warm pizza and then got out, locked the doors behind him and slipped down the rocks to the shore. He made his way carefully around the saltwater pool while the waves vaulted the concrete walls and wet his shoes. There was no one on the beach, not even a dog. He climbed the path on the far side, searching for her amongst the yellow canna lillies. Then he saw her standing out on Shark Point, standing on the very edge of the sandstone cliff.

Slowly he moved towards her. The wind was clawing at her Levis and billowing out the sleeves of her blue corduroy jacket while the sea below frothed and boiled. Spray shot up all around her ankles but she didn't seem to notice. She just stood there, staring down at the water as if she was hypnotised.

Jack reached out and grabbed her by the elbow. He

plucked her back from the edge. 'What the hell are you doing?'

Angela blinked at him. Her hair was sticking up at the front. Her lips were blood red lines across her pale drawn face. She shook her head and shuddered. A huge sheet of seawater rose up and slammed against the Point where she'd been standing. 'I've got to finish this, Jack,' she said. 'You understand that don't you?'

He nodded, put his arms around her and held her tight. For a long while they stayed locked together while the sky darkened and small yellow lights flickered back up along the ridge.

She said, 'We're gonna need help. You know anyone we could get?'

'Yeah,' Jack nodded slowly, 'I know some people.'

34

In the car park Angela threw him the keys. Jack opened the driver's door and got in behind the wheel. He backed the EH out and spun it around. The headlights picked out a pair of lovers thrashing about like dolphins in the front seat of a Peugeot. The road climbed towards the city and he felt her eyes watching him closely as if she were waiting for him to speak.

He skidded through a roundabout and changed down. He looked out the window. The city was dark out there and big and hostile and if you had even one person that you could trust in it then you were lucky. He reached over and took her hand. It was wide open.

Jack said, 'Quarrell killed a mate of mine – Nepo Kemp. He shot him in the throat at close range. It was murder,

but the coroner exonerated him.' He took a long breath
and wrapped his fingers around the knob of the gearstick.

'It started back in Darlinghurst when I was working
the bar there. Me and Vick'd just had Toby and I was
only clearing two eighty, three hundred a week. Anyway
I started selling, a few sticks wrapped in al-foil, small
time shit. Then I sold 100 gram bags. The Roberts was a
roughhouse back then. We used to get in prostitutes from
William Street, tow-truck operators, bikies, cops. A lot of
cops liked to wet their whistles there. Detective Sergeant
Quarrell was a regular – always drank OP rum chasers
with his schooner.

'One night after work I go out into Stanley Street and
there's Quarrell and two armed hold-up detectives waiting for me. Turns out they knew where I kept my stash,
who I got it from, everything. Been watching me for
weeks. So I'm sitting in an unmarked cop car expecting
to go down, when Quarrell sticks his face over the seat
and says, 'From now on, Butorov, you're working for me.'

Angela said, 'Dealing?'

Jack stared at Centennial Park closing in on his right;
it was thick and dark with trees and there were large
gaps like missing teeth in the iron rail. 'It sounds crazy,
but the police were organising a plantation on the South
Coast, growing it in a joint operation to snare the big
distributors. Only trouble is, Quarrell and a couple of
smart New South Wales detectives are skimming off kilos
of the stuff. At one point he was delivering to half the
pubs between Woolloomooloo and Redfern. Used to come
in the Roberts every second Friday and toss a Dunlop
sports bag over the bar. Like he's been to football training
– 'cept the only gear inside was green and full of heads.
Top quality stuff. Quarrell used to boast about it, called
it Federal grass.'

The car's headlights arced across the racecourse fence
and Jack swung the Holden right. He said, 'That's when
Nepo got involved. He was working the Railway View in

Redfern then. I used to box with Kempie. Drank with him. We even started working pubs round about the same time. Tough little nut.'

Angela shifted in her seat. 'So why'd Quarrell shoot him for?'

Jack said, 'Me and Nepo are making a hundred, hundred and twenty a week tops, while Quarrell and his pals are raking in thousands. Had a string of barmen all over town workin for em. I never met a man who liked money much as Lindsay. Liked the smell of it, liked the feel of it. You'd see him counting out a big roll, staring at those crisp new fifties like he was going to eat em.' Jack worked his bottom lip hard against the edge of his teeth.

'One Thursday night Nepo bowls into the Roberts with a map. All fired up because he's found the forest where the police crop's growing. Wants me to go down there, rip a load of it off. He's even hired a Hertz van, but I couldn't go cause Toby was in St Vincent's having his first bunch of tests. So Nepo went by himself. I never saw him again.'

Angela said, 'Did it get into the papers?'

'Yeah,' Jack said. 'It made the papers alright, and the TV. Know how the *Sun*, or *Mirror* I think it was, wrote it up: *Drug dealer shot dead in plantation bust*.' He rolled his window open and looked out at the coloured lights of the Lebanese takeaways on Cleveland Street. 'At the inquest the cops produced a pistol they reckon Nep had on him. Said he tried to kill Detective Quarrell with it. Said it was self-defence. Nepo never owned a pistol in his life. Doubt if he'd even fired one. Guy was a boxer.'

Angela chewed silently on her lip.

Turning into Regent Street, Jack said, 'This is where Nep used to hang out.' He pulled up outside a run-down hotel with barred windows and rolled up shutters. He cut the lights and they got out of the car. An alsatian on the second floor started barking as they approached the pub doors. Music was thumping from a jukebox inside and George Thorogood was singing, 'I'm bad, bad to the bone.'

Eyes watched them come in. A dozen dark men and a couple of tough-looking women standing around a worn pool table under the dim light. Hard set faces scowling through a pall of blue smoke. Jack and Angela edged towards the taps on the narrow bar, Angela glancing down at her Doc Martens as if she wanted to scuff them up a bit. The barman was working a dirty grey sponge into the cracked bar top while Jack leaned on the rail feeling two dozen eyes crawling over his back. He waited for the barman to ash his cigarette out and limp over.

'Two midis a new,' Jack shouted over George Thorogood and the Destroyers. 'Irene Kemp, she still come in here?'

The barman looked at Jack like he was new furniture they hadn't ordered. He sloshed two headless beers down on the wet bar towel. 'Three eighty.'

A young Koori with a Bonds blue singlet, curly black hair and biceps the size of rockmelons drifted up close to Jack. Pool sticks stopped clicking at the table. The Koori was clutching an empty schooner tight in his fist and holding the rim of the glass out at a 45-degree angle.

'What do you want here, maggot?'

Jack saw red streaks in the man's dark eyes. He stiffened, trying not to show fear. He'd seen a man get glassed once: 24 stitches to sew his cheek back on. 'I'm looking for Irene Kemp,' he went, keeping his voice steady.

'You some kinda TV journo?'

'No,' Jack said, 'just a friend.'

The young Koori thrust a forearm in between Jack and Angela, dropped the schooner glass down on the bar. His stomach was as flat and hard as slate. 'Wanna see me Auntie eh?' Staring at Jack real closely now. 'I'm Brick.' He grinned and flashed strong white teeth. 'You wuz a mate of Neppy's right?'

Jack nodded.

'I remember you now. Used to box with him up Newtown. Neppy was good huh?'

'Yeah,' Jack said. 'He was special.'

Brick's dark eyes flicked to Angela. 'Cops shot mu cuz,' he said. 'White cunts.'

Angela met his gaze. She didn't blink. 'Some of us white cunts,' she said softly, 'are on your side.'

Brick pressed a knuckle to the side of his jaw and rubbed.

'Don't write us all off just yet,' she said, then turned and walked away.

'Who's the dubay?' Brick watched her leaning over the cracked face of the jukebox.

Jack said, 'That's Angela. Her brother was murdered too.'

'Gunjies do it?'

'No,' Jack said, 'Chinese gang. That's why I'm looking for Irene's boys. We need back-up. They still living up in Lawson Street?'

Brick said, 'Whole family moved outta the Fern. Stevie and Ewan got a place out at Campbelltown, and Auntie's gone back up to Coonabarabran. She's been real crook.'

Jack pictured a short woman in her fifties, eyes like saucers, strong wide face.

'After the inquest we got the vultures flying through, sticking their TV cameras down our throats. Make you sick those creeps. Auntie got nothin out of it but, just a lotta fuckin handwringin. Probably sold a few To'tas for em.' Brick chewed on a pale scar on his lip.

Yothu Yindi started singing, 'Treaty yeah, treaty now,' as Angela walked away from the jukebox with everyone's eyes pinned on her. She came up alongside of Brick and tilted her head back at the crowded pool table. 'That your mob over there?'

Brick said, 'Why?'

'How would you and your friends like to earn some money?'

35

Two big Kooris crammed into the back seat of the Holden next to Jack, while Brick and a girl with wild black eyes slid into the front. The doors slammed and Angela hit the pedal, turned left and drove past the courthouse. It was quiet out on the street. A full moon hung low over the twin TNT towers like an enormous wet paint lid. The wild-eyed girl in the front handed a bottle of VB over the back seat. She was as thin as a shadow, her frizzy hair cut short around her ears. Jack could smell dried sweat in the car mingled with strong tobacco. He took a long swig of beer and passed it to the Koori wearing the ochre, yellow and black beanie, the one they called Big Trap. On the backs of his hands were tattooed the words, 'Our Land, our Country'. In the pub he'd said to Jack, 'Why you gubbs only come around when you got trouble eh?' and shifted his thick eyebrows over at Angela. 'How much we getting paid for this sister?'

Angela said, 'I've got two hundred and fifty dollars in cash and my Mastercard. But I got to warn you. This Chinese gang are tough and it could get dangerous tonight.'

Brick and Big Trap and the other Kooris watched her, their lips curling back over their teeth to form identical grins.

'She's right,' Jack went. 'This crew know how to turn it on. Plus there's a chance they'll be packing.'

Angela nodded. 'I can understand if you guys don't want to get involved.'

Brick looked up from the cigarette he was building. The muscles on his chest ridged. 'How many of them?'

'I don't know, ten or more. But they're martial arts experts.'

Big Trap laughed. 'Look, sister, when you've had yer bedroom door kicked in at dawn by the TRG squad and all you've got between you and half a dozen itchy triggers is a pair of cotton sheets, then ten Chinamen don't seem much at all.' He snatched the pool cues off the rack and stood there clenching a stack of them in his tattooed fist.

'Okay,' Brick said, 'we're gonna come along.'

Angela nodded rapidly; her hand dug into her purse.

'Save it,' Brick said, 'to the job's over. We know what it's like when one of your family gets shot.'

Jack watched the shine spread across her face, trying to figure what it was that attracted him the most about her – the line of her cheekbones or those violet-blue eyes. When he looked into them sometimes he caught a glimpse of what it might be like to get lost in another person again.

He squashed his shoulder against the door and watched the shadows from the park flick past his window. The Holden slowed at Central and there was a tightening in his bowels. They were going up against the Sun Sai Gei armed with pool sticks, and who knows what kind of shit they'd meet – knives, machetes, .32s. It didn't seem to worry the Regent Street mob any, Big Trap and the one called Charlie laughing as they passed the VB around, the wild-eyed girl in the front saying, 'Naragar, naragar, Brick!' Nepo was like that. Didn't fear nobody. Even that day he was going down to rip Quarrell off he was joking about it. A cab blew past on the inside lane doing ninety-five k's. Fear was like a spiked prison wall that you carried around with you. And once you were over the top of it, you were free. Jack wrenched his window open and thrust his big head out, the veins on his neck bulging as he let loose with a yell into the night, then slumped back against the car seat and wound the window up tight.

Angela's eyes met his in the mirror. 'You alright, Jack?'

'Yeah.' Jack nodded. Just scared that was all, but you couldn't tell people that. The Kooris were grinning at him as he took the bottle out of Big Trap's hands, felt the man's heavy rings scrape against his knuckles. They turned into Campbell Street and cruised past the Woo Ling Barbecue Shop. Lights were burning on the top two floors. Angela pulled into the narrow street opposite, backed the EH into a drive and turned the headlights off.

'What you want us to do, cuz?' Big Trap said.

'Ask Angela,' Jack told him. 'It's her play.'

Angela unclipped her safety belt. 'See the white Hiace out front. That's Fang's van. We wait until he comes out and then we grab him.'

Brick said, 'What if he don't come out?'

'Then we flush him out.' She placed her hands back up on top of the wheel. The skin on her face was stretched as tight as a drumhead.

Jack stared at the steel security door at the side of the barbecue shop. Big black cockroaches ran up and down the road in the moonlight, and the air smelled of rotting vegetables. In the distance he could hear the rumble of the city like some huge relentless press.

Angela leaned forward suddenly and tapped the windscreen with her nails. 'In the van,' she went, 'there's someone there in the van.'

A cigarette glowed faintly on the driver's side.

'A lookout,' Brick said. He had his arm around the wild-eyed girl in the front like the two of them were at the drive-in. 'Reckon you can take him, Charlie?'

Charlie's thick curly hair stood up on top like a palm cockatoo's. Without a word he unscrewed the small interior globe overhead, passed it to Jack and slipped a long leather-stitched sap out of his Levis pocket. He cracked the car door open quietly and stole across the alleyway, stepping between the garbage lids. When he reached the corner he paused, then shot across Campbell Street and came up around the rear of the Hiace. A minute later the driver's door swung open and Charlie jumped out alone. The faint glow in the van had been extinguished. He crossed the street quickly, sticking to the shadows and slipped into the back seat of the Holden. In his hand he clutched a black plastic contraption the size of a thick envelope.

'You don't muck about Charlie,' Jack said, 'do yer?'

Charlie's hard brown eyes stared at Jack intently, but he didn't speak. He let Brick take the plastic device from him and hold it up in the moonlight. 'Looks like a remote control,' Brick said. 'Press this button here and it sets off an infra-red alarm in the building. Taiwan shit. You can buy them for twenty bucks at Dick Smith's.'

'How do you know all this?' Angela asked.

Brick's lips drew back over his strong white teeth. 'Last job I had was working with alarms.'

Big Trap laughed and shoved Brick's arm.

'Okay,' Jack said, 'what we need is a decoy. Someone very fast on their feet.' He looked at Charlie, but Brick said, 'Na, my turn now.' And tossed the plastic alarm over the seat to Jack.

'I'm coming with you,' the wild-eyed girl said.

'It could get dangerous,' Jack warned her. 'Once I hit this button these guys're gonna come streaming outta that door like rats.'

'This is my man,' the girl said. 'Where Brick goes I go.'

Brick smiled and pushed at the end of his nose. 'Kara never trusts me on my own, do you girl?'

'We'll pick you up at Belmore Park,' Angela said. 'Just make it there in one piece, okay.' She touched the accelerator with her foot and the motor growled in response.

The air was cool outside, but Jack was sweating under his arms and between his legs. He wiped his brow and lifted the pool sticks out of the boot, passed two of them through to Charlie and took one himself while Brick and Kara walked slowly towards the front of the Hiace. Jack slid in beside Angela and closed his eyes for a moment.

When he opened them again, heads were moving about
on the floor above the barbecue shop. He watched as
Brick sprung the catch on the van's bonnet, yanked out
the coil lead and flung it into the gutter. Then the young
Koori turned to them and waved.

'Now,' Angela said.

Jack pressed the button on the alarm. All eyes went to
the security door. The seconds ticked past.

'Nothing happen, cuz.'

Angela's fingers were wrapped tight round the knob of
the gearstick. She pressed the clutch in and Jack could
feel the 179 engine straining under her feet. The smell of
petrol filled the car. He opened his window and pointed
the alarm directly at the building opposite, pressed his
thumb down and kept on pressing.

Faces appeared suddenly at the second and third floor
windows. Jack gripped the smooth neck of the pool cue
hard in his right hand. Then the security door swung
open and seven young bucks wearing cut-off T-shirts and
black kung fu pants poured out. When they spotted Brick
they ran towards the van, wielding nunchakus and
double dragon fighting sticks. Brick slammed down the
bonnet, grabbed Kara's hand and tore off towards Central
with a mob of them in pursuit. Other fighters were still
streaming out of the building, tattoos of blue unicorns
visible in the moonlight on their well-muscled arms.

'We gotta help Brick.' Big Trap said.

'Not yet,' Angela murmured, 'we wait for Fang.' She
was scouring the faces of the Blue Unicorn Gang as they
milled about in the street. One of them tried to start the
van's engine; several more were yelling in Cantonese as
they pulled their unconscious companion out by the arms
and legs.

Big Trap pushed against the back of Angela's seat.
'Come on, sister, let's go!'

Jack's eyes were on the doorway. A short, shaven-
headed man rushed out onto the footpath. His face was

purple and twisted with anger; he waved his arms furiously at his men.

'That's him,' Angela said and stamped the accelerator to the floor. The Holden shot out of the laneway and sped across Campbell Street without lights. At the last moment she braked and jerked the wheel firmly to the right – the back end of the Holden mounted the pavement and the tyres scudded to a halt beside the plate-glass window. Jack leapt out, swinging his pool cue overhead. The wooden butt cannoned into the side of Fang's head. The 'thwock' sound it made was like a cricket ball struck plumb in the middle of the bat. Fang's head jerked back and when Big Trap's fist clunked into his temple the Triad enforcer hit the pavement. Angela jumped out and sprung the boot lid open. She and Jack and Big Trap dragged Lee Fang over by the collar and heaved him in on top of the spare tyre. She slammed the lid down hard on his fingers and jumped back in behind the wheel.

The other Blue Unicorns were standing around the van gaping – it had happened so quick. Then one with a stringy moustache rushed at the Holden, his hand reaching into the waistband of his trousers. Jack and Big Trap dived into the back seat beside Charlie as Angela took off in reverse, swerving the wheel violently down the narrow street. A muzzle flashed twice and a bullet ricocheted off the bonnet. Another man burst out of the Woo Ling doorway, raised a sawn-off shotgun and blasted. Glass shattered on a red Tarago parked alongside as its side windows caved in.

'Shit!' Jack blinked.

The Holden slid out backwards into George Street, tyres smoking. An RSL taxi blasted its horn as Angela rammed the gears into first, stomped on the pedal and accelerated through two sets of red lights.

When she turned into Eddy Avenue she said, 'Anyone behind us?'

Jack shook his head. He couldn't stop his hands from

shaking. He stared out into the darkness of Belmore Park and it occurred to him suddenly that he was in this right up to his ears.

The Holden braked outside the bus shelter. Big Trap wound the window down, placed his thumbs together, cupped his hands and gave a short, high-pitched whistle. A figure jumped out from behind the trees followed by another. Angela popped the button on the door and Brick and Kara slid into the front seat.

'We nearly got cut,' Brick said. 'Four of them.' Globs of sweat rolled down his dark muscular neck and he was panting hard. Kara's frizzy hair was wet around her ears and her eyes were big and black and beautiful.

The Holden wheeled away from the kerb without any power, like it was towing a Viscount caravan. From the boot there came a muffled, but persistent thumping.

'What you gonna do with him, titta,' Big Trap said, 'roast him?'

'I'm gonna make him talk,' Angela said. In Redfern she parked the car in a laneway running off Lawson Street. She took out her purse and handed Brick two hundred and fifty dollars.

Brick grinned and counted the money. Charlie's brown eyes were gleaming in the back seat.

'I want to thank you four for what you did tonight,' Angela said. 'We've got a lot to learn from you Kooris.'

'That's right, ta.' Brick laughed. 'And don't you gubbs forget it.' He climbed out of the car with Kara and slapped Jack's palm through the back window. 'Come round when this is over cuz, we'll go up the gym for a workout.'

'Thanks, fellas,' Jack said. 'I will.'

Big Trap nodded towards Angela. 'Gunyum gwarnie,' he said.

Outside the air smelled of grime and dust and diesel fumes. The Holden pulled away and Jack watched the Kooris melt into the night, his fingers playing with the lip of an empty beer bottle.

Angela drove fast through the quiet streets of Redfern, past the shuttered stores and barred windows. 'You learn Koori from your friend?'

'Just a little,' Jack said, 'yeah.'

'What's gunyum gwarnie mean?'

'Crazy arse.' He cocked an ear and listened. He could hear something rolling about back behind the seat, something heavy and loose and dangerous.

36

For forty-five minutes they hammered south-west along Highway 31 until the suburbs began to thin out and pastureland popped up on either side of the blacktop. She turned into Camden Valley Way and drove into a caravan park that backed onto a golf course. Jack stayed with the car while Angela walked up the path and rapped on the aluminium siding. There were no lights on in the office and even though it was not yet twelve the whole park seemed bathed in a silvery moonlit silence. All the way down he'd worried about what he'd have to do when they stopped; now they were here there was no sound at all from the boot. Lee Fang was probably saving his energy. A light came on and an elderly man in bicycle-patterned pyjamas stood behind the screen door talking sternly at Angela. 'You know what time it is?' Jack heard him say. For caravan-dwellers this was late, but for doormen it was early. If he hadn't met her he'd be getting ready to knock off at the club now. Instead, he was sitting in a 1964 Holden, on the outskirts of town with a Triad enforcer, a 426, stuffed into their boot. Some people could just walk into your life like that and change it forever.

Keys rattled on the path and the driver's door opened. Angela slid in behind the wheel and said, 'Lend me forty dollars.'

Jack scowled and rubbed his neck.

'I've got us a cabin right off the road. Mr and Mrs Jones. It's got its own cooking facilities.'

'That's good,' Jack said, 'I'm starved.'

'There's no food I'm afraid. We'll have to get some tomorrow. I meant to thank you for tonight. You've been fabulous.'

Jack stared at her. She was acting as if they were on some kind of holiday. He kept his eyes fixed on her right fist as she walked over to the office clutching his two twenties. When she came back, she got in and steered them down past a line of tents and vans, the headlights picking out kids' tricycles on the grass strips outside. At the end of a gravelled road she stopped beside a cluster of pine cabins, cut the engine and then the lights.

'How we gonna get him out,' Jack said. 'We should've tied him up in the first place.'

'We didn't have time did we?'

'There's no way I'm opening that boot without a weapon, preferably an automatic.'

'Don't open it then. It's too quiet anyway. We'll get up early tomorrow. Right now we need some sleep, both of us, Jack.'

A muffled thumping started up in the boot, like a shoe beating on metal.

'You think he can hear us?'

'We'll leave him in there until he's ready to talk,' she said loudly and climbed out. She banged the car door shut behind her and went up the steps.

Number 3 cabin had an electric stove, a small bar fridge, plates, cutlery, but no sheets. They undressed to their underwear and slipped into bed. The army blankets prickled his skin as he worked a hand up under her black camisole and over the soft mound of her breast. The moment her head touched the pillow she was out to it, but he lay there, curled up like a worm, wondering whether the boot lid would hold, listening for the sound of creaking floorboards as he drifted down a long winding canal at the edge of a river.

They were searching for her keys in a strange black room. Rain dribbled across the windows. He helped her pull away the dusty sheets that shrouded queer lumps of furniture. Outside it was grey and cold and the room smelled of silt from the river. An old fur coat was draped over a black wooden trunk and there were noises coming from within, high-pitched screeches. She held up a heavy iron key. The screeching grew louder and he knew then that he didn't want to see inside. He tried to stop her, but she was too strong. She brushed him off as if he were a fly and bent over the trunk. The hinges creaked as she lifted the lid. He tried to back away, but she grabbed his arm tightly and he yelled, 'No!'

'Only a dream, Jack. Wake up.'

He jerked his head off the pillow and blinked at her. She was kneeling fully dressed on the bed, one hand on his wrist while behind her the cabin door stood wide open. 'You alright?' she said.

He nodded. He could hear birds squawking, dozens of them. A splash of green and crimson flashed past the open door.

'Fang,' he remembered. 'Where's Fang?'

'Still in the boot. I think we should bring him in before everyone's awake. There's some rope in the car. If you stun him I'll tie him up.' She handed Jack a length of 4 by 2 timber. 'I found this out back.'

He rubbed at his eyes. His pillow was wet and stained like rust had leached from his head. He wanted a lot of things right now, but most of all he wanted a drink. 'Breakfast?'

'After, Jack. We have to hurry. Come on.'

He staggered to his feet and pulled on his trousers. It

was not quite light outside and the links behind the caravan park were cloaked in a fine mist. A flock of Rainbow Lorikeets carried on in the branches of a silky oak. Jack put an ear to the boot: it was quiet in there. Too quiet. He gripped the length of hardwood so tight he could feel splinters digging into his fingers.

Angela looked over at him; Jack nodded. She inserted her key in the lock and turned it. The lid of the boot kicked open and Fang tried to leap out at them. His eyes were red and glaring, his lips were drawn back over the gold caps of his teeth.

Jack brought the lump of wood down quickly. He saw the whites of Lee Fang's eyes roll upwards and hit him again hard on top of his shaven skull.

'That's enough. We don't want to kill him!'

Jack leaned against the car door, letting the lump of wood slip from his grasp, feeling his heart beat like a disco drum machine.

Fang was slumped over the spare tyre, a gash running diagonally across the crown of his head and both eyes closed, but he was breathing. Angela covered him with a dirty blanket and they carried him inside, propped him up in the sturdiest chair they could find and secured his ankles and arms behind with tow rope.

'Get some water.' Angela tugged on the rope until it cut into Fang's wrists. There was a look of determination in her eyes, as if she was going to follow this through whatever the cost.

Jack went over to the tap and filled a big tall glass. He downed it in one gulp, watching her dig a Sony tape-recorder out from her bag and place it beside a pair of metal coat-hangers on the table.

'The water, Jack, the water.'

She took the fresh glass and flung its contents into Fang's face. Water dripped off his nose and chin. His red-rimmed eyes shot open and he struggled furiously against the rope.

'You know who I am?' Fang spat. 'The Hung Kwan.'

'We know,' Angela said. 'We know you invaded my house. We know you murdered my brother.'

'My soldiers come after you.' Fang's gold teeth gleamed. 'Your daughter, your little son – ' He looked to Jack and clicked his tongue like a lizard.

Jack moved towards him, balling his fists. 'You threatening my kid?'

Blood trickled down the centre of Fang's shaven skull and into his smooth eyelids. 'If you want to see your family grow old, you untie me now.'

Angela grabbed Jack's raised arm. 'Let me handle this.' She turned to Fang. 'Who paid you to kill my brother?'

Fang's dark eyes glared at them contemptuously. 'Amateurs. You know nothing. You will get nothing.'

Angela picked up the two coat-hangers, walked over to the stove and turned the hotplate on high. She bent the metal necks of the hooks out straight and laid their sharp edged points over the heat. She made sure that Fang could see everything. 'Take his trousers down, Jack. Underpants, too.'

Jack wrenched off Fang's leather belt and ripped his trousers and Y-fronts down over his hairless white legs. A large blue unicorn was tattooed on Fang's right arm and a green and red snake was coiled around his left thigh.

Jack watched her go into the bathroom and come out with a face towel. She tossed it over to him and he stuffed it into Fang's mouth, wondering how far she meant to push this.

She picked up one of the coat-hangers. Its sharp end was glowing red hot. Fang writhed and twisted on his chair as she came towards him, but the rope held firm. She grabbed his flaccid penis with her left hand and brought the scorching metal up close to it. She prised the eye of his penis open with her thumb and fingers. At the last moment Jack looked away.

He heard the sizzle of flesh. Fang bucked violently and the legs of his chair scraped on the wooden floor.

'Why'd you kill my brother for? Why'd you do it?' She was shaking him.

The smell of burning skin filled the small cabin. Jack got up and opened a window. He pictured Clea trembling on this man's knee while her mother lay unconscious on the kitchen floor. He tried to think of Damian lying in lower Pitt Street with his eyes shot out.

Angela turned her face away. Her broad shoulders were trembling. 'I want to know who ordered it done.' She clicked the tape recorder on and Jack jerked the towel out of the killer's mouth.

Fang's eyes bulged white and saliva gathered like foam at the corners of his lips.

'You gonna talk now,' Jack said, 'or I'm gonna ram the next one down your throat.' He walked over and picked the second coat-hanger up off the stove.

Fang looked at him and then at the smoking hot wire in his hand. His face was covered in a thick film of sweat. 'Hospital,' he blurted, 'you take me to hospital now.'

'Name first,' Jack said. 'Then we take you. Give us a name.'

'Callagher,' Fang blurted. 'Callagher paid for the job.'

'Why?' Angela said.

'Your brother stole his disc.'

'And you killed him for that?' she yelled.

'What about your boss,' Jack said. 'What about Tony Chiu?'

'Mr Chiu have nothing to do with this.'

'You're lying. Chiu's the 489 – your Dragon Head. He gives the orders. You're just the triggerman.'

Fang clamped his gold capped teeth together. His eyes had sunk further back into his head and Jack got the feeling that whatever they did to him now Fang wouldn't say anymore. He let the wire slip from his fingers and clatter onto the floor.

Angela turned and strode across to the bathroom, banged the door shut behind her. Pipes hammered behind the walls as she wrenched on the shower taps and Jack could hear her throwing up in there. He looked down at Fang with his genitals exposed and the neck of that coat-hanger jammed deep into his urethra.

'Hospital,' Fang said.

'Yeah,' Jack muttered. It was starting to spit outside and he stood for a moment staring at the curtained window, listening to the rain brush lightly across the roof. He walked over to the bathroom and opened the door. She was squatting on the edge of the toilet seat with her head clutched in her hands and even through the blanket of steam he could tell she was crying. He turned off the hotwater and waited for the tiny room to clear. He put an arm around her back and felt the tightness like a hook in her spine.

'You think I'm crazy, don't you?' she said. 'You think I'm mad?'

Jack didn't say anything.

'I wanted to kill him. I wanted to burn him inside. I thought I'd feel better for it, but I don't. I loved my brother. Does that sound sentimental to you?'

'No.' Jack moved some muscles about in his face.

'When your own life is dark, you pin your hopes on others and I guess I thought that if things were bad for me then they'd turn out good for Damian. I could tell you about my father, drugs – all that boring crap, but I won't. I just want to see this thing through to the end and then I want to get back to some ordinary living.' Her eyes glistened and she wiped her cheek quickly with the blade of her hand. 'Don't judge me on this Jack, please.'

'I don't,' he said, 'I couldn't.' He squeezed her ribs hard with his fingers. Her face was flushed and for the first time since he'd known her she seemed open and vulner-able. 'Hey, I'm on your side.'

She stood up, nodding, and pulled down the hem of her black skirt. 'We'd better get him to a hospital.'

Boards creaked out in the cabin and Jack stiffened. His eyes went straight to hers and a whole range of terrifying possibilities tumbled through his mind. Silently he eased the bathroom door open and stepped out. The moment he saw the frayed rope strewn across the cabin floor, he ducked his head. Something sharp and pointy glinted in the morning light and flashed past his face. Fang came at him fast, hissing. Jack stumbled back against the laminex table, searching for a weapon. He saw the coat-hangers lying near his feet and the red stain on the front of Fang's trousers. A roundhouse kick ripped into his kidney and a back spinning hook kick slammed him up against the wall. Fingers jabbed at his eyeballs and the sharp point of a can-opener dug into the meat of his arm. He yelled with pain and thrust a forearm up to protect his face from Fang's chopping fists. There was a crash of crockery and green chips of porcelain flew off the top of Fang's skull. His mouth dropped open and a big glob of spit bungied off his bottom lip as the Triad enforcer hit the deck.

Angela stood over him, clutching the remains of an electric jug.

'Hit him again,' Jack cried. Fang was lying face down on the cabin floor, a strong smell of cigar-smoke and sweat seeping from the pores of his skin.

'He's unconscious,' she said, bending over him.

'Are you sure?' He wrenched the can-opener out of his arm and flung it across the room. 'That guy's indestructible.'

'You alright, Jack?'

Blood dribbled down his good white shirt. 'Terrific,' he said, 'just terrific.' If Fang so much as moved he'd hit him with the fridge. 'I tell you one thing,' he said, 'no way am I touching this fucker again.' He'd heard about Triad enforcers – how if you chopped their legs off, they'd come at you on their stumps.

'What are we going to do with him?'

'We can either kill him or leave him here.'

Angela shook her head. 'Leave him.'

'Okay, I'll back the car up.'

Outside it was drizzling and long black clouds pushed across the sky. Plovers called out to each other on the golf course and he remembered how as a boy in Eden their click click sound always signalled rain. Casuarinas whispered to each other in the wind and drops of water hung like pearls from their leaves. He jammed the Holden quickly up against the cabin door and started throwing in her tape recorder and clothes while she walked down to the office. When he'd finished he went inside, dragged the kitchen table over and wedged the back of it firmly on top of Fang's shoulders. One thing was sure – Lee Fang wasn't going to forget them in a hurry. He punched on the TV, waded through the channels until he got the news. The man reading had a face like a frog and a voice like a wobble board: *'Police say there were several reports of firecrackers being let off last night as part of traditional wedding celebrations. In other news the Prime Minister met with senior advisors and key ministers in Canberra today as the government gears up to go to the polls.'* Journalists shadowed a bunch of grim-faced powerbrokers up the steps of parliament.

Something moved behind Jack and his heart jumped in his chest.

Angela was standing there in the cabin doorway, staring at the screen as the TV cameras closed in on a large man in a double-breasted suit and red tie limping down a labyrinthian corridor deep inside the Big House.

Jack looked at Angela and her eyes flicked back at his. Rain streaked her cheeks and glistened in her shiny black hair. There was no need for words; he knew what she was thinking. The weatherman came on, forecasting a sunny outlook for Sydney and Southern New South

Wales, but the cries of plovers in the distance and the dark swollen clouds massing across the sky said otherwise. They went outside and got into the car. A peacock was dragging its dirty tail feathers behind in the mud. It stopped, cocked its fan-shaped crest to the side and watched them out of one eye. Jack heard the crash of furniture as gravel crunched underneath the tyres. The peacock took off, running straight at the wire fence. Trees flicked past their windows and they were rolling south towards the capital.

37

On a long flat stretch outside of Campbelltown Angela opened it up. Rain was coming down heavily and the wipers flailed against the windscreen as the needle climbed. Trucks and semitrailers raced to stay alongside, rain steaming off their huge arrowed treads. At Goulburn the storm cleared a little. Four Japanese men in suits posed outside the Big Merino. Newly-shorn sheep dotted the plains beyond the township and a pair of fat crows drifted low overhead. There was something special about the smell of rain in the air, the feel of it on your skin, the drumming sound it made against the windscreen. The road curved between bare brown hills enshrouded in mist. They pulled into an Ampol service station to fill up on warm pies, Milo bars and cans of mineral water. He stared at the soft fine hair on her arms while he ate, the sleeves of her red mohair cardigan pushed back to her elbows, the hem of her black skirt just touching her knees, and he realised how much she interested him.

Coming into Canberra was like driving into someone's private estate. Pines and eucalypts lined the road rather than the car yards, KFC outlets and industrial estates that greeted you in Sydney. The national capital was well-planned, clean as a pin and surrounded by bushland, and although many people said the place had no soul, Jack and Vick had once wanted to live here. But when Toby came along that all changed and they started blaming themselves for the child and then blaming each other. Even now a part of him couldn't help thinking that his son's sickness was a payback for something he'd done wrong in his past. He prodded at a crack in the dash with his fingers, watching Angela frown behind her Ray-Bans, her lips pressed together as if her thoughts were a thousand miles away. Maybe when this was all finished he'd tell her about Toby. The trouble with this life was you only got one crack at it, and it was so easy to botch that.

She turned off Northbourne Avenue and they climbed a hill to the Motor Village, the engine whining like a tired old spaniel, rain stroking the windows. She drove a hundred metres past the office and killed the motor.

'Don't forget that forty,' Jack told her. He wondered whether Fang would have called the police. No, that wasn't the way these gangs worked, but there was going to be hell to pay. You didn't snatch a 426 Triad headbanger off the streets of Sydney's Chinatown without consequences. Jack watched her come out of the office, tucking her Mastercard into her purse. The motel room she'd scored was nothing special, the cigarette burns in the beige carpet and the dripping shower tap a blunt reminder that they were just another link in the company's daisy chain. Rain played loudly on the iron roof and washed down the tall narrow window that looked out onto a spread of blackbutts and further on towards the winding road. She kicked off her black Reeboks with the pink tongues and dropped onto the bed. She unhitched her skirt at the back and slid it down over her hips. Her panties were light blue and he could see the dark hair pressing through the lace inserts. He stared at her smooth legs and then walked over awkwardly to pull the curtains.

'Leave them,' she said, 'I want to watch the rain.'

He unbuckled his belt, heard it clank against the wardrobe, rolled his trousers off and then his socks. He knelt in front of her and felt her hand go inside his boxers. 'God,' he said. He unbuttoned her mohair cardigan and her top and let out her breasts. He sucked on the nipples and ran his hands up the bony ladder of her ribs.

'Kiss them, Jack, kiss them.'

He could smell her skin, a mixture of fragrance, soap and sweat. With his thumbs he peeled off her cotton panties and slipped his tongue up between her legs. He licked her until saliva dripped from his chin.

'From behind,' she whispered.

The rain was sweeping across the window as he pushed inside her, his palms clasped round the curve of her hips, watching the branches lifting in the wind, water flying off the sickle-shaped leaves. Her back arched and she shuddered. A red pulsing light seemed to pass in front of his eyes, a door opened up and he was sucked through. The backs of his thighs twitched, he groaned and sank back on his ankles, wondering why if making love was this damned good, they didn't do it more often. She rolled over onto her side and looked across at him, her pupils dilated.

'Tired?' she said.

His eyelids drooped as if all the energy had drained out of him. The stab wound in his arm throbbed like crazy.

She pulled the sheet and the woollen bedcover over the top of them and they curled up, arm over arm, smelling of sex and listening to the roar of thunder in the sky.

* * *

He sat up with a jolt. The room was dark and he felt on the dresser for his watch, saw it was only ten past two in the afternoon. Voices were moaning in the adjoining unit, an older man and a younger woman's. He wondered if they were fucking too? Maybe that's what they did down here in Canberra – public servants and politicians – screwed each other in their lunch breaks. He rubbed at his grainy eyes with the heel of his hand and checking that Angela was sound asleep, slipped out of bed, grabbed the phone by the tail and took it into the bathroom. There was something working at the back of his mind like a sliver of glass, a thought that wouldn't go away. He squatted in the doorway – the cord didn't stretch far enough – and dialled a number, waited as it rang and rang, drumming on the cold blue tiles with his fingers. A woman finally answered as he was about to hang up.

'It's Jack,' he said. 'Everything alright there?'

'What?'

'You haven't seen any strangers hanging about, no weird phone calls?'

'What are you playing at?'

'I'm in some trouble, Vick. I'm worried they might try and get to me through Toby.'

'You bastard. You keep away from us. Just stay away.'

'He's my son too, remember.'

'I hate you, I hate you. You're a jinx on our lives.'

The phone went dead in his ear, a dull burr. He held the receiver up to his face and closed his eyes tight, breathing in through his teeth. A hand touched the top of his head.

'Something wrong?' Angela said. She was naked except for the red mohair cardigan unbuttoned around her firm breasts. 'Who were you talking to?'

He looked up at her body with affection, like he was seeing it with fresh eyes. 'I think we should ring Lam. Maybe he knows something, maybe there's been a new development.'

'You kidding?' she said. 'Those Feds couldn't find their backsides with both hands. What have they done for us so far?' She stepped around him, walked over and squatted above the toilet bowl, her bum just lifting off the seat.

He listened to her piss, thinking how Vick always used to shut the door, even after fourteen years together. Angela wiped herself, dropped the toilet paper into the bowl and flushed. When she reached out to turn on the taps, he saw the scar tissue ridged on the insides of her arms, little whitish lumps round the main cables, and he wondered why he had never noticed them before. Maybe you only saw what you wanted to see in your partner. Maybe that was it.

She pulled off her mohair cardigan, folded it neatly over the towel rail and turned to face him. 'Okay, ring Lam, if that's what you want.' She lifted her shoulders. 'If you think it's going to do us any good, but I don't want to talk to him, alright.'

He watched her step under the hot water, take the soap and start to lather between her legs. He watched her breasts pinken and the steam close in around her like a fist, then he scooped up the phone and took it outside and dialled. The woman on the switch connected him straight through as soon as he gave his name. Jack got the feeling he was expected.

'Christ almighty!' Detective Superintendent Lam said. 'What the hell have you two idiots been doing?'

'We snatched Fang,' Jack said. 'We've got his confession down on tape to murder. Bryan Callagher ordered it done.'

'You can't just kidnap suspects off the streets, beat the shit out of them and then expect to use that as evidence.'

'Why not?' Jack said.

'Because it won't stand up in court. Any confession which is obtained by threat, promise or inducement is inadmissible. Chiu's silk'd have Fang loose in two seconds flat even if you could find a prosecutor dumb enough to take it that far. As it is you two'll probably be charged with assault. Right now the New South Wales police are looking for you as well as every soldier in the Sun Sai Gei. The Triad are chopping at their own shadows. We've had to pull our men out of Chinatown and cut surveillance. You realise you've jeopardised a six-month operation involving two police forces and fifteen detectives.'

'What about Callagher?' Jack said. 'What about the big fish? Aren't you going to go after him?'

'Listen, Butorov. Bryan Callagher's a New South Wales power broker wired directly into Capital Hill. He isn't just some two-bob Tasmanian senator come up for a term. When he pulls strings, a lot of shirt collars in this town start to tighten.'

'But the disc,' Jack said, 'the donations from Chiu. Callagher's taking Triad money. The guy's involved up to his neck in murder.'

'Proof,' Lam said. 'Where's the proof?'

'I've seen it. There's a connection, you know that. Where's your copper's nose? Where's your instincts, Lam? I thought you were going to run with this.'

'I did,' Mick Lam said. 'We've been in contact with Senator Callagher and we warned him that we have Tony Chiu presently under Federal Police investigation.'

'Warned him,' Jack said. 'You fucking warned him!'

Lam's voice didn't waver. 'The A C deemed it the appropriate course under the circumstances.'

Jack held the phone away from his ear; the realisation hit him like a smack in the teeth that he and Angela were in this on their own. The Feds were going to play it by the book and doing that with first division crims was like giving Ben Johnson a hundred metres start. From the bathroom he heard the taps shudder and the shower curtain clink back. When he turned around he saw Angela standing in the bathroom doorway, those blue eyes narrowed on him.

'You there, Butorov?' Lam was saying.

'Yeah,' Jack said, 'I'm here. So what did he have to say?'

'That's confidential. The Senator acknowledged receipt of a small donation to the government's election fund from Mr Chiu's restaurant business.'

'How small?'

'Twenty five thou. I can't reveal anymore, except the Senator assured us he had no idea Mr Tony Chiu was involved in any illegal activities.'

'And you bought that?' Jack said.

'Listen, Butorov. If you can come up with anything solid that I can take to the DPP, that's fine. Because right now all I got is your word against an important Goverment Senator's in an election year.'

'I'm not the fucking policeman,' Jack said, 'remember. Besides, I'm more worried about these Sun Sai Gei arseholes getting at my kid. I want a man stuck on 44 Loftus Crescent, Homebush. Will you do that for me?'

'I'll see what can be arranged.' Detective Superintendent Lam's tone was distant, as if he was already thinking of something else. 'Now put Angela on.'

'She doesn't want to speak to you.'

'Put her on!' Mick Lam ordered.

Angela took the receiver like it was contaminated, murmuring: 'I hope he's paying for this call.' Lines tracked across her forehead while she listened to Detective Lam in silence. Finally she said, 'I understand that, but I'm going after him anyway, Superintendent.' She threw the phone back at Jack. 'Here, he wants to speak to you again.'

Jack fixed his gaze on the light-blue veins forking beneath the pale skin of her breasts. He heard the edge of frustration in Lam's voice:

'You're staying at the Motor Village Motel in Canberra. Now listen good. I want you to get in touch immediately with Harvey Madden. Got that?'

'The Independent MP?'

'Mention my name,' Lam said, 'tell him what you told me about Senator Callagher. You can trust Madden. And Butorov?'

'Yeah.'

'Don't make things any worse for yourself.'

'How the hell could I do that?' Jack said. He hung up on Detective Mun Bun Lam, walked over to the window and looked out into the driving rain as if he half expected to see a black Berlina parked behind the eucalypts. Angela was towelling herself down in front of the wardrobe mirror, her hair wet and spiky at the front and the motel room smelling of her body oil.

Jack said, 'So what did Lam want to tell you?'

She pulled on a pair of blue and white hipster briefs. 'He wanted to warn me that's all.' Her eyes evaded his. 'I think he's worried someone's going to get killed.'

38

Driving into the city with a map of Canberra between them on the front seat, the brakes squealing at every little roundabout and the wipers toiling ineffectively against the rain, Jack wondered whether the Holden would make it back to Sydney. The EH Premier might've been a good car in its day, but 1964 was long gone. A yellow vein of lightning flashed across the sky revealing the inner fleshy folds of the clouds and the engine knocked loudly as they accelerated over Commonwealth Avenue bridge. A Mynah bird was trying to raise itself off the middle of the road, its broken left wing flapping uselessly at its side while its frantic relatives circled overhead, then the Mynah's feathers disappeared under the wheels of an envelope manufacturer's truck. Angela turned sharply into King Edward Terrace and pulled up outside the National library.

'Okay, I'll meet you back here in an hour.'

'You're not coming with me?' Jack stared at her, incredulous.

Her fingers gripped the wheel tightly as if it were all she could do just to hold on. She turned her head away and looked out over Lake Burley Griffin. She said, 'I've got some people to see first.'

He poked the ashtray in roughly with his fingers. 'I thought you wanted all the cards out on the table.'

'It's only some old acquaintances, Jack. They wouldn't interest you.'

'Yeah, so how would I know if you don't tell me their names.' He slid across the seat, banged the door shut behind him and heard the swish of the tyres as she wheeled away. So that's how she wanted to play it. Fine with him. He'd look after his own tail. He ran up the steps in the rain and in through the library doors. The place was big and airy and the walls were lined with antique books and glossy posters behind glass display cases. The occupants of the reading room were either ANU students or else snowy-haired Canberrans scribbling down on fat foolscap pads what appeared to be their memoirs.

Like most people who read the political pages Jack had heard of Harvey Douglas Madden. An anti-corruption crusader and one of only two independent MPs in the Federal Parliament, Madden had gained national prominence by receiving death threats from both criminals and serving members of the New South Wales police force in the early 90s.

A small bald man with a white Abe Lincoln beard and long bat ears sat behind the magazine section. He looked up blinking over the book he was reading. Jack saw it

was written in a foreign language with upside down Vs
and back to front Es.

'Thucydides,' the small bald man said, tapping the
spine. 'The Peloponnesian Wars. Are you acquainted with
the ancient Greeks, Mr Butorov?'

'Just a few from Enmore and Newtown,' Jack said, 'but
the really old ones've moved out.'

Harvey Madden smiled. 'Do you have some
identification?'

Jack produced his driver's licence and pulled a chair up
alongside the MP's desk. 'Thanks for meeting me on such
short notice, Mr Madden. As I said on the phone, Mick
Lam thought you might be able to help.'

'Mun Bun's a fine police officer. We used to pray
together at St Thomas's. So how can I be of assistance?'

'A young friend of mine got killed.' Jack glanced over at
the magazine racks. A blowzy woman was reading *The
Economist* and he dropped his voice to a whisper. 'The
man who ordered it done is a cabinet minister.'

'Go on.' Harvey Madden's ice-blue eyes flickered with
interest and his long ears seemed to quiver like antennae.
He listened intently while Jack talked, his concentration
never wavering for a second. 'This computer disc,'
Madden said, 'who else was on it?'

'Frank Frick.'

'The developer?'

'Yeah,' Jack said, 'and Tony Chiu as I said on the
phone.'

Madden fingered his bald crown. 'I'm familiar with Mr
Chiu's formidable reputation in the east coast import
business.'

'That's why Lam put me on to you. The Minister
admitted receiving a twenty-five thousand dollar donation from Chiu, but what I saw on that disc was well over
three million bucks.'

'You're certain.'

'I saw it alright and so did Angela. You don't forget

those kinds of figures. Not six-wheelers. They weren't all donations either, I mean most of them were, but there were smaller sums, payouts for forty and fifty thousand bucks.'

'Do you recall any of the names?'

'Max Cham was one,' Jack said. 'Des Roberts. They ring a bell?'

Harvey Madden shook his head and then wrote the two names down in a green Quill memo book. 'If what you say is correct, then this Minister of yours is either diverting campaign funds for his own purposes or else he's taking enormous bribes.'

'Or both.' Jack looked at the little man with the white beard, thinking all Madden needed was a red cap and you could've stuck him in a rock garden.

'The new Political Disclosures Act,' Madden said, 'makes it very difficult for any party to fund a campaign with secret donations. Perhaps they're doing something else with the money?'

'All I know,' Jack said, 'is my friend was killed for that disc. And I've been slugged, kicked and stabbed with a rusty-can opener.'

'I think you're fortunate to be alive, Mr Butorov. Who's the Minister involved?'

Jack glanced around the library. The woman reading *The Economist* had edged closer. She hitched up her skirt and adjusted the front of her pantyhose. 'Callagher,' Jack whispered, 'Bryan Callagher.'

Harvey Madden removed his specs and wiped the lenses vigorously on a wrinkled handkerchief.

Jack stared at the woman. She smiled back at him and moved off, swinging her hips. 'That surprise you, Mr Madden?' he said.

Madden slid his glasses back along his nose. 'I've never liked Bryan Callagher's arrogance, nor the manner in which he operates in the Parliament, but to hear that one of the most powerful figures in this government is involved in murder. . .'

'I know,' Jack said, 'it sounds crazy doesn't it.'

Madden stroked his beard with his fingers. 'Who's investigating your friend's homicide up in Sydney?'

'South West Region,' Jack said. 'I've no idea who's handling it now, but it was Detective Quarrell.'

'Good God,' Madden said. 'Not Lindsay Quarrell!'

'You know him?' Jack pushed forward in his chair. 'I'm pretty sure he's mixed up in this somehow.'

Madden snapped Thucydides shut. 'My advice to you, Mr Buturov, is to leave Canberra immediately. Your life is in great danger if you remain here.'

'Can you do anything?' Jack said. 'Can you help us at all?'

'I intend to make some inquiries in the parliament. In the meantime you should lay low and keep in constant touch with Superintendent Lam, but don't return to Sydney. I'll see if the AFP can put you in their witness protection program.' The Member for Northbridge reached out and touched Jack's arm gently. There were small brown stains on the cuffs of his shirt and he smelled musty, like a book that had got damp. He stood up. 'Be careful won't you? We don't want to fish you and your friend out of Lake Burley Griffin.'

39

Standing on the National Library steps with the rain falling like a slow handclap, Jack decided he had never known it to rain so much. He stared out at the eleven kilometres of man-made lake which reminded him of a moat set around a medieval city. Jack had no intention of going on any witness protection scheme, spending his days bailed up in front of the midday movie with a couple of cheese-eating cops. For a moment he pictured Harvey Madden with his Bic biros poking out of the top pocket of his baggy suit and then Senator Bryan Callagher in his smooth Italian threads looming behind a big bank of phones. And he knew – Callagher would eat Madden alive. Whatever happened now Jack didn't intend coming out of this empty-handed. Not after all he'd been through. He had a son to think of. He had a life to straighten out. He saw the creamy roof of the two-tone EH glide into view. She was forty-five minutes late, but who was counting. He went down the steps to the car park and slid in beside her. She leaned over and brushed his cheek with her lips. 'Were you waiting long?'

Jack shook the water off his hair. She smelled different. He didn't know much about fragrances, but that seemed like an expensive scent she was wearing.

'How was your MP? Any help?'

'Not much,' Jack said, 'but the old boy means well. What about your little rendezvous?'

She stiffened at the tone in his voice, shoved the car into gear and hit the pedal. They cruised on past the High Court where a pedestrian bridge linked up with the National Gallery so that the judges could stroll over for a peek at the canvasses whenever they felt the urge. It was a good life down here, Jack figured, if a man could just buy into it. 'So how'd it go?' he said.

'Alright.' She kept her eyes fixed on the traffic.

'These buddies of yours,' he said. 'Who'd you say their names were again?'

Angela braked hard and swung the wheel to the right. A stick reared in the middle of the road and skittered off between the tyres. Jack glanced out the back window at the long brown tail of a lizard.

'Something big's going down, Jack,' Angela said. 'A lot of local businesses are being bought up.'

'What sort of businesses?' Jack said.

'Massage parlors, restaurants, nightclubs. A friend of mine, she works for one of the classier escort agencies in Red Hill – Shangri-La.'

'She a close friend?'

Angela ignored him. 'Apparently a month ago Shangri-La was taken over. Want to guess the name of the new owner.'

'Tony Chiu?' Jack said.

'You got it.' She fished a small plastic packet out of her purse, tossed it down on the seat between them.

Jack held the empty packet up to the windscreen. Chinese characters were stamped on one side underneath a blue unicorn logo.

'Rock heroin – sixty to eighty per cent pure.' Angela looked over at him. 'There's a heap of it just hit the streets.'

'Sounds like the Sun Sai Gei's moving into town in a big way. Buying up Canberra's knocking shops – I mean that's prime real estate, and it'll give them access to a lot of pollies and diplomats. Maybe that's what Chiu's paying Callagher for – social introductions? I tell you one thing,' Jack said. 'You can't help feeling there's a ton of dough stacked up behind all this.'

Angela said, 'I want you to ring Callagher today. Tell him we've got Fang's confession down on tape, tell him that he's implicated in my brother's murder.'

Jack thought this over. 'Then what?' he said.

'Then we arrange a meeting. But first we make him sweat. I want this bastard to pay.'

Jack looked out the car window at the rain stirring up the lake. He could swear they had been down this same road before. They were driving around in circles, like Canberra was just one big roundabout.

40

He stood at the open window watching the streetlights reflected on the wet road outside. Now and then a car hissed by and braked loudly as it hit the bend. He could smell dampness in the air, see water angling across the outside of the glass. The rain kept falling and the lights strung out along the roof of the motel units looked yellow and dirty. He took a flask of Wild Turkey off the table beside the phone, swigged on it and let the bourbon fumes run around the back of his nose. He wiped his lips once with his fingers and turned to face her. She was sitting cross-legged on the edge of the bed in black footless tights and a black ribbed top eating from a tub of Akiki yoghurt.

She held the tub out. 'Want some?'

He shook his head, took another long swig of bourbon and waited until his eyes had stopped blinking, then he said, 'This friend of yours, what's her name?'

Angela looked at him. 'Gabby. Gabrielle Bunce.'

'You two ever work together?'

'We did some acting once, a long time ago, why?'

'Acting.' Jack kept his eyes fixed on her. 'What sort of acting?'

'Videos mainly.'

Jack nodded slowly.

'Everyone's got things in their past they regret, Jack.'

'Yeah,' he said, 'but some more than others.'

'You're such a prude deep down aren't you?' She swung her long legs off the edge of the queen-sized bed. 'Anyone ever tell you that?'

'All my life,' Jack said, 'people have been telling me stuff.' He glanced over at the phone. 'Most of it shit.'

A truck growled off in the distance. His eyes went to the window and then back to the telephone on the table. He said, 'Mind if I ask you something personal?'

Angela put down her yoghurt carton on the carpet. Her shoulders tensed.

'Why do you want to nail Callagher so bad?'

'Are you serious?'

'Revenge won't bring Damian back. You could let Lam and the Feds handle this from here.'

'I want to see it out to the end,' she said, 'I told you before.'

'Sure that's the only reason?'

'What are you getting at, Jack?'

'This,' Jack said. He pulled out of his pocket the photo of Damian with his cock sticking up like a boomerang, laid it on the edge of the table right in front of her. He watched the skin tighten around those blue eyes.

'You bastard,' she said. 'You sneaking bastard.'

'This is a guilt trip isn't it? You're carrying around a trailer full of the stuff about your brother, and you want to dump your load.'

She snatched the Polaroid back. 'Fuck you, Jack,' she said.

'Yeah, whatever you say. But when Callagher's made to pay for it all, then you can go back to your daughter and your little house and your second-hand clothes business in Newtown. But what about me?' Jack said. 'I haven't got any job, I haven't got any little house, I haven't got my kid.'

'I'll pay you some extra money,' she said, 'if that's what you want.'

'How much? A couple of hundred, a thousand maybe. Trouble is I'm playing this for peanuts and you're playing for keeps.' He looked down suddenly as the phone started to ring. It sounded loud in the small motel room. As Angela reached out to take it he grabbed her wrist.

'Not so fast. Don't want the man to think we're in any rush.'

She threw him a look which didn't need translating. The phone kept on ringing, like it had a mind of its own.

On the seventh buzz he lifted the receiver and said, 'Butorov here.' The female voice on the other end was efficient and extremely businesslike. He listened to her instructions and said, 'Yeah, yeah, okay, yeah.' And clunked the receiver down. He searched Angela's face for a sign that she had forgiven him, but could see nothing but anger in her eyes.

'That was Callagher's personal secretary. She said he'll fit me in tomorrow at noon.'

'Just you alone is it, Jack?' Angela's tone was cold as a freezer.

'You want me to ring her back? Ask if you can come too?'

She shrugged her shoulders, but he could tell she wasn't keen on the arrangement. Then he yanked the phone out of the wall and dragged the three-legged table over and jammed it against the motel door. Sweat trickled down his brow as he leaned an elbow against the gyprock wall.

'What the hell are you doing?'

'Watching my arse,' Jack said. 'From here on in we can't be too careful who we trust.'

41

Parliament House wasn't the kind of building you could easily miss, not even in a downpour. It stuck out on

Capital Hill like a set of antlers on a bald man's head. Angela parked the Holden in the cavernous lot underneath the Big House and cut the engine. In the last twelve hours she'd hardly spoken to him. Even now she kept her eyes averted, watching the tourist coaches manoeuvre noisily in beside the elevators.

'You know what to do then?'

'He's not going to fall for it,' Jack said. 'I give you the tip.'

'Tell him I'm taking Fang's confession round to every media outlet in town, tell him if he doesn't want the publicity he's going to have to come get the tape personally.'

'The man's a politician, he'll be suspicious as hell.'

'Just do it, Jack, please.' She almost looked directly at him then, but turned her head away at the last moment as if he was one of the Gorgons' sons.

Jack got out of the car and walked across the parking lot to the stairs. Not once did he look back. He wondered what kind of fantasy books she had read as a kid. Snatching a Triad killer off the streets of Sydney's Chinatown was crazy enough, but kidnapping a Government Senator only weeks before a Federal election – that was lunacy. Callagher'd know that Fang's forced confession was worthless in a court of law. He'd know they had nothing on him that would stick. It was only their word against his, so why the hell was Callagher so willing to see him at such short notice? That's what he couldn't figure.

At the top of the steps Jack paused and gazed out over the forecourt at Canberra's skyline. A party of senior citizens were being led through the glass entrance doors to steal a closer look at what 1.5 billion of tax payers' dollars had bought. Jack followed them in, past the Cipollini marble clad columns and up the flecked marble stairs. Jarrah and coachwood panelling decorated the foyer. Giant oil paintings by Roberts and Streeton lined the upstairs walls. He went down a long glassed walkway that was lit so well and felt so warm you could hardly tell it was cold and wet outside. Three attendants stopped him at the end of the passageway and relieved him of his keys. When Jack stepped through the metal detector the alarm rang. The attendants eyed him closely while he shook coins out of his pockets into a plastic box and tried the ramp again. This time the metal detector stayed quiet. Pocketing his gear, Jack strode into the public gallery. He grabbed a seat at the front and ran his eyes over the handful of silver-haired men sprinkled around the red benches below, but Callagher wasn't among them. Jack glanced at a pair of clocks – five past twelve. An opposition Senator was speaking in a soporific voice, but no-one seemed to be paying him any attention. Then a door opened on the left and Callagher in a double-breasted suit and red striped tie limped slowly into the chamber and took his seat. Jack saw the respectful unease with which his colleagues greeted him. A female attendant came up with a glass of water and passed it to Senator Bryan Callagher who drank it slowly.

Fascinated, Jack watched as the big man pushed himself up out of his chair and addressed the Acting President on a point of procedure. And as Callagher sat down again his eyes swung round the public galleries and met Jack's. There was no sign of recognition in them, just a hard stare over the top of his half-moon glasses, as if, Jack thought later, he was regarding some minor obstacle on the freeway. It lasted no more than a second, and then the Senator unfolded the *Guardian Weekly* on the desk in front of him.

Jack leaned back in his seat. He had a nasty feeling in his gut. Maybe it was the six McNuggets he'd eaten for breakfast or the flask of bourbon last night.

A hand tapped on his shoulder and his heart jumped like a fish. He jerked his head around. A man in a plain black suit stood in the aisle. Average height. No distinguishing features. The type of face that was easy to forget.

'Would you accompany me, please, sir.' A mobile phone antenna poked out of his left fist.

'Me,' Jack said. 'Where?'

'Your appointment, Mr Butorov?'

Jack got up slowly. Every nerve in his body was telling him to deck this guy and run. But Angela had said his intuition was no good. They wouldn't do anything to him here. Not in the Parliament surely.

'This way, sir.'

'You can drop the sir, mate,' Jack said. 'I haven't been knighted yet.'

The man smiled and held the public gallery door open.

Jack saw calluses on the tips of his fingers. Some sort of hot-shot security cowboy. He wondered if there was anyone over the age of twelve nowadays who didn't do karate. He'd have to whack this chump good and hard if it came to it. The thought played on the edge of his mind as he was led down a long corridor and through an enormous hall supported by columns. He could smell hot meat and baked bread from a busy kitchen. They passed a Turkish baths and sauna. He'd never realised the Federal Palace was so big. They were heading south, he knew that much. Through a courtyard and down another long corridor. The plain-clothes guard stopped outside a door, turned to Jack and frisked him thoroughly, running his fingers up between his legs.

Jack said, 'This part of your duties, pal, or just relaxation?'

'Routine, Mr Butorov. This way.'

They went into a magnificent private suite. How many rooms it contained altogether, Jack couldn't tell, but the large room the guard shepherded him into had silver ash panelling, a bare cedar desk and four wine-coloured chairs. He dropped into one shaped like a magnet; the smell of tanned leather hit the air. The monitor on the wall was tuned to the House of Reps and the PM was up on his feet jabbing his finger.

Jack turned to the guard. 'You a cop? Or d'you do one of those special defence courses?'

The Security face stood rigid by the door. 'Won't be long, sir.'

'Lighten up, pal. You only get one innings and it's too short to spend it as a robot.'

Male voices rose and subsided outside. Jack let his shoulders relax. If they'd wanted to do him in they would've taken him somewhere quiet. He unloosened a notch on his belt. His damned stomach wouldn't stop rumbling.

The door opened and Senator Callagher limped into the room. His big ruddy face was strained. He nodded at the guard who slipped outside and shut the door quietly. Jack listened for footsteps, but didn't hear any.

The Senator leaned his weight on the edge of the desk and his large lips moved. 'What are we going to do with you, Jack?'

Jack didn't say anything.

'Stirring up old Harvey Madden like that.' He stared at Jack over the top of his glasses. 'This isn't Athens 430 BC, but Australia going into the new century with twenty million people on board. We can't cling to the old-fashioned notions anymore. Not if we're to survive.'

Jack could smell the Senator's aftershave from where he sat.

'The Australian people want growth. We can't afford to jeopardise investment.'

Jack said, 'What investment?'

'Billions of dollars, Jack.' The Senator lifted his thick-soled shoe up onto the rail underneath.

'You're talking about Triad money, that it?'

The Senator didn't blink. 'I'm talking about a relationship that shall benefit our nation greatly. Mr Chiu is a remarkable businessman.'

'But this is drug money,' Jack said.

The Senator smiled faintly. 'Many of the great commercial institutions of Hong Kong were founded on opium – Dent and Co, Hutchinson, Jardine and Matheson – the British upper classes made vast fortunes from the opium trade. But no, this is more than just drugs.' He pushed himself off the edge of the desk and advanced towards Jack slowly.

'Crime, Jack. Crime is one of the most profitable industries in Australia and growing rapidly. In the US the proceeds from crime are greater than those of the aerospace and entertainment industries combined. Now we either fight crime and waste a great deal of our precious resources like the Americans, or we manage it like our neighbours. We control crime from within and we take a percentage.' The Senator stopped. 'I want you to come and work for us.'

Jack sat up in his chair. The palms of his hands were sticky wet and he ran them along the soft red leather. 'Why me?'

'We could use your skills.'

'What skills?' Jack said, 'I'm a doorman.'

'You understand how it works out there in the real world, Jack. Everyone's a harlot at heart, everyone's got their price.' The Senator arched his thick eyebrows. 'Besides, we can't just let you go.'

A fist banged on the door and the Senator called, 'Hold!' His eyes went to the monitor on the wall, then back to Jack.

'What about Lam?' Jack said.

'A fine police officer. He thoroughly deserves his promotion.'

'Promotion?' Jack heard the rise in his own voice.

'I believe he's been attached to Scotland Yard. A real step-up for his career.'

'And Madden – Madden knows everything.'

'Poor old Harvey. Without your corroboration I don't

think anyone will take him too seriously. I'd be surprised if he's returned after this election. Independents are so unreliable.'

Jack stared at the Senator's jutting lower lip. The sheer bulk of the man was intimidating.

'Well, Jack?'

Jack could hear voices outside. He rubbed at the bristles on his chin. He couldn't go back to the Club – not now. Maybe the Senator was right. Who cared where the money came from. He had to think of his own future, his own flesh and blood.

'Okay,' Jack said slowly. 'But I want a senior position in security. I want a house in Canberra and a new car, either a Falcon XR or a Commodore Calais. And I want to arrange for a neurosurgeon to see my son.'

The Senator stroked the wide knot on his silk tie. He turned away and limped over to the desk, took out a sheet of blue paper from the second drawer and wrote some instructions on it. 'One more thing.' He peered over his half-moon glasses. 'Your friend, Angela. I'm concerned about her health.'

Jack locked eyes with him.

'We can't just let her run around loose. She's a very unstable woman.'

'I don't want her harmed.'

The Senator said quietly, 'Angela will receive the best medical treatment. Her father'll see to that. You know about Damian and the daughter of course?'

Jack didn't answer.

'Such a shame when a family becomes in-grown. I was very close to that young man.'

'But you had him killed,' Jack said.

'I pulled that boy up out of the gutter, I paid his rent, I gave him money and he tried to blackmail me. After all I'd done. Young people are so cruel. He used to laugh about you, Jack.' The Senator nodded his big head slowly. 'I never wanted him dead. I wanted him frightened, that's all. There was an unfortunate misunderstanding that's since been rectified. Where's his sister?'

'I want your guarantee she won't be hurt, Senator.'

The Senator pushed out his jaw. 'I give you my word.'

'She's downstairs in the parking lot.'

'And her daughter?'

'Up the coast somewhere. Why?'

Bells rang from a hidden speaker in the room and a red light on the clock face started flashing. The Senator picked up a phone on his desk and said, 'Take Mr Butorov down to the parking area. Pick the Frick girl up, but she's not to be harmed.'

Jack got slowly up out of his chair. The whiff of leather lingered in the Minister's suite. Angela would never forgive him for what he was doing. He was real sorry, but he had to look out for his own.

A fist rapped on a door behind him and Jack heard footsteps enter. The smell in the air grew faintly putrid and the Senator said, 'You know Lindsay, Jack.'

Jack slewed around. Two men in dark-brown suits stood inside the doorway. They weren't wearing hats, but they had little bulges under their jackets. The tall lean man was chewing something and his dead-grey eyes showed no expression. Jack stepped back. He could feel his heart thumping in his chest. 'No way, Senator.' He shook his head firmly. 'No way am I working with these two creeps.'

The division bells kept ringing and the red light on the clock flashed. The Senator picked up a slim attaché case with gold lettering and limped past the two detectives in the doorway. 'You must excuse me, Jack,' he said. 'We can discuss the full conditions of your employment later.'

And Senator Bryan Callagher shut the door quietly behind him.

42

Jack stood with his tailbone pressed hard against the ridge of the desk and Detectives Quarrell and Brown looking at him like two crows eyeing a sick calf. The Senate division bells stopped ringing and Brown took out a key ring with a little plastic square that said *Billy*, and started cleaning his nails with the clippers. For several long seconds nobody spoke, then Quarrell quit chewing and his fingers went up to his mouth and he flicked something wet and sharp into Jack's cheek.

'So what's new, shitbag?'

Jack brushed the toothpick off his collar and stared into the grey, buckled face.

'The doormouse's lost his voice, Billy.'

Brown grinned and dropped his clippers into his suit pocket.

Quarrell reached a hand in under his jacket and slid a .38 S & W Special out of its metal-reinforced holster. He moved close to Jack with the top of his thumb rubbing gently on the concealed hammer. 'Not scared are ya?'

Jack jerked his face away.

'We're here to protect you, arsehole.'

'Who from?'

'From yourself.' Quarrell jammed the muzzle of his .38 into Jack's sternum. 'So I'm going to tell you this once and once only. You fuck up on us or try on any kind of shit and that's it. No second warning. No two weeks' notice. I'll put a bullet in your apple, just like I did your boong friend.'

Jack looked past him, at the muted blues of a water-colour on the wall.

'You read me, Butorov?'

'I read you.'

'Good.' Quarrell worked his tongue in around the back of his teeth. 'Now show us where the bint is.'

They went out into the corridor and through the executive courtyard. The south wing was quieter than a morgue before Easter. Two parliamentary attendants passed them and avoided Jack's begging eyes. He wondered if they could smell fear on him. Every nerve in his body was telling him to run, to get out fast, but where? He had no money. No car. The chances of him getting more than twenty-five yards without a hail of wad-cutter bullets peppering his spine were a thousand to one. He could feel the two detectives' shoulders rubbing up on either side of him, hear the echo of shoes on the parquetry floor. The stink from Quarrell's breath was more than Jack could bear and he wondered how Brown put up with it. They strode through the Members' hall, past a mob of pensioners, Brown shifting his eyes from left to right and Quarrell looking straight ahead.

'Haven't run out of sick-leave yet?' Jack asked.

'Didn't you hear, Butorov? They offered me the Commissioner's job, but I had to knock it back on account of the take-home bag weren't good enough.'

Brown laughed. He had a pudgy nose set in a round barrelled face and teeth you could fit a spoon between.

Jack said, 'I bet they're real sad to see you boys go.'

'What the fuck would you know.' And Quarrell shoved him in the spine.

Going down in the elevator, Jack realised he had done some pretty low things in his life, but what he was about to do to her was probably the lowest. He was selling her out. He was doing it for a house, a job, a new car and the faint chance of getting his son back. He wanted those things so bad it hurt. If he blew this now, he could kiss goodbye to the lot. Quarrell would shoot him; he had not the slightest doubt of that. He was a dead man if he didn't give her up.

The lift doors slid open and Jack stepped out into the underground parking cavern sandwiched between the two ex-detectives. The dim light seemed to make Quarrell relax. He said,

'So what's the bitch like to bang, Butorov?'

Jack looked straight ahead. Sixty metres away to the left of the ramp Angela was sitting in the car with her hands bunched on top of the wheel. The two-tone Holden stood out among the late model Nissans and Mitsubishis.

'Wave her over,' Quarrell murmured, 'nice and friendly.'

Jack could see Angela staring back at him. He wondered what she was doing. Couldn't she see these two creeps. Why was she acting so cool for? He glanced down at Brown's suede boots and then back at Angela and it struck him that she knew – she knew he was about to betray her. And she was just waiting for him to follow through with it. Her eyes never left his face.

'Now,' Quarrell snarled.

Jack remembered what McCredie had taught him about handguns. That only an expert had any real accuracy with them over fifty metres. If he could make it to that car before Quarrell fired off his first round then his odds were better than average. It all depended on what kind of marksman Quarrell was. He'd take the punt. There was no way he was going to deliver her up now.

He raised a hand slowly in the air, then twisted around and crunched the heel of his shoe down on Brown's big toe. Jack heard the bone split and a shriek of pain from Brown as he slammed the blade of his hand across the bridge of Quarrell's nose. He felt the cartilage give like soft rubber tubing and saw a spurt of bright red blood.

Then he ran. He ran for the Holden, his heart pumping, his legs flying underneath him and his elbows going like crazy. He ran screaming out for her to start the engine. He saw her big blue eyes widen and her shoulder drop as she worked the key in the ignition. In his mind he pictured Quarrell, feet apart, raising the .38 to eye level. And Jack waited for the flat-nosed bullet to rip through the back of his skull. The shots, when they came, were much louder than he'd expected. Angela ducked behind the wheel as chips of glass flew off the windscreen. She had the engine running and she kicked open the passenger's door. He was nearly there, five, ten metres, his heart going like a racehorse. He wanted to live, he wanted to live so bad. And then something exploded between his ribs and hip and a searing pain tore through his left side like the flesh and muscles had been splashed with white hot metal. He fell into the front seat of the Holden, clutching at his back, as she took off in reverse, tyres screeching up the concrete ramp. Quarrell was down on one knee, hand cupped over his nose, the muzzle of his revolver flashing.

'Jack!' Angela swerved the wheel wildly, her left arm hooked over the back of the seat.

'I'm shot,' Jack said. 'He shot me!'

'Christ,' she said.

He sucked in air and watched a dark red stain spread slowly across the front of his pale blue shirt. The pain was steady in his back, but tolerable. He wrenched his shirt-tail out from his trousers and pressed the heel of his hand up against the new hole in his gut. He felt the warm blood trickle between his fingers and down into his pubic hair.

'We've got to get you to a hospital, Jack, now!'

'That's the first place they'll look. Head for Sydney,' he said. 'I know someone there who can help.'

Sparks flew off the back door as the Holden scraped against the concrete walls of the parking lot. She drove backwards at top speed, jabbing her thumb on the horn until they broke through into the light of day and she spun the Holden around. Rain was falling on the hill and thunder rolled across the washed-out sky.

He said, 'You reckon this tub can make it?'

The road curved in a circle and the engine sputtered under the hood. Angela swept him a quick look. 'Callagher arranged to have Damian killed didn't he?'

Jack nodded.

She pressed her forehead against the steering wheel for a second. 'I wanted to be sure. I'm sorry, Jack. Sorry that I dragged you into all this.'

Jack stared at the dark cherry lipstick on her lips.

'Back there at the elevator, I thought that you had – '

'What?' Jack said.

She gave her head a shake. 'Nothing.' Her hand reached over and touched his belt.

Jack winced.

'Did I hurt you?'

'Forget about it.' He leaned his head against the door. He felt surprisingly calm for someone who'd just been shot. He couldn't help feeling he was moving towards something, some point in his life he'd known was there all along. A wave of gladness overtook him and he smiled across at her. Except for the burning pain in his side he felt pretty good. 'Way too close, huh?'

'I think I could grow to like you, Jack,' she said.

Her eyes met his and he knew there was no need for her to say anymore.

43

For three and a half hours she drove through the rain. Water dripped down the inside of the punctured windscreen forming a pool on the rubber mat on the floor. Jack lay stretched out in the back seat, trying not to move his legs. It wasn't just the pain that bugged him, though that had got worse, but the stickiness of the blood inside his undies. He tried to think of all the organs the bullet might have hit. It had missed the major blood vessels, Jack knew that. Otherwise he'd already be dead. Losing a kidney worried him the most; he didn't think he had it in him to give up drinking. He lifted his head over the front seat and saw the petrol gauge was showing empty. It was dark outside and he could taste the lead fumes in the air, hear the heavy pulse of big city traffic.

'Hang in there, babe,' Angela murmured.

Gently he fingered the ruptured wall of his abdomen as the Holden shuddered and a thundering sound drowned out everything, even his thoughts. Jack looked up into the protruding black wheels of a Qantas 747 as it streaked low overhead.

'What's the street number?' she shouted.

He told her and lay his head back on her bolero jacket. He felt weak and tired like all the punch had gone from him. As a kid when he'd fought in the amateur ranks he always got his second wind just when he was right out of breath and could hardly lift his eight ounce gloves above his belt. He'd won over half his fights, a quarter on KO, but in the end he'd lacked that real desire to punish his opponents which separates the future pro from the rest.

She braked suddenly and nosed the car in against the kerb. She cut the engine, but left the lights on. Then she came round and opened his door.

'Can you walk?'

Pain shot through his side as he tried to slide his legs out of the car and he gritted his back teeth.

She said, 'We gotta get you to a hospital, honey.'

Jack shook his head. It had been a long time since any woman had called him that. It sounded fine. He leaned his right arm across her shoulder and felt her knees buckle under his weight. She smelled warm and he could see the soft round nipples down the inside of her pink cotton dress.

'You won't believe this,' he said, 'but I'd really like a fuck.'

'When you're patched up, Jack, you'll get all the sex you can handle.'

'Incentives,' he said, 'that's what I want.'

Rain made the paint factory at the end of the street look grey and hunched. The Cyclone fence out the front of the bare weatherboard house had blue plastic bags sucked in between the wires. Angela and Jack staggered up the broken path between the rusting motorbike wheels and banged on the front door.

Dogs howled at the back of the house and voices shouted angrily at each other. Minutes passed, but nobody answered.

Angela hammered again with the meat of her fist.

A light came on over the porch and Killer McCredie stood there in a red silk dressing-gown with beads of sweat running down his temples. His good eye went to Jack's blood-splashed clothes and then to Angela who was propping Jack up against the architrave.

'Marilyn home?' Jack blurted.

Killer didn't answer. He stared long and hard at Angela, adjusting the cord on his robe with his big gnarled fingers.

'He's hurt bad,' Angela said.

Killer opened the door up and they stumbled into the dark-brown hall. The carpet was thick underfoot and grabbed at Jack's shoes. Through a crack in the bedroom doorway he caught sight of Marilyn peeling off a skin-tight leather suit and hood.

'We got visitors, pigeon,' Killer called out. The barking of dogs grew louder.

Jack stopped at the end of the hall and peered into the lounge cautiously. Thick drapes covered the windows. A

TV was snowing in a corner with the volume turned down and a red light underneath showed the VCR was on. Jack held a hand up to his leaking side. From out in the yard came a frenzied snarling.

'What's wrong with your mutts?' Jack said, 'they're going crazy.'

'They smell blood, Butorov.' Killer padded through into the kitchen in his bare feet and pounded on the back door with a lump of wood. The dogs quietened at once. When he came back, Angela asked,

'Don't your neighbours ever complain about the noise?'

'One did.' Killer took a cassette out from the VCR, switched off the TV.

Jack could smell lubricants in the room, some kind of body oil. He turned and saw Marilyn standing in the doorway doing up her blouse.

'Good God, Jack. What's happened to you?'

'Shot,' Jack said.

Marilyn ran her eyes over the pair of them. 'Take him through into the kitchen,' she ordered. 'Kelvin, go bring my kit.'

Leaning heavily on Angela, Jack dragged himself through into the next room and fell onto a dark bench beside the table. Marilyn pulled off his shirt and threw it on the floor. She unbuckled his belt, undid his zipper and moved her cold fingers down over his stomach. Jack looked up and saw Killer watching them.

'Quarrell do this?'

Jack grunted as Marilyn cleaned around the exit wound with a handful of cotton balls soaked in antiseptic. She rolled him onto his right side and worked away at the smaller tear in his back. At least the bullet had gone straight through; he was thankful for that much. He flinched as Marilyn applied the dressing and taped it tightly around his waist.

'How is it?' Angela asked.

'With any penetrating abdominal injury,' Marilyn said,

'especially a gunshot wound, there's a strong chance of internal haemorrhaging. He'll need a CT scan.'

'A what?' Jack said.

Marilyn stood up straight and wiped hair from her eyes. 'They'll need to check you thoroughly at the hospital.'

'I told you that,' Angela blinked.

Jack sunk back on his elbows. There was no way he could go anywhere near a hospital. Not with two former Homicide detectives gunning for him. He'd be a dead duck. If he wanted to go on living he'd have to find some other plan. He looked up into Marilyn's angular face. She was much thinner than she used to be. 'What happens if I leave it a few days?'

'Maybe you're lucky, Jack, or maybe that bullet's already sliced off a piece of your bowel and you're bleeding into your abdomen.'

'Lovely,' Jack said. He turned to Killer who was standing very close to Angela. 'I need to use your phone.'

Marilyn and Angela helped him to his feet. The stabbing pain in his side was identical to when he'd had his appendix out. He wasn't looking forward to taking a crap. 'Thanks, Marilyn.' Jack squeezed her bony wrist.

Marilyn bent down and picked up his shirt. 'I'll wash this for you.'

'Please don't,' he said.

'It's no trouble, Jack.' She carried it out to the laundry and Jack felt Killer's eyes crawling all over him as he hobbled into the loungeroom.

Killer switched on a mushroom-shaped lamp beside the phone and scratched at his mangled ear. 'You were never here, got that?'

'Of course.' Jack watched Killer go out of the room, the dragon pattern rippling across the back of his silk robe.

Angela placed a hand on Jack's thigh as he picked up the receiver and dialled. A woman answered and he asked for Superintendent Mick Lam. 'It's an emergency,' Jack said and spelt out his name. After several moments the woman came back on the line with a message for him to ring Lam urgently at home. Jack hung up and dialled the number she'd given him. The phone rang twice before he heard the Superintendent's broad New South Wales vowels.

'Listen, Lam,' Jack said, 'I can't talk for long, but I'm in deep shit.'

'Where are you, Butorov?'

'Callagher's working with the Sun Sai Gei for God's sake. The man's taking Triad money –'

'Just cool it,' Lam said. 'Where are you exactly?'

Jack wiped a fresh web of spit off the mouthpiece. 'Look, I want a guarantee of protection for Angela and me and our two kids. Think you can arrange that?' He looked to Angela who gripped his leg tightly and nodded. 'Second I've copped a slug in the side. So I'm going to need medical treatment.'

'Okay,' Lam said. 'Now hang on a moment. I've got some news –'

'Congratulations on your transfer.'

'Christ,' Lam said. 'That attachment's just come through. How the hell'd you hear?'

'Guess,' Jack said.

The phone went silent at the other end and then the loungeroom window rattled and the dogs out in the yard began to bay as a tremendous roar enveloped the house and every stick of furniture shook. Jack caught the words 'nobbled upstairs' as he waited for the passenger jet to pass over. He heard Lam take a long deep breath and he wondered if the Superintendent had somebody there with him.

'Listen to me, Butorov. This task force's still operational and I'm not due into Heathrow for another ten days. So I'm willing to stick my neck out if you're prepared to give evidence.'

Jack smothered the mouthpiece with a sweating palm. He said, 'Hear that?'

Angela looked at him. Her big blue eyes were distant and he didn't need to be a mind-reader to tell she was missing her kid bad. 'Whatever we have to do, Jack, we do, okay.'

Jack nodded and brought the receiver close to his lips. Angela stood up suddenly. 'I forgot the headlights.' She ran down the hall.

'By the way,' Lam said. 'Those two names you gave Madden. It may be a coincidence, but he's turned up a couple of bods down in Canberra who match.'

'Say where they worked?'

'Constitution Avenue, Building 3. Both very senior public servants in the Australian Customs Service.

Jack whistled through his teeth. He could hear Killer prowling about in the kitchen, opening drawers. 'Look,' he said. 'You arrange for us to come in and we'll make out a statement.' The front door slammed and Angela came rushing down the hall.

'One more thing,' Lam said, 'I thought you'd want to know.'

Pain tore into Jack's side and he clutched at his dressing while Lam kept on talking in a flat tone. Jack waited for the pain to peter out and then said, 'When'd it happen?'

Angela's hands flew to her mouth. 'It's not Clea?'

Jack shook his head. 'Look, I gotta go, Mun Bun.'

'Wherever you are, Butorov, just stay put! Don't –'

Jack hung up in the Superintendent's ear. He leaned back against the stucco wall and closed his eyes. 'Cops,' he said, 'they're harder to get out of your hair than chewing gum.'

Angela stood there watching him. 'Tell me, Jack.'

'The Feds found Lee Fang this morning in Darling Harbour. Three bullets drilled into his forehead, .32 calibre.'

'They killed their own man, why?'

'Fang was the only direct link to Damian's murder. Plus he'd talked to us. Either way Chiu and Callagher are cleaning up loose ends.'

'What about Lam, do you trust him?'

'My guess is that Mun Bun's on the level. But I'm more worried about his superiors.'

Angela sat down beside him on the vinyl sofa. Drops of water clung to the short hair at the back of her neck.

'In two weeks' time Lam's out of the country – where does that leave us?' Jack placed a hand over Angela's knee. He said, 'Ever been in a really strong rip?'

She shook her head. Her eyes were streaked red from the long drive.

'It happened to me once at Crescent Head. And I got the same feeling right now.' He looked up and saw Killer standing in the kitchen doorway, wiping a carving knife on a Sea-World tea-towel.

'Finished with my telephone?' Killer said.

Jack nodded and took his hand off Angela's knee. 'You got any whisky round here?'

Angela said, 'Don't be stupid, Jack. You can't drink alcohol after you've been shot.'

Killer flipped the tea-towel over his shoulder. 'It's your funeral, pal.' He went out to the kitchen. Cupboard doors banged and voices rose in argument. A tap turned on and a moment later Marilyn came in with a glass of water and two Panadeine. Her lips were shiny with lipstick. 'I washed your shirt, Jack. It's in the dryer. Now I'll call an ambulance.'

'No ambulance,' Jack said.

'Don't be ridiculous. You need an ambulance.'

'We need to stay here tonight.'

'There's only one spare bed.' Killer looked at Angela.

'I can sleep in the car,' Angela said quickly.

Marilyn touched the point of her husband's elbow.

'They can have our bed, Kelvin. I'll sleep on the floor. It's better for my back.'

'We can't take *your* bed,' Jack said.

'Take the bloody bed,' Killer said. He turned and walked off down the hall.

'You sure?' Jack called out. He started to get up off the couch. 'He doesn't mind, Marilyn?'

In the master bedroom, Jack leaned against the king-sized water bed and wondered how the hell he'd manage to climb up onto it.

'I don't like the way he stares at me,' Angela whispered. She peeled off her dress.

'Killer's alright. He's just worked up the Cross too long.' Jack leaned a hand on her broad shoulder, placed one leg awkwardly on the corner of the bed, eased his hip up and rolled over. For several minutes he lay on his side with the sweat pouring out of him while the waves in the bed settled underneath.

'Jack, you gotta see somebody,' Angela said. She tucked her body in behind his. She wasn't wearing any clothes and he liked her best that way. A few moments later he felt her arm twitch, then the phone rang in the loungeroom and he heard Killer pad down the hall to answer it.

Jack lay there in the dark waiting for the Panadeine to take effect and wondering if Damian had really laughed about him.

44

The room was hot and Angela was gone. Her scent lingered on the black cotton sheets. Her twisted up pillow was jammed halfway down the bed like she'd been wrestling with it in her sleep. Jack gazed up at the mirror on the ceiling. The house was too quiet. It took him a moment to realise what was missing – the rain. It had stopped raining out there. He could feel the sun trying to break in through the thick drapes. He rolled over onto his back and examined the fresh bloodstains on his dressing. Red-hot needles burned in his side and he felt sick in the bowels. He wondered where the hell she'd gone without him. He pulled himself up onto his elbows as the bedroom door kicked open and Killer came in wearing Levis 501s and a pair of ranch boots.

Jack said, 'You seen Angela?'

Killer studied him in silence. The hair on his chest was as thick as a mat. 'Your girlfriend took off half an hour ago.'

'Say where?'

'Nope.' Killer shrugged his shoulders. 'Can you walk, Butorov?'

'Not real good,' Jack said. 'Why?'

'I got some bad news for you. Wanna hear it in the kitchen?'

Jack couldn't see that it mattered a shit where he heard it, but he took hold of Killer's outstretched arm. His friend was as strong as an ox and he didn't smell much better. A pot of scrambled eggs simmered on the stove in the kitchen next to a frying pan filled with strips of burnt bacon. Killer lowered Jack into a chair at the table and poured him out a mug of steaming coffee.

'No eggs,' Jack said. 'Don't think I could hold them down.' He watched Killer pile his own plate high and tuck in while the dogs growled out in the yard.

Killer fixed Jack with his good eye, the muscles in his jaw moving as he chewed. 'Word on the street is they're offering ten thou for you and fifteen for the girl.'

Jack stared. 'Who are?'

'Who the hell do you think?' Killer loaded his fork up

with more bacon. 'Quarrell's the contact, but word is the money's being paid out of Chinatown.'

'How'd you hear this?' Jack said. 'Somebody rang you last night, didn't they?' He watched the food go round in the old bouncer's mouth like clothes in a tumbler. 'Why they paying fifteen grand for Angela? I don't understand.'

Killer waited until he'd finished eating, then stuck his elbows on either side of his greasy plate. 'Because they want her alive.'

Jack spilled coffee down his chin. He wiped at it hastily, wondering if he could trust Killer for twenty-five big ones. 'What am I going to do?'

'You're going to need protection.' Killer stood up. 'I want to show you something out in the shed.'

Jack's eyes went to the door.

'Don't worry, Butorov. I've chained the dogs up.' Killer grabbed Jack under the arm and wrenched him onto his feet. They went out through the back door. Razor wire topped the two-metre high corrugated-iron fence that bordered the bare concrete yard. From out of the shadows a huge black dog rushed at them. The chain on its collar jerked suddenly and pulled the animal up centimetres short of Jack's groin. 'Seth likes you, don't you boy?' Killer said. The alsation bared its sharp white teeth. Two more black dogs watched red-eyed from the far side of the yard as their master unlocked the shed. Jack could smell the heat from their bodies. He followed Killer inside and shut the door quickly behind him. Some kind of heavy-duty press was mounted on a rough wooden bench and a number of specialised steel tools were laid out in a pattern alongside. The only thing that Jack recognised in the dim light was a batch of cartridges in a plastic ammunition box. Killer stretched up and unwrapped a long canvas bag on the overhead shelf. Inside, Jack saw, were more than a dozen automatics and revolvers. Killer took out a .44 Magnum Ruger Redhawk and passed it down. He said, 'I thought you might need some armour this time.'

Jack weighed the revolver in his hand. It was big and heavy with a barrel half a foot long. And in his heart he knew that this is what he'd come for.

Killer said, 'You ever fired one of these fellas?'

Jack shook his head.

'It'll stop a freight train, but it's got a kick on it.' Killer reached up and grabbed a box of shells from the shelf. 'These are soft points, 240 grain bullets – I make my own ammo. It's cheaper.' He put the Ruger and the ammunition in a black and white David Jones bag and gave it to Jack. 'You know what you're doing, Butorov?'

'Yeah,' Jack said, 'I know.' He hoped he wouldn't have to fire this revolver, but he was tired of running. He stepped out into the white concrete yard and the glare of the sun blinded him. He could hear the dogs panting and the clanking of their chains as they paced up and down. He leaned on Killer's bare shoulder, shielding his eyes with the David Jones food bag. The pain in his gut wouldn't go away.

In the kitchen he steadied himself on the Kelvinator fridge and looked across at Killer's big rugged head. 'Thanks, mate,' he said. 'Where's Marilyn?'

'Working.'

A fist beat urgently on the front door and Jack stiffened. He dropped onto a rickety chair, thrust his hands inside the bag and started loading the chambers of the revolver while Killer went down the hall. When Jack looked up again Angela was standing there in a short dark blue dress and black pumps. Her top lip was trembling and she was out of breath like she'd run from Bondi.

'Where the hell've you been?' Jack yelled. 'I was worried sick.'

'I went home.' She swept him a quick look, but her hands wouldn't stay still.

'You realise that's the first place they'd look for us.'

'It's Clea,' Angela said. 'I think something's happened to Clea.' She took a couple of steps towards him and her big blue eyes were blinking like crazy. 'I've been ringing and ringing the house for an hour, but all I get is the engaged signal. The phone's been taken off the hook.'

'Maybe Helen took it off,' Jack said. 'Maybe she's talking to some girl.'

'She wouldn't; Helen knows I ring Clea every morning at this time.'

'You never told me.'

'You never asked.'

Killer came into the kitchen and stood in the doorway with his burly arms folded. From the loungeroom came the raw steady beat of rock music.

Angela went up to Jack and brushed her lips against his mouth. She said, 'I've got the car running outside. I'm driving up to Seal Rocks now.' She turned to Killer. 'He needs to see a doctor right away.'

Jack climbed up out of his seat. 'I'm coming with you.'

'Don't be ridiculous, Jack.'

'Don't argue,' he said. 'It hurts my belly.'

'You can't go anywhere, you're bleeding. Look at your bandage, for God's sake.' She spun round. 'Tell him, Killer, if that's your name.'

Killer stared at her long legs. 'Butorov's a big boy, sweetheart.'

'I'm not your sweetheart.' She shook her head fiercely. 'I'm going, Jack, I'll be back soon as I can.'

'This is our fight.' Jack reached out and touched her neck with his fingers. 'You and me, remember.' He picked up his bag, went out to the laundry and lifted his shirt out of the dryer. For a moment he had to grip hold of the tub with both hands. He threw his shirt over his shoulder and went back into the kitchen where Angela was standing next to the wooden chopping block staring at Killer coolly. The Pretty Things were singing, 'I ain't gonna quit yer, get the picture.' And Jack leaned on her as they went down the dark hall. 'Listen to me, Jack, please,' Angela murmured in his ear. But Jack wouldn't listen. Out in the car she quit talking to him as if she realised it was futile. Jack rolled his window down and watched Killer press against the cyclone fence, his heavily tattooed arms looking like they'd been dipped in woad.

'Keep your head down, Butorov,' Killer called.

45

An old woman was sweeping dead leaves out through the iron lace on her balcony into the sunlight. The light was so strong that it hurt Jack's eyes to look into it. It bounced off the windows and the chrome strips of cars. Angela drove fast through the backstreets of South Sydney, cutting in front of trucks, squealing round corners. 'I thought Clea'd be safe up there,' she said. 'Whenever Helen's parents use the cottage they don't even bother to lock their doors at night.'

'Maybe there's a fault in the line,' Jack said. 'I'm sure she'll be alright.'

'I hope so, Jack, I hope so. If anything happened to Clea I don't think I could go on.' Her eyes flicked at his and her fingers tightened around the thin black wheel.

Jack leaned his shoulder against the door, holding onto his stomach. The road darkened underneath a huge concrete overpass and then curved towards the bridge. Steel and glass towers looked down upon them, crammed together like teeth.

'What's in the bag?'

'A gun,' Jack said. He took the DJ's bag off his lap and placed it carefully on the seat between them.

'I thought you were against guns.'

'I'm against other people having them.'

A train raced alongside trying to keep abreast and then the road dipped suddenly and Angela swung the car left onto the Pacific Highway. She pushed at her fringe with her hand, the skin across her forehead was bunched up. 'I'm frightened, Jack,' she said, 'not for me, but for Clea.'

'I told you in the beginning this wasn't a game.' Jack closed his eyes for a second and gripped the back of the seat. When he opened them again he saw the huddled glassy towers of North Sydney shimmering in the light.

'Yesterday after you were shot I realised I didn't want to go on with this whole business anymore. We've found Damian's murderer and now he's dead.'

'And the man who ordered it done,' Jack said, 'we haven't laid a glove on.'

Angela stared at the road ahead as if she were reading something off it. 'I don't care any longer,' she said. 'I just want my life to be how it was before. I want to bring up my daughter, I want the small things back, the important things.' She flattened a palm against the wheel. 'This morning I made myself a promise that if Clea was unharmed, I'd go away somewhere, take her north, to Queensland, walk away from this nightmare.'

Jack fiddled with his bandage. He tried to keep his voice on an even keel. 'That right?'

'And I want you to come with us.'

Jack looked at her.

'I know Clea likes you.' Angela reached over and touched the back of his wrist with her small warm hand. Her nails were bitten to the pink.

'And you,' he said. 'What's your opinion?'

Angela laughed. 'You're growing on me, Jack.'

He saw the muscles in her face relax and thought how attractive she looked when she smiled. He didn't know if what he was feeling for her was love. He only knew that he cared for her a great deal and that whatever happened now he wouldn't let any harm come her way.

The air was warm in the car and the whirr of the engine encased them like a membrane. She turned and held his gaze for a moment. 'Well?'

'I'd like that,' Jack said, 'but I don't think Callagher's going to let us go that easily. There's too much riding on this for him to risk it.'

'He won't find us, Jack,' she said. 'Anyway he has enough to deal with. Seen the paper?' She reached behind her into the back seat and dropped the *Herald* beside his leg. 'You're hot,' she said.

Sweat was running down the side of his neck. He wiped it away with his hand, rolled the window down and let the air rush at him. Now they were driving through the North Shore, melaleucas and plane trees screening the grand homes of Lindfield and Killara. Mercs and Saabs gleamed like family silver in the driveways. He had always wondered what it would be like to be stinking rich, but it didn't seem to matter anymore. He'd made his choice. He picked up the newspaper. The wind tugged at the pages as he fought to keep them open. A headline on page three grabbed his attention.

Prominent Businessman Named in Parliament

CANBERRA: Senator Callagher last night challenged the Independent MP, Mr Harvey Madden, to 'put up or shut up' over sensational allegations of corruption. His challenge came only hours after Mr Madden in the House of Representatives had accused Senator Callagher 'of conspiring to conceal and divert political donations for his own use.' A prominent Sydney businessman was named in what Mr Madden, amidst rowdy interjections, described as a 'collusion between a cabinet minister and a Triad gang leader.'

Senator Callagher said afterwards that Mr Madden's allegations were 'absolutely ludicrous and a farrago of lies. What's more I regard this cowardly attack under privilege

on a respected member of the Chinese business community,
a man I have never even met, as a reflection of the Member's
own deep-seated racial prejudices.'

'Did you read this?' Jack said.

Angela nodded.

'Madden's going to have to come up with some hard
facts pretty soon. I think we should make that statement.'

'Just as soon as we get Clea. Then we'll go to the police.'

'Maybe we make our statement to Lam then disappear.'
Jack folded the newspaper in half and ran his eyes over
a small article at the bottom of the page.

Body found in Darling Harbour. A man fished out of the
harbour early yesterday morning had multiple gunshot
wounds to the face and neck. Police as yet have established
no motives for the murder of Lee Fang, 39, of Surry Hills.

Jack flicked the *Herald* off his knee and leaned his head
against the car door, thinking of Nepo Kemp and Damian.
Trees threw their shadows across the highway as they
sped north away from the maw of the city. He had to
hope that Quarrell hadn't got to the kid yet. He didn't
dare tell her what he'd done. Didn't want to frighten her.
Most of all he didn't want her to change her opinion of
him. The wound in his abdomen burned like hell. There
was nothing like pain to concentrate the mind. He had no
illusions of what Quarrell would do to him next time.
None at all. He pressed one hand against his sticky
bandage while the other moved over the DJ's bag on the
seat and his fingers fastened around the long barrel of
the Ruger.

46

It was hot inside the car and Jack dozed fitfully while the wind worked away at the plastic windshield. Now and then he opened his eyes and looked up at her pale drawn face behind the wheel. Once he heard her murmuring to herself and he wondered if she was praying.

'Did Callagher tell you about me and Damian?' she said.

Jack nodded. He could smell petrol in the air, hear the engine straining as they flew along in the fast lane.

Angela fixed her eyes on the three-laned highway as it climbed between two huge walls of rust red sandstone and then plunged towards the Hawkesbury. Jack held onto the broken strap of the safety belt with one hand.

Angela said quietly, 'You know I've been in Rozelle Hospital don't you?'

The wind rattled the hood and shook the doorhandles. 'I don't care about that,' Jack said.

'Damian and me – we needed each other. How could it be wrong to have Clea?' She looked at him quickly and then looked back at the road. 'Did you tell them where she is?'

Jack shook his head.

'But you think Quarrell knows, don't you?'

'It's possible. The man was a cop for fifteen years. It wouldn't be too hard for him to trace this shack. It's in the name of Helen's parents right?'

Angela reached out and touched his hand. 'There's something you're not telling me, Jack. I can feel it.'

He gazed out the window. Trees thickened on either

side of the road and the wind tore at the coat-hanger she used as an aerial.

'You've got a fever,' she said. 'Soon as I pick up Clea, I'm taking you to a hospital.' She took her hand off his wrist and placed it back on the curving wheel.

'Remember I told you how Quarrell killed a mate of mine?'

'Nepo,' she said. 'Your Koori friend.'

'Well I was there. I saw Quarrell do it.'

She swept him a quick look.

'That night Nep came into the bar with a map, I drove down with him to Braidwood. We got in just before dawn and took this dirt road out into the forest. We left the Hertz van underneath some trees and had to walk three k's through the bush until we came to a huge plantation. I'd never seen so many dope plants before, there were thousands and thousands of them; all these irrigation pipes running parallel. There was a little drying shed at the far end of the clearing, but no-one else around, so we started ripping plants out of the ground and carting them back to the van.' Jack took a deep breath.

'I was coming back for another load when I saw Nepo in the middle of the clearing with an armful and three men walking towards him.' Jack stopped, watched a biker fly across the concrete overpass. Angela waited for him to go on.

'Nepo just stood there as Quarrell came up with his revolver out and when he got real close he shot him in the throat. Not even a word.'

Angela said very softly, 'What did you do?'

'I ran,' Jack said. 'There was nothing I could do. Nothing.'

'You didn't go to the police?'

'Those were police,' Jack said. 'Next morning Quarrell and two others come up to the hotel looking for me.

'So what happened?'

'I went to Spain.' He wiped his mouth on the back of

his hand. His throat was dry and his forehead felt on fire. 'I never told you this, but that night I met Damian in Oxford Street when those kids were bashing him, I was going to walk on by, but he just reminded me of Nep.'

Without moving her eyes off the road Angela said, 'Were you and Nepo lovers?'

Jack threw her a glance. 'No. We were friends. I was never anything special with the gloves, but Nep had class. We used to hang out, but we never used to talk that much. In the best friendships you don't need to.'

Angela stared straight ahead. 'Quarrell's going to kill us isn't he?'

'They want you alive,' Jack said, 'twenty-five grand's riding on our heads right now, but Quarrell'd do me for free.' He stretched himself in the seat, reached over and laid a hand on her muscled arm. 'Clea'll be alright, I promise you that.'

Angela pressed her shoe down on the accelerator and a billboard whizzed past showing two happy faces in a creamy-white sports car. 'Mazda,' Jack said, 'that was the name of the old Persian God of Light. Mazda.'

'What are you talking about?'

'Zoroastrianism.' He clamped his teeth tight and took long breaths through his nose until the waves of pain had passed. The sun beat down on his drooping lids and he could smell his own sour sweat, feel the grit of the road sticking to his skin.

'We're nearly there,' she said. 'Not far now.'

There were so many little things he wanted to tell her. Bits of useless information he wanted to share. She switched on the radio and got an election broadcast, tried for some music down the band and kept picking up politicians. She hit the off button and placed her hand back on top of the wheel.

Tall flooded gums brushed the sky, the pure white lines of their trunks as smooth as bone. Jack listened to the swish of the tyres on the hot blue bitumen and watched the light shimmer on the leaves. Angela turned off after the small township of Bulahdelah and sped east along a narrow sealed road. Trees hemmed them in, bloodwoods and ironbarks. Maybe, Jack was thinking, just maybe they'd got here first. Angela pushed at her sunglasses with a finger, her dress hitched up over her knees. The bitumen gave way to dirt and then they were flying down a hill, Angela trying to steer between the potholes while the back wheels kicked out dust and stones. Jack clutched at his stomach as the Holden swept around a bend and there, before them, lay the great blue ocean.

47

Seal Rocks, the sign said, and underneath it somebody had sprayed in red paint – *the last frontier*. Fibro cottages looked down over a curving bay. Fishermen were folding up nets on the clean white sand while petrels and pelicans circled overhead. Jack stared out the window. This was how it used to be. Waves crashed and foamed on the shore as the Holden climbed the ridge and for a moment he forgot all about his bullet wound.

Angela swung the wheel and pulled into a makeshift driveway. She jumped out and ran up the path to a green and yellow cottage that was all windows. Jack watched her push the front door open and then tried to ease his legs out after her. He leaned on the hood, feeling the heat from the engine. A child's bathers and pink towel stirred on a rope strung up between the water tank and a melaleuca. Jack reached his hand inside the David Jones bag and closed his fingers tight around the butt of the revolver. Holding it in his hand like that, he moved slowly towards the cottage. The air tasted clean and the breakers roared in his ears. Fresh tyre marks had been dug into the soft lawn and he kept his eyes glued to the front door. He wasn't intending to fire this gun until he had to. Angela rushed out onto the patio calling, 'The phone's been taken off the hook and the back door's wide open.'

Jack leaned against an old man banksia as a bolt of pain ripped through his gut.

'Clea's clothes, her toothbrush, everything else's here.' She placed a hand over her mouth and blinked her eyes rapidly. For a moment Jack thought she was going to cry and then she seemed to gather control of herself. She came down the steps and got in behind the wheel, waited for him to shut his door.

'Maybe they've gone for a walk,' Jack said.

Angela didn't speak.

He touched her arm gently. 'Don't worry yet.'

'I'll do anything if Clea's alright. Anything they say.' She shoved the gears into reverse, swung the car out and drove back down to the store-cum-post office that was the only shop in town. She parked in the shade beside a rusty anchor, got out and went inside. Through the window, Jack saw her talking to an old woman who must've been ninety or more. A few moments later Angela came running out of the store and jumped into the front seat. She had the motor going and the tyres kicking up dirt before Jack could get a word out.

'What happened?'

'Helen and Clea bought bread and milk in there yesterday. That old lady knows the names of everybody in Seal Rocks. She even knows the names of their dogs and cats.'

'That's good. That means they're alright.'

'No.' Angela shook her head. 'Two men were in this morning asking where Helen Kofler lived. They said they were policemen.'

Jack shut his eyes as they bounced along the dirt road. When he opened them again he saw fishermen's shacks flying past, and down below, the white foam riding the flat blue sea.

Angela's hands gripped the wheel tight as the dirt road climbed and narrowed through the bush. Branches scraped at the car doors. The engine rattled and pinged.

'Where you taking us?'

'There's only one road into Seal Rocks,' Angela said. 'That old woman in the post office saw the two men drive in, but she never saw them drive out.'

Jack glanced at her, a heap of thoughts running through his mind. If Quarrell did have the kid, he was only using her to get to them. He hoped she realised that. The track turned sharply and the glaring white walls and roof of the lighthouse keeper's residence rose in front of their eyes. Beyond the point, the ocean slammed against a nest of rocks.

Angela spun the Holden around in the turning circle and cut the motor. A gate barred the driveway and she got out and walked towards the lighthouse. Jack stayed in the car listening to the wind fanning the tops of the trees. Something moved in the bushes off to his right. He slipped the revolver out of the DJ's bag and placed it on his knee. He waited, watching the light flicker on the silvery banksias. Two shapes burst out of the bushes. For a second he didn't recognise Helen. Her face was tanned, her jeans were ripped at the crutch and she'd lost weight. Clea had hold of Helen's hand and when the child saw her mother's car she broke free.

Jack shoved the Ruger into the glove box just as Clea leapt into the front seat and threw her arms around his neck. She squeezed him so tight that he grunted with pain. She pressed her mouth up against his cheek and he could feel her heart thumping.

'Hullo little goat.'

'Where's Mum, Jack? Where's she gone?'

Jack tooted the horn twice. Angela came rushing down the hill from the lighthouse and the instant Clea spotted her mother she ran towards her like a rabbit.

'Two men,' Helen panted, tumbling into the back seat. 'Down on the beach . . . they tried to grab Clea.' Dirt and sand streaked her clothes and Jack could smell the sweat on her.

He put a hand on her wrist. 'Where are they?'

'We lost them in the bush.'

Jack stared at the new silver ring inserted through Helen's lower lip. It looked painful. He said, 'One a tall lean guy with a busted up nose?'

Helen nodded, swallowing hard while she caught her breath. She squeezed his arm with affection. The car door flew open and Angela reached in, hugged Helen tightly and kissed her.

'Let's get the hell out of here,' Jack said as Angela slid in behind the wheel and turned the key. Clea hopped into the front beside him and slipped her hand inside his. 'What happened to your stomach, Jack?'

'Nothin hon, just a cut.' He covered the blood stain on the front of his shirt with his arm. Clea's small hand was warm and her brown skinny legs dangled over the edge of the front seat. He liked the kid. The kid was ace.

'Get in the back, sweetheart,' her mother said. Clea climbed over the seat and clicked her safety belt on as they sped down the dirt track past some old dinghies anchored on the front lawns and a handful of fishermen's shacks hidden in behind the trees.

Jack peered out the window. This was where he should've taken Toby. Shown him a chunk of New South Wales paradise while it lasted. He hoped his son would meet Clea one day. A burgundy-coloured Falcon swept down a steep driveway on the left.

'That's them!' Helen cried.

The Falcon locked onto their back bumper bar. Jack turned his head and saw Brown in a pair of shades hunched over the wheel and next to him, Lindsay Quarrell with a white plaster cast on his nose.

Angela jammed the stick into second and stamped on the accelerator. A cloud of dust kicked up behind them as the Holden pulled away. They tore past the post office and along the narrow dirt road that led back to the highway. Trees whipped past their windows. The suspension shook. Clea started whimpering and Helen put her arm around the kid's shoulders.

'It's alright, honey.' Jack leaned over and touched her cheek. Whatever happened now he wasn't letting Quarrell get to them. The Falcon was gaining fast. They hit a hairpin bend in the road; the back wheels started to drift. Angela pressed her foot down on the pedal, steering them out the other side. Jack saw the Falcon behind go into a 180 degree skid, flatten a low spiky bush and end up in a shallow ditch pointing the other way.

'Won't be so easy doing a U-ey there,' Angela said. 'Once we hit the T-junction they won't know if we've gone north or south.'

Jack slapped his window open. The wind smelled of eucalypts and the light was trying to break in through the trees. The road turned and climbed sharply. Jack checked the mirror twice. There was no burgundy-coloured Falcon in sight.

'You've done it, Angela!' His heart lifted in his chest. Beyond the hill, just a few kilometres away, lay the Great Lakes highway. Clea leaned forward and pointed at the red oil light. 'Mum,' she said.

The engine sputtered suddenly and gave a loud bang. Bluish-black smoke trickled out from under the hood. Angela pumped at the accelerator fiercely as the motor cut out and a foul smell of burning rubber blew in through the vents.

Jack rolled his window up and pressed his hands hard against his face. The old Holden slowed and a hundred metres short of the crest of the hill it stopped completely and began to roll backwards. Angela threw on the handbrake.

'Block the road,' Jack said to her. Helen and Clea jumped out and Angela angled the car back across the narrow dirt road. He reached into the glove-box and took out the Ruger. Angela locked the other doors and came round to his side.

'C'mon,' she said. 'Put your arm around me.'

He was standing by the hood holding the revolver in one hand. He looked up through the trees and the light dazzled his eyes. A kookaburra was balanced finely on a wire.

'I'm not coming with you, Angel,' he said softly.

'Don't be stupid, Jack.'

He looked over at Clea who was clutching Helen's hand, her wide blue eyes jittery and that blonde hair all messed up. The kid was scared stiff, but trying not to show it. Jack caught a flash of Damian around her mouth, saw the young man lean back frightened against a window in Oxford Street. 'I want you three to go on ahead,' he said. 'I'll hold Quarrell off here.'

'No,' Angela said.

'Go on. There isn't time to argue.'

'I'm not going without you.'

'I wouldn't make it to the highway on foot.'

'I'm not leaving you here alone.' She stood in front of him on the dirt road with her black pumps planted firmly apart.

Jack reached out and touched the side of her neck. 'Listen to me,' he said, 'you're my girl, and I'm real glad we met up, but this is the only way out. I'm through with running and you've got your daughter to think of.'

A car engine whined in the distance. Angela flung her arms around his neck.

'Go on,' he said, 'take her out of here.'

'I love you, Jack.'

'Go north, get as far away as you can.'

The whine of the engine grew louder.

'I'll come back for you,' she said. 'I'll get help. I promise.' The wind tugged at her dark-blue dress as she turned and grabbed Clea's other hand and with her daughter in the middle, she and Helen ran towards the top of the hill. Jack followed them with his eyes and when the child, the girl and the woman had disappeared from view, he tucked the Ruger into his belt and leaned his fist on the boot of the Holden. He waited until the wine-coloured Falcon was only fifty metres away and as soon as he was certain that Quarrell had sighted him he staggered off the road into the National Park. He heard the Ford's brakes squeal and two doors slam in succession as he zigzagged through a thick stand of bloodwoods and ironbarks. Bark crunched under his shoes and bushes tore at his bare arms. He clutched at his side, stepping between the tall straight trees. When he could go no further, he stopped and picked out a pink-tinged angophora, leaned his back up against its smooth cold trunk and slid down onto his arse. Panting, he took the revolver out from his belt and held it in both hands over his knees. He waited, facing the direction he had come and listening to the wind blow the leaves about. Footsteps grew closer and a grisly voice called,

'We gonna skin your fucking hide, Butorov, you don't come out now.'

Jack lifted his revolver to eye-level. He had to remember not to flinch when he fired.

'You want this done quick, or you want it slow and painful?'

For a second he couldn't figure out where the voice was coming from and then he saw Quarrell in a grey cardigan ten metres off to his right, gripping a police special in two hands as he came on.

Jack held his breath. He waited until ex-Detective Sergeant Quarrell was almost on top of him and shot him in the chest. The force didn't hurl Quarrell backwards.

He just stood there swaying on the spot, and then he lifted a hand and groped at the round hole punched into his breastbone, before dropping face down where he'd stood.

A voice yelled off to the left and Brown came running through the trees, a muzzle flashing in his hand. Jack's head banged against the angophora as a bullet ripped open his thigh. He brought his revolver up fast, aimed it at the middle of Brown's chest and fired. Brown pitched forward in the dirt and lay there with his short legs twitching and half his jaw blown off. Jack shot him again through the top of the head. He tossed the Ruger into the ferns and watched the curled up strips of bark between his legs turn red.

He'd often wondered what it would feel like to kill a man, but he didn't feel anything much. Only the throbbing pain in his right thigh. The bullet had cut deep into muscle; blood oozed from the wound like the blood from a bull's neck. Jack was sweating now, his head rested on a thick trail of sap that seeped down the trunk. He stared out at the straight line of trees, the wind lifting their branches. The air smelled of the earth. He pressed his fingers down into the hard stony soil. All around him the bush rippled and quivered with enormous energy. He heard the wind grow faint overhead and footsteps crackling the leaves. He watched her bend down over him, felt her breath soft against his lips.

EPILOGUE

MINISTER PREDICTS MASSIVE INVESTMENT BOOM

Senator Bryan Callagher predicted today that record amounts of overseas investment would start to flood into Australia during the next three years. 'Boom times for all Australians are just around the corner,' the Minister said.

Speaking from the Hyatt Hotel in Kowloon, where he is holidaying with friends before undertaking official government business in Hong Kong and Taiwan, the newly-appointed Minister for Finance totally rejected allegations of discrepancies in the Federal Government's recent election campaign funding and said, 'that every single donation over $1,500 has been fully disclosed and the Australian Electoral Commission has found no impropriety whatsoever with regard to any aspect of electoral funding.'

Senator Callagher has begun legal proceedings in Sydney against a former Independent MP, Harvey Madden, for comments he made to reporters outside Parliament earlier this year in regard to Government campaign donations. The Minister was unable to comment further on the matter, but told journalists today that he was 'absolutely delighted' with his new portfolio.

IN BRIEF

BODIES FOUND IN NATIONAL PARK

Police are investigating the discovery of two male bodies
found in thick scrub in Myall Lakes National Park, 20
kilometres east of Bulahdelah. Bushwalkers stumbled across
the badly decomposed remains yesterday about 4 pm. Forensic medical officers were still examining the scene early this
morning. Detectives are treating the deaths as suspicious.

Founded in 1986, Serpent's Tail publishes the innovative and the challenging.

If you would like to receive a catalogue of our current publications please write to:

FREEPOST
Serpent's Tail
4 Blackstock Mews
LONDON N4 2BR

(No stamp necessary if your letter is posted in the United Kingdom.)